The Length of a String

ELISSA BRENT WEISSMAN

PUFFIN BOOKS

PUFFIN BOOKS
An imprint of Penguin Random House LLC, New York

First published in the United States of America by Dial Books for Young Readers
Published by Puffin Books, an imprint of Penguin Random House LLC, 2019

Visit us online at penguinrandomhouse.com

THE LIBRARY OF CONGRESS HAS CATALOGED THE DIAL EDITION AS FOLLOWS:
Names: Weissman, Elissa Brent, author.
Title: The length of a string / by Elissa Brent Weissman.
Description: New York, NY : Dial Books, [2018] | Summary: Twelve-year-old Imani, the only
black girl in Hebrew school, is preparing for her bat mitzvah and hoping to find her birth
parents when she discovers the history of adoption in her own family through her great-
grandma Anna's Holocaust-era diary. Identifiers: LCCN 2017043498 |
ISBN 9780735229471 (hardback) | ISBN 9780735229495 (epub)
Subjects: | CYAC: Adoption—Fiction. | Identity—Fiction. | Families—Fiction. | Jews—United
States—Fiction. | African Americans—Fiction. | Holocaust, Jewish (1939-1945)—Fiction. |
BISAC: JUVENILE FICTION / Family / Adoption. | JUVENILE FICTION / People & Places /
United States / African American. | JUVENILE FICTION / Historical / Holocaust.
Classification: LCC PZ7.W448182 Le 2018 | DDC [Fic]—dc23
LC record available at https://lccn.loc.gov/2017043498

Puffin Books ISBN 9780735229488

Printed in the United States of America

Design by Jennifer Kelly
Text set in Sabon LT Std

5 7 9 10 8 6

FOR MY BROTHERS,
MATT AND MIKE

Dear Belle,

All my life I've shared with you. Before we were born, we shared Mama's belly, splitting the resources so equally that we weighed the exact same amount at birth. The story of our arrival was our bedtime story for years and years. How the doctor didn't realize there were two of us until nine minutes after I was born, when you followed me into life. (How you have always loved a good surprise!) How in those nine minutes, Mama and Papa had already named me Annabelle. How they were so shocked at your arrival, they didn't think to come up with a second name. Instead, they split mine in two. I became Anna, you Belle.

Twelve years later, we share more than a name. To strangers, we're identical. We have the same straight brown hair cropped to the same place beneath our ears, the same gray-green eyes, the same pattern to our forehead wrinkles when we squint without our same-prescription glasses. We have the same height, the same weight, the same narrow heels that make buying shoes the same type of challenge. Save the mole on my left elbow that you lack, we are mirror replicas. So, like a name, we share our appearance.

We certainly don't share a personality. You are carefree and adventurous, while I am careful and cautious. You are quick to laugh, but also quick to cry. Your emotions flap back and forth like clothes drying on the line. We are both 12 but in many ways you are like our baby sister Mina, lashing out in anger in one moment, then jumping with delight the next, your hurt erased at the sight of something pretty.

Don't be angry at that comparison. You are the fun twin, the mischievous twin, the reckless and funny and passionate twin. I am the dull twin, the quiet twin, the responsible and reserved twin. I'm more careful than you, and more deliberate. I compared you to Mina, but you always compare me to Oliver. That is a compliment as well. Oliver is only 4, but he's wiser than most adults. We all love his story too. How he had so many ear infections as a baby that Mama used to worry he wouldn't hear. How he now hears every whisper, and how nothing escapes his big blue eyes. We know it's more than that, however. He understands. People, ideas, feelings . . . it's as though the tubes the doctor put in his ears made a path all the way to his heart. I am quiet like Oliver, and I like to think I share at least some of his intuition.

Of course I've arrived back at sharing. With so many brothers and sisters, we know nothing besides sharing. Me, you, Oliver, Mina, Greta (who is every bit 9), and Kurt, now 14 . . . Our house was quite full enough with 8 people. When the occupation pushed Grandmother and Grandfather to move in, it became nearly unbearable for us all. I know you too have wished to have something for yourself . . . a bed, a hairbrush, a whole potato, or an entire magazine. The only thing I've ever had for me and me alone are my thoughts. I try to keep them for just me, but in that I even fail, for you, Belle, know me to my core. You speak for me and through me, and often (does this happen to you?) it's as though I don't know my own opinion until I hear you speak yours.

I've often wished for some time alone . . . some moments, belongings, or experiences just for me. I wanted to be like the magician who performs at the Luxembourg Fair and make my 5 siblings, even you, even Oliver, vanish.

Now here I am, crossing the ocean, my wish come regrettably true. Who is vanishing, you or me?

CHAPTER 1
October 2014

Y ou're invited!"
      Parker Applebaum dangled two postcards over the low shelves in the synagogue library. Even though I couldn't see her from my spot on the floor with Madeline, I knew it was Parker because there was a giant photo of her face taking up half the post-card. Madeline and I looked at each other and suppressed giggles. The picture looked like it was meant for a department store ad. Parker's long red hair was blowing in the wind, and her mouth was open in a hearty grin, like the photographer—no doubt a professional one—had caught her mid-laugh.

Madeline squinted at the postcard. "Where are her braces?"

Parker's actual face appeared over the bookshelf.

"Photoshopped out," she explained. "This photographer's amazing. He doesn't usually do bat mitzvahs, but he's willing to do mine because we used him for my modeling portfolio. Let me know if you want his number. I can probably get you guys in too. *And*," Parker sang, her lips curling up, "guess who else is invited." She cocked her head in the direction of the tables in the center of the library.

"The whole class?" Madeline deadpanned.

The corners of Parker's lips dropped. "I was talking to Imani," she said. She smiled at me and did a double-raise of her eyebrows. "I'm inviting Ethan Bloom."

"Okay," I said, trying to sound casual. Ethan and I are both on our school tennis team, and ever since Parker heard him compliment my backhand a couple weeks ago, she's been convinced that he likes me. I'm not as convinced. It's not like he complimented my serve (which stinks). Everyone compliments my backhand, because it's killer.

"I'm going to sit you and Ethan at the same table," Parker said with some more eyebrow wiggling.

Mrs. Coleman's face appeared above Parker's. "Girls," she said. "Back to your projects, please."

Parker smiled and handed Mrs. Coleman a postcard. "You're invited, Mrs. Coleman."

"December sixth," our teacher said without needing to look. "Will you have your haftorah ready by then? How about the research project you're supposed to be working on as we speak?"

"Yeah, yeah." Parker rolled her eyes and reminded us, "December sixth," before walking away.

Madeline and I went back to our Holocaust books. As if we didn't have to do enough to prepare for our bat mitzvahs (write a speech, know all the prayers, read nine lines of Torah, *sing* a long haftorah portion . . .), we each had to research some aspect of the Holocaust. Like we hadn't heard enough about the Holocaust every year of our lives. I'm usually pretty good about doing classwork, even for Hebrew school, but this assignment was seriously uninspiring. We couldn't even use the internet to look stuff up the easy way; Mrs. Coleman was making us use actual books, which was why our Hebrew school class had permanently relocated from a classroom to the synagogue library.

Not wanting to think about Ethan or my Holocaust project, I waited till Mrs. Coleman was out of earshot and then poked Madeline with Parker's postcard. "Are you going to have your photo on your invitations?" I whispered.

Madeline blew air through her lips, like a bike tire deflating. "I don't think so. We're not even going to do paper invites; wastes too many trees."

Figures. Madeline's parents are green to the extreme.

"When are you going to tell your parents what you want for your present?" she asked.

I sighed and leaned back into the bookshelf. Instead of having a blowout party for my bat mitzvah (like Parker) or a tasteful luncheon (like Madeline), I'm going to get a big present. My parents said they'd get me whatever gift I want, within reason. I know exactly what I want, but so far I've only worked up the nerve to tell Madeline. I also told Madeline to make sure I don't chicken out of asking, and boy, was she keeping that promise.

"Imani." She poked my arm with her pointer finger. "Just tell them. They said you can have anything."

"Within reason," I reminded her.

"What could be more reasonable than wanting to know who you are?" Madeline flipped through the pages of the book she was holding. It was full of old pictures of white people, emaciated, with sunken cheeks and resigned eyes. "Remember when we used to look at that *Children of the World* book? The one with the people from all different countries?"

"Oh yeah," I said, as though just now remembering. "You used to hold it up next to me and try to see which country my ancestors might be from." This was always a one-way game, since there's nothing mysterious about where Madeline gets her appearance. She looks exactly like her mom, only shorter.

"We thought that girl from Ghana could be your twin!" Madeline laughed, which made Mrs. Coleman appear again.

"Mayim. Emunah." She said our Hebrew names like she was too tired to be stern, which made me feel worse than if she'd just yelled at us.

"Sorry," I said.

We looked back at our books, but now my mind was with the *Children of the World*. That book was about how everyone's the same on the inside, but I always liked it more for how different everyone looks on the outside. In my town, everyone looks pretty much the same, and it's not like me. Nobody in my own family even looks like me. My mom is tall and sturdy, like she's built to survive a Nordic winter. My dad is also tall, but angular and spindly, like he'd have to spend that Nordic winter huddled close to the fireplace (probably stocked with wood my mom had chopped). They both have fair skin, thick brown hair, and icy blue eyes.

My brother Jaime's skin is a shade darker. His eyes are brown, and his hair is a shiny black. Not surprising, given that he's adopted from Guatemala.

Then there's me. I'm short and skinny. My arms and legs look like toothpicks no matter how much tennis I play or how many bowls of tortellini I eat. (My records, by the way, are fifteen hours of tennis in one week and five bowls of tortellini in one sitting. I like tennis, but I'm obsessed with tortellini.) My complexion's a little darker than Jaime's, but my light brown eyes are flecked with green. My hair is soft and springy, with tight coils that extend up and out, challenging gravity. Parker says I look "exotic"—she's actually used that word, straight out of an ad for some honeymoon resort—and she's always lamenting that she doesn't. She says I'd get a ton of modeling jobs if I wanted them. Apparently, talent agents want people whose ethnicity "keeps you guessing."

I'm no stranger to guessing. I know I was born in Philadelphia, and I know my birth mother was black. The rest has been left to my imagination, and boy, has my imagination embraced the challenge. Long after Madeline outgrew *Children of the World,* I kept playing on my own, holding up pages next to my reflection in the mirror. Picture by picture, I'd compare the tone of my skin, the shape of my nose, lips, eyes. Is my father Irish or Italian? Am I a quarter Filipino? Part Indian or Latina or Arab? I never have an answer when people ask, "What are you?" I usually tell them I'm human, but sometimes I also add that I'm Jewish, just to make them more confused.

When Madeline and I were in third grade, and she said that Ghanaian girl looked like my twin, I started to wonder if I really might have a twin somewhere in the world. I imagined that my mother gave birth to twins, but she could only afford to keep one child, so she placed me for adoption. Unlikely, I know, and not the happiest story. But even if it were true—that I was a twin and my birth mother kept my sister but not me—I told myself I could handle it. I just wanted to know.

I still want to know.

That's why, for my bat mitzvah gift, I want to find my family. My *first* family. My blood-and-guts, double-helix, you're-as-stubborn-as-your-father family.

Does that sound reasonable?

My phone vibrated in my pocket, and I nearly jumped. I glanced around to make sure Mrs. Coleman was out of sight, then I took it out. A text from Madeline, who was still, like, twenty inches away. I rolled my eyes at her, but she was pretending to be very interested in Kristallnacht. (Like, too interested. She was pointing at something in the book and nodding and saying "hmm.")

I opened her text. *Tell your parents tonight.*

I sighed again. Maybe I shouldn't have asked Madeline to make sure I do this. She wants to be an investigative reporter when she grows up—like one of the people on NPR, this boring radio station her parents always have on in the car—and I was starting to wonder if she was in this for me, or if she was just hoping for her first big story: *From NPR News in Baltimore, I'm Madeline Winter with the latest on Imani's adoption story.*

I guess I could tell her to back off, but I *do* want to investigate this too. More than anything. I just wish I could do it in a way that won't hurt my parents beyond repair.

Another vibration. Another text from the reporter-in-training. *Play the bat mitzvah card. Adult in Judaism, etc. etc.*

This was a convincing point. When we turn thirteen and have our bat mitzvahs, we'll be considered adults in the Jewish religion. It doesn't get us much in the real world—I won't be able to see R-rated movies or buy a scratch-off lotto ticket or anything—but Mrs. Coleman and Rabbi Seider like to remind us that it does mean something symbolically. The symbolism seems extra applicable to me, since the odds that I'm genetically Jewish are probably, like, zero. Madeline thinks I should milk that symbolism for all it's worth. I'm the only black girl in Hebrew school, gamely researching a heritage that has no biological connection to me. The least my parents can do is let me research my real history too, right? If I'm considered an adult in Judaism, I should be old enough to deal with whatever I discover.

Ok, I texted back. *I will*. I was feeling strong and sure. I was really going to do it. That night.

I watched Madeline's eyes move down to the phone hidden in her book. Then she looked up at me and nodded, her freckled face lit up with satisfaction. "Just don't run away and live with your biological family, wherever they are, okay?" she whispered.

"No way," I said. I held up Parker's invitation. "Then I'd miss the event of the century."

Madeline shook her head. I thought she might bring up Ethan, who I could see cleaning his glasses with the bottom of his T-shirt, but instead she said, "I can't believe her braces are Photoshopped out."

"Parker always looks good in pictures," I said, "even without Photoshop. How come I always look like I'm about to sneeze?"

"You look great in pictures," Madeline insisted. "I'm the one who always has, like, one eye half blinking and the other looking at the wrong camera."

She made a face, trying to demonstrate, and I let out a laugh so loud, the entire class—including Ethan—looked our way. Mrs. Coleman did not look happy. Luckily, the bell rang at that exact moment, and Madeline and I bolted before we could get in trouble. We ran, laughing and puffing, out the side door of the temple and to the corner, where we had to wait for our younger brothers so we could all walk home together.

"Let me know what your parents say," Madeline said, catching her breath.

"I will," I promised. "Tonight."

CHAPTER 2

When Jaime and I got home, my mom was standing at the stove, crying. This wasn't too shocking a scene; Mom's a crier. For all I knew, these tears could be because we ran out of chicken broth. Even so, the odds of me keeping my promise to Madeline were looking slim. I was already worried that my request would break my mom's heart. It would not be smart to bring it up when she's sobbing into a pot of soup.

"Hi, Mom," Jaime said. He put his backpack down on a kitchen chair and approached her cautiously.

Mom turned around. "Hi, sweetie," she said with a sniffle. Her eyes were all pink and puffy. Maybe this wasn't about chicken broth.

"What happened?" I asked.

Mom swallowed and gave me a sad smile. "Grandma Anna died."

"Whoa," I said. Is it bad that my first thought was that I definitely shouldn't ask about finding my birth parents tonight? Is it worse that I felt relieved about that instead of sad about Grandma Anna? In my defense, Grandma Anna is actually my *great-grandmother*—my mom's grandma—and I didn't know her very well. She lives—lived, I guess—up in New York, and we live in a suburb of Baltimore. Mom's always saying we should go visit her more, and we were actually planning to go see her in New York next month, around Thanksgiving. I guess we wouldn't get to see her now. It hit me that that was probably making Mom extra sad. I thought about going over to hug her, but for some reason it seemed weird. The mom's supposed to comfort the kid, not the other way around.

"I'm sorry," I said, tentatively.

Mom sniffled again, and I could see that fresh tears were about to fall.

Jaime was starting to get sad too. He's super tuned in to Mom's emotions.

I moved to put my arm around Jaime, and Mom came over and hugged us both. "It's okay," she said, restoring the proper giving-comfort order. She gave Jaime a kiss on the forehead. "She was eighty-five. She lived a very full life."

"How did she die?" Jaime asked.

"Peacefully," Mom said. "In her sleep."

That's how I want to die too. Asleep. I've thought about this before. "That's good," I said.

"Very good," Mom agreed.

I heard the front door. Dad was home. He came into the kitchen and wrapped his skinny arms around Mom and, by default, Jaime and me.

Mom sighed and pulled out of the full-family hug. She wiped her eyes, sniffed, and stood up straight. "The funeral's tomorrow," she told us. "We're going to have to drive to New York tonight, after dinner."

"Tonight?" Jaime said.

"Tonight," Dad confirmed. "We'll probably stay through the weekend, so figure three or four days. Why don't you two go pack?"

Three or four days in New York. Funeral, family, sad stuff. There was no way I'd be able to bring up anything about searching for my birth family until this whole thing was over. Off the hook for now, and with a perfectly good excuse.

I climbed the stairs slowly. What sort of clothes do you wear to a funeral? I wasn't sure Dad would know, and I couldn't exactly ask Mom. I figured I'd text Madeline—she could ask her mom—but when I got to my room, I found my black skirt and blue collared shirt already on my bed. I peeked in Jaime's room. Mom had laid out his suit.

That was just so Mom, to think of *us*, even when her grandma had just died. I thought about her downstairs, and Dad hugging her, and I got this warm pang in my chest. The kind of pang that made me feel guilty that I want to know about my biological family at all.

CHAPTER 3

The hardest part about the funeral was seeing so many grown-ups cry. My mom always cries, so that wasn't particularly sad. But my grandpa Fred, who's never greeted me without a goofy grin or a new magic trick, sobbed into his handkerchief. (I guess I shouldn't have been surprised, since this funeral was for his mom.) My great-aunt Janet (Grandpa Fred's sister) buried her wet face in Grandpa Fred's shoulder. Even Aunt Jess—who arrived at the cemetery on her Harley, her Mohawk freshly dyed black—was dripping tears that made her thick eyeliner run down her otherwise stony face.

Jaime and I stayed close to Dad. I was by his left pocket, which was unusually flat, meaning Dad hadn't brought his video camera. That thing was usually strapped to his hand. I guess a funeral was the one thing he didn't want to record and relive later.

I heard a couple sniffles from Jaime and a glance confirmed that he was, in fact, crying. Why? Was it because all the adults were so upset? Or did he feel some deep connection to Great-Grandma Anna that I couldn't?

I got a lump in my throat, as if I'd swallowed a gumball whole, but it still wasn't about Grandma Anna. I was worrying about myself. Am I some kind of cold, unfeeling monster? Jaime's so sensitive, like Mom and the rest of her family. It's almost like he inherited it for real instead of being adopted. I guess I could add "heartlessness" to the list of ways I'm different from my family. Does Jaime even feel different at all? If he does, he sure doesn't show it. Add that to the list too.

Maybe, somewhere, I have a biological brother, and he's just as cold-hearted as I am. Like me, he'd be more creeped out than sad about the big coffin right there, with our great-grandma in it, dead. We'd whisper to each other about there being people in coffins underneath all of this grass, and we'd both curl our toes in our stiff black shoes.

But in my actual life, the rabbi was talking about how hard it is to say goodbye to people we love. "Anna was no stranger to goodbyes herself. She had to say goodbye to everyone and everything she knew when she was just twelve years old. A child! But this brave child became part of a new family, and she grew up to create her own."

What? I thought. *A new family?* I knew, vaguely, that Grandma Anna had an interesting history. She was born in Luxembourg, a tiny little country in Europe that I picked for International Day in fourth grade. (I wasn't going to bother fighting for one of the popular countries like Italy or Australia.) I knew she came to America when she was a kid, maybe close to my age. But I didn't know she'd gotten a new family. Was Grandma Anna adopted, like me?

I listened hard, blocking out the sniffling sounds, but the rabbi had moved on to naming Grandma Anna's descendants. Then he switched to Hebrew for the Mourner's Kaddish, one of the prayers I knew well from my bat mitzvah lessons. After that, Grandpa Fred shoveled some dirt onto the coffin, and my other relatives followed. Dad leaned down and asked quietly if Jaime or I wanted to do it too. We looked at each other hesitantly and both shook our heads. I knew it wasn't the time or place to whisper back asking if Grandma Anna had been adopted. Dad probably didn't know anyway. And then everyone was hugging and getting into cars for a silent ride to Grandma Anna's apartment.

When Madeline's grandfather died a couple years

ago, my whole family went to pay a shiva call. I was really nervous on the short walk over, thinking everybody would be all sad and quiet, and I wouldn't know what to say or do. But it was nothing like that. There were tons of people gathered, and everybody was sharing funny stories about her grandpa. Family photos—old-timey ones and new ones too—were laid out around the whole living room. The TV was even playing an old video, one where Madeline's aunts and uncles had ugly clothes and goofy haircuts that made everybody laugh. There was tons of food too, and everybody kept telling me to eat more, so I did. Madeline's family was sad, I'm sure, but someone passing by an open window would've thought they were gathered for a birthday party rather than a mourning ritual.

So this time, I thought I knew what to expect. But leave it to my mom's family: It was the exact opposite. Great-Aunt Janet was a wreck. Grandpa Fred tried to be cheerful, but he just couldn't muster it. Aunt Jess didn't even come.

Even some of Grandma Anna's elderly friends thought the whole thing was too big of a downer. "What's with all the sadness?" an old lady whispered to me near the tray of bakery cookies (the kind that crumble into a thousand pieces on the way to your mouth). "Anna was eighty-five. I'm only eighty-two, and every day I don't see my name on the obituary page, I consider it a success."

I gave a weak chuckle, not knowing the polite response to an old lady telling you she might croak at any moment.

The lady pointed to the tray of cookies. "Are these sugar-free?" she asked me.

"I don't know," I said.

"Ask your boss."

I wrinkled my forehead. Then I looked where the lady's bony chin was pointing, and saw a woman putting out more napkins. She was wearing dress pants and a collared shirt, and she was the only other person in the room with skin as dark as mine.

"I'm not working here," I said dryly. "I'm Anna's great-granddaughter."

Now it was the old lady's turn to chuckle weakly. I walked away and sat by Jaime on the plastic-covered sofa, leaving the lady to feel awkward.

"This sucks," I muttered.

Saving grace: My parents felt the same way. Mom was going to stay and mourn with her family for the whole seven days of shiva. But Dad, Jaime, and I only stuck around for another lousy half hour. Then we put the giant bowl of uneaten tortellini salad in the trunk with our unopened weekend bags. We kissed everyone goodbye and took off for home. It was going to take all night to get there, though. The Holland Tunnel was an ocean of brake lights. "Who are all these people," Dad said, "and where are they going?"

I looked at the people in the next car and wondered the same thing.

"Hey Imani," said Jaime, "you want to play Pickle?"

"Not really," I said.

"Picnic?"

"Nah."

"The movie game?"

I sighed. Jaime always wants to do this little-kid stuff. "Can't you just listen to your iPod or something?"

"I want to play with you."

I leaned my head against the window. "Maybe when we get to New Jersey."

Jaime groaned. "How long will that take?"

Dad sat back in his seat and shook his head. "How long is a piece of string?"

"What does that mean?" I asked.

"It means," Dad said with a chuckle, "that I have no idea."

CHAPTER 4

Mom might have been in New York all week, but only her body was missing. She called and texted me constantly, not wanting to miss a moment of my life. I'm used to it from when she goes on business trips, this constant checking in. I've tried to use it to my advantage, pointing out that if I had a phone from this century, I could text her pictures of my life while she's away, but so far it hasn't worked. I still have this ancient phone that doesn't have a camera or even a touchscreen. And all week, it chimed with texts from my mom, trying to make sure I wasn't hitting any major milestones without her, I guess.

In reality, she only missed one important thing: My tennis match against Central. I normally play doubles, but Sophie Volk got sick, so I got to play singles for the first time. My dad and Jaime came, and they cheered when Coach called my name for fourth singles. Dad had his video camera, of course, so Mom could watch the match when she got back, even if I double-faulted the whole thing.

My opponent was a tall, muscular girl with blond hair and red braces. We met at the net to determine who'd serve first, and she pointed with her racquet to my family. "Who are they?"

"My dad and my brother."

Her face contorted with confusion. "Is your mom black?"

I'm used to strangers asking me obnoxious questions that are none of their business. What I'm not used to is playing singles, and fielding obnoxious questions right now could mess with my head. I needed to shut this down, but I was too nervous for the game to do anything but tell the truth. "I'm adopted," I said. "Heads or tails?"

But she couldn't have cared less about tossing the coin for that first serve. "That's so cool! Have you ever met your real parents?"

"I live with them," I said coldly.

"No, like your *real* parents. You know. Biologically or whatever. Do you know them?"

"No."

"You should find them!" suggested this total

stranger. "You might have this amazing history you don't know about."

Thank you! I thought sarcastically. *That never occurred to me until* you *brought it up.* "Heads or tails?" I asked again.

"Where are you from?" the girl asked. "Like, what are you?"

My fist tightened around my racquet. *I'm* allowed to wonder about that because it's my life. But what's it to this girl? Why would she care? It's not like she should aim for my forehand if I'm Puerto Rican and play at the net if I'm part Chippewa.

"Tell her, Imani," came a voice from the side of the court. It was Ethan, with his racquet and his sport goggles instead of glasses, on his way to his own singles match. "Don't be modest."

I looked at him. Waited.

"Imani's really a Williams," he told my opponent. "You've probably heard of her sisters, Venus and Serena?"

The blonde's mouth dropped open, showing her full mouth of metal. "For real?"

I suppressed a smile and shrugged, trying to appear as Williams-like as I could. "They had to place me for adoption so they could focus on my sisters' training."

"No way . . ." the girl said.

"Watch out for her backhand!" Ethan called before jogging over to his court.

"You're kidding, right?" the girl said. But I could tell she still wasn't sure. And now I wasn't sure how wrong Parker was about Ethan liking me.

My face got warm, and this time I couldn't keep my lips from curling up. I hoped my nosy opponent thought it was because I was embarrassed that my true lineage had been revealed. Now I just had to play well enough to convince her. I drew up my shoulders and prepared, again, to flip the coin. "Heads or tails?"

CHAPTER 5

So, did you win?" Grandpa Fred asked.

Dad and Jaime and I were back in New York, and I knew Grandpa would appreciate the story Ethan told that girl. I made sure to tell it to him while my mom was busy with something else; she wouldn't have appreciated it at all. We *never* talk about my adoption—a major reason I'm so nervous to tell her what I want for my bat mitzvah.

"I lost," I told Grandpa.

"No!"

"Yeah. I won a few games, but she took the match. I kept double-faulting."

"Eh," Grandpa said. "You gave her the story of her life. One day she'll tell her grandkids she won against a Williams."

I laughed. "I guess I did her a favor."

"That's right." Grandpa patted me on the shoulder. "You did a mitzvah."

The sounds coming from the second bedroom started getting louder, and Grandpa's smile turned into a frown. My mom and her siblings were arguing again. My dad had said there'd be a different vibe here after shiva, and he was right. Instead of sobbing or being somber, now everyone was fighting. Over Grandma Anna's stuff.

"Why do *you* need a sterling silver gravy spoon?" Aunt Jess asked my uncle Dan.

"I'm an adult," Uncle Dan said. "I might host dinner parties."

"Oh yeah?" Aunt Jess snorted. "In your cabin in the woods? Who's going to come, grizzly bears?"

"Better than biker dudes who look like grizzly bears."

"My friends do not look like grizzly bears!"

My mom stifled a laugh. When Aunt Jess turned to glare at her, Uncle Dan tucked the big silver spoon in a side pocket of his cargo pants. It was so heavy it made the whole pant leg droop. Uncle Dan wasn't wearing a belt, so he had to grab the waist to keep his underwear from showing. Now my mom laughed at that. Jess whirled around and shook her head at Dan. "*That* is exactly why *you* shouldn't get all the valuable things."

"Jess," Mom said seriously. "There's a whole closet of valuable fur coats that you don't want any part of."

"That's right. Because fur is murder."

"I don't blame you for thinking that," Dan said. "It'd be like making a coat out of one of your hairy biker friends."

Jess lunged at Dan, and my mom jumped in the middle, and Grandpa sighed and said, "Excuse me, Imani. My grown children are acting like toddlers."

I had no desire to watch the fight unfold, so I decided to go back to my own inheritance. Even though there seemed to be no instructions as to who could claim the expensive things like fur coats and gravy spoons, Grandma Anna did specify that certain things were meant for her great-grandchildren. Jaime got an ancient baseball glove and a collection of marbles in a small wooden box. My cousin Isabel, who's only five, got the stuffed bear that always sat on a high shelf above Grandma Anna's bed. And I got a big box of chemistry equipment. Some of it was really old, but some looked brand-new. I chuckled, picturing my eighty-five-year-old great-grandmother wearing safety goggles, conducting experiments in this small, musty apartment.

According to Grandpa, her will also stated that us three great-grandchildren were to inherit all of her books. When I first heard that, the lump from the funeral returned to my throat, and this time it *was* about Grandma Anna. We didn't visit her that often, but whenever we did, she'd stock the living room bookshelf with books just for us. If it had been the kind of shiva where people shared happy memories of the deceased, I'd have shared that whenever we arrived at Grandma Anna's apartment, she'd first sit us at her kitchen table and say, "Eat." Once we were full, she'd lead us to the living room bookshelf and say, "Read." Those two words were among the only ones I ever heard her say. Grandma Anna was pretty quiet, around me and Jaime at least. She definitely never talked about being adopted, if she was. Maybe that's where my mom gets it.

I have to say, we kids handled our inheritance more responsibly than the adults. Isabel wasn't there, so I got the teddy bear down from the shelf and placed it carefully in a corner. (It could have used a spin—or two, or five—in the washing machine, but it was so old, it would probably come out as a pile of stuffing, and I was determined to treat Grandma Anna's belongings with more respect than the grown-ups.) Jaime and I had already put aside some books for Isabel too: all of the ones with pictures and a few novels we thought she'd enjoy when she got a little older. Then, while the adults were arguing about jewelry and china patterns, we had gone through the living room bookshelves, making four piles: "Imani," "Jaime," "Talk about," "Donate."

All that was left was the big bookshelf in Grandma Anna's bedroom. It was stuffed to the max. Grandma must have been quite the reader.

"Hey, Jaime," I said.

"Yeah?" I found him in the kitchen, drinking some flat ginger ale from a bottle that had been in Grandma Anna's fridge. The lack of carbonation didn't bother him. Neither did the fact that it belonged to a dead person. Boys.

"Let's go through the books in the bedroom," I said.

"Are those for us too?"

"Grandpa Fred said yeah."

"Is there anything good," Jaime asked, "or just boring grown-up stuff?"

I held out my hands. "How should I know? That's why we have to go through it."

Jaime took another swig from the ginger ale bottle. "Let's play with the marble thing I got instead. Want to have a competition? It can be me, you, and that old teddy bear."

There he goes with the kid stuff again. I'm in

junior high. Why would I play marbles with a stuffed animal? "No," I said, "I want to see what's on the bookshelf. We have to figure out who gets what."

"You're not fun anymore." He frowned, twisted the cap back onto the bottle. "Go do the books. The bear and I will play marbles without you."

I was annoyed for about half a second before realizing I didn't care. I'm *lots* of fun when I want to be, so whatever. And it'd probably be easier to do the books on my own anyway. This way I'd be sure to keep anything cool for myself. Who knows, there might be some information about her past in there—maybe even her adoption papers. Maybe I'd find something about Grandma Anna's adoption that I could use when asking about my own. Maybe it'd give me the courage to actually do it too.

Armed with purpose, I walked to the bedroom and piled up some dictionaries to stand on and tackle the shelf from the top.

This collection was more varied than the one in the living room. There were worn classics, newer novels without a single crease, and a range of stuff in between. I decided to keep every Agatha Christie book—there must be something to them if Grandma Anna owned twenty. She had a decent number of chemistry books, which I decided to keep too, to go with my new set of beakers and burners. Some books were in other languages; I recognized French and what I guessed was German or maybe Dutch. *Cool,* I thought. Was Grandma Anna learning new languages? Or maybe she still knew them from when she was a kid in Europe. I tried to think back to my fourth-grade project on Luxembourg, but I couldn't remember what language they speak there. (Could I be part French or German or Dutch? If I hadn't been placed for adoption, would I speak a different language? If I found my birth parents, would we even be able to communicate?)

The third shelf down had a bunch of old user's manuals for outdated technology, which were funny to read. How to program your VCR, how to load "film" into something called a Polaroid camera . . . When I pulled out a guide to "using your new icebox," another book fell to the floor. It was small and thick, and the cover was solid, though faded, black. I picked it up. The binding was soft but flat, like a couch cushion that had been sat on for too long. A frayed green ribbon hung from the top. My heart fluttered and my fingers knew to handle this book gently. It clearly wasn't a user's guide. It wasn't like any of the other books on the shelf.

The cover stretched and creaked as I opened it, as though nobody had done so in years. I felt like I was in one of the fantasy books from the other book-shelf, about to discover a portal to some magical world. But the page I opened—a random one, in the middle—had no stardust or spells, just small, careful writing. The cursive letters were precise, every line straight and every loop perfectly circular.

I ran my hand over the old paper until my eyes stopped on a familiar word. A name: Anna. It was at the bottom of the page on the right, the way you'd sign a letter or a diary. My fingers jumped back as though the ink were hot.

A diary! I thought. *Oh my God, I found Grandma Anna's diary.*

I went to the very first page, hoping to confirm my hunch. It had a date in the corner from 1941. But the rest was in a different language. The letters were normal—well, normal for English—but they formed words that I had no way of translating. But that random page I'd found first . . . that one hadn't been in this strange language, had it? I turned the pages one by one, careful not to rip anything. Page after page of this other language. Just when I was starting to doubt whether I'd been right about seeing English at all, the strange writing stopped. There was one blank page, and then the writing started up again, this time in English. The date was the same as on the very first page and it began:

Dear Belle,

All my life I've shared with you. Before we were born, we shared Mama's belly, splitting the resources so equally we weighed the exact same amount at birth. The story of our arrival was our bedtime story for years and years. How the doctor didn't realize there were two of us until nine minutes after I was born, when you followed me into life. (How you have always loved a good surprise!) How in those nine minutes, Mama and Papa had already named me Annabelle. How they were so shocked at your arrival, they didn't think to invent a second name. Instead, they split mine in two. I became Anna, you Belle.

"Imani!"

I snapped my head up and the book shut.

"Pizza or Greek for lunch?" Grandpa asked from the doorway.

"Um. Pizza, I guess. No mushrooms."

"No mushrooms," he repeated. "You finding anything worth keeping?"

"Maybe," I said, my face making the world's most awkward smile.

"Great. I'm going to go order the pizza."

Grandpa left, and I swallowed, wondering if this diary was rightly his. He was Grandma Anna's son, but she did leave me (and my brother and cousin) all of her books. Then again, this wasn't an ordinary book. I don't have a diary, but if I did, I wouldn't want *anybody* reading it. Even if I was dead, though? Even if my great-granddaughter had a pressing reason to learn about my past? I don't know. I *do* know that I wouldn't want my grandkids fighting over it like money-hungry monsters.

I obviously needed more time to figure this out. I wasn't going to tell anybody just yet. Unfortunately, that meant I wouldn't be able to look at it until I was back home, away from people who might barge in at any moment and ask what I was reading. For now, I was going to keep this secret between Great-Grandma Anna and me.

CHAPTER 6

Okay, for now I'm going to keep this secret between Great-Grandma Anna, me . . . and Madeline.

It was so hard to keep the diary hidden from my family, but I had no choice. I initially brought it with me in the car, but there was no way to even take it out without everyone seeing and getting curious, so I transferred it to my bag in the trunk when we stopped at a rest stop in New Jersey. By the time we got home, I was dying to get back to it. Madeline texted when she saw our car pass her house, asking if I could hang out. I wanted to see her, but I couldn't wait another second to look at the diary again, and I was itching to share this discovery with someone anyway. So I brought it with me.

In her basement, Madeline turned the diary over in her hands and gingerly flipped through the pages. She said, "This is so. Freaking. Awesome."

"I know, right?"

"What do you think this language is?"

"I don't know, but she translated it into English as an adult," I said. "See how the dates are the same on all those entries, and then she put a new date underneath? I think that *t* means 'translated.'"

"Look at her handwriting," Madeline said. "It's like the sample handwriting in cursive books."

"Seriously. This is the first time I'm actually glad I can read cursive."

Madeline started reading the first English page. I watched as her eyes ran across the page and zigzagged back down, reading the words that my great-grandmother wrote. I had the urge to reach out and snatch the book back. This wasn't Madeline's story to investigate, for the radio or anywhere. I didn't even know if it was rightly mine.

"Did you know that your great-grandma was a twin?" Madeline asked.

I didn't. I wondered if my mom knew, or even Grandpa Fred.

"I wonder what happened to her family," Madeline said. "All those siblings she left behind. Can you imagine growing up somewhere, not knowing what happened to your family? Your twin? Your *parents?* You'd probably be always wondering, forever."

I looked at Madeline, waiting for it to sink in. That I could imagine it, very well. That she was right: You'd always be wondering, forever. Maybe I did have a right to this story after all.

I saw Madeline get it, an invisible lightbulb dinging on above her head. She handed the diary back to me. But what was I going to do? Make my best friend sit there and watch me read? I opened the diary and held it between us so we could both read together.

Dear Belle,

I am aboard a ship called the S.S. Mouzinho.
It is a big and fat thing that by the strange beauty
of science can float. You are at home I suppose,
with a whole bed to yourself now. You are the only
12-year-old in our family. I am jealous. Yet you are
jealous of me, I know. I wish we could be jealous
together.

Everything happened so quickly, I still cannot
understand it. Twins are not meant to be apart. We
are, and it is done for now, but I can barely add
2 and 2 without you beside me, reading my mind
and telling your own. That's why I'm addressing
this journal to you. Paper and ink are no substitute
for my twin sister, of course, but until you follow
me to this new life, what choice do I have? I
cannot mail these letters, not with the war and the
censors. But addressing them to you, pretending
I am telling you everything as we lay side by side
in our bed . . . it's the only way for me to try and
make sense of it all.

Just two weeks ago you were sitting on the

floor of our room with your legs stretched out long as you painted your toenails red. (Ever since the occupation, we've had little bread and only powdered milk and that horrid black soap, but you, Belle, have enough polish to make your nails a different color every day until the Germans surrender.) I was standing in our doorway watching the adults have one of their late-night conversations. I am imagining them now, hunched over the table, rubbing their temples and whispering in Yiddish. I can still smell that odd combination of grass and herbs Grandfather has been putting in his pipe since the tobacco ran out. I was straining to hear them but could make out few words. (What they wanted, of course. Speaking in Yiddish means their words are not meant for "die kinder.") No matter, we both knew what they were discussing . . . the war, the Nazis, our miserable life in occupation. How the Nazis were taking apart the Great Synagogue stone by stone. How we needed to get out. It is all they've talked of for months, ever since Rabbi Serebrenik was attacked and not even Papa and his rosy glasses could ignore what was happening.

Do you remember what I said to you that night,

just two weeks ago? I said, "Where do you think we will go?"

You guessed France, to Mama's family. I said, "It's even worse there," and you said, "Belgium, then." But we both knew Belgium wasn't safe either.

Then Oliver came into our room. He was wearing his pajamas . . . the ones that were once Greta's, pale blue with dots of pink hearts . . . and dragging his bear along by one paw. He knew where we were going . . . America.

Maybe Oliver could hear better from his and Kurt's room, but he can't know more Yiddish than we do. He was likely just being Oliver . . . picking up on all the small clues the rest of us missed. I had no doubt he was right. Neither did you . . . I could see stars in your eyes. You said, "I hope we go to Georgia, like in 'Gone with the Wind.' Or Hollywood! That's even better, because that's where they made 'Gone with the Wind.'" You said (remember?), "Golly Anna, we could be discovered!"

I get a stone in my throat now, to think of it, my movie star sister.

You said, "We must practice our English!" very slowly, in English.

Is this why Papa has always spent the money on our English lessons, a language so useless in Luxembourg, except at his university? Why we kept up the lessons even in secret, after the Nazis insisted on nothing but German? Was he preparing us for America all this time? Is this why I was sent away, because I take more naturally to languages? You must practice, Belle. No one knows Luxembourgish outside of home, and you will not be able to use your beloved French in America. You must teach Oliver too. It should be an easy task. Our clever Oliver can likely learn to pass for an American in a few short weeks.

We talked a bit about America that night, the three of us. When Oliver gave a big yawn I noticed the time, 10:30, so late. I took his hand and began to walk him down the hall. That's when I heard Mama say "Anna." Looking back now, it was the very first sign of what was to come. Papa cut in, hissing in Yiddish, so fast and fiery his words were like steam from a kettle. The only thing I could make out was "Belle."

Oliver pulled on my sleeve, his face a portrait of worry. I held him close and touched the soft curls of his hair. I did not want him to be scared. The adults kept arguing, talking over each other, as we tiptoed to the boys' room. Kurt was spread all over his bed, fast asleep. Oliver climbed into his own bed and snuggled with Bier on his pillow. I pulled the old blanket up to his nose and tucked the sides under his small body (I hope you remember, since I am not there, that he likes to be wrapped tight like a bug) and kissed him good-night.

I was back in the hall when I saw your head out of our door. You were listening to the adults and put a finger to your lips. Mama and Grandmother were still talking, but very softly now . . . calm. All I knew then was that their argument was settled.

I heard Mama say "Anna" again. Then "Anna un Kurt."

Believe me, Belle, at that time I did not know the question, but I knew the answer was Kurt . . . and me.

CHAPTER 7

When I finished the page, I glanced at Madeline to gauge her reaction and make sure she wanted to keep going. She didn't even notice me looking at her, she was so sucked in to the story. Good, because I definitely wanted to keep reading. I wanted to know what Anna's parents and grandparents were whispering about in Yiddish, what secrets they were keeping from their children and grandchildren. It made me think of my own parents and the big secrets about my past that they're keeping from me. They don't stay up late having conversations in a language I can't understand—as far as I know, anyway—but they are keeping information from me. Things I'm dying to know but can't find the courage to ask.

"You ready?" Madeline asked.

"Huh?"

"Can I turn the page?"

"Oh. Yeah," I said. "I want to see what happens."

24 August 1941
t. July 1950

Dear Belle,

The sea is rough today . . . many people have taken ill. My stomach is as rolling as the water out my tiny window. ("Porthole," I am told it is called.) Am I so ill from the sea or from missing home? I cannot say. I cannot stop thinking about my last days at home. I did not appreciate it enough, and you and I barely talked . . . forgive me, I was just so worried about the future.

After I heard Mama say my name that night (with Kurt's), you fell asleep right away but I did not. I could not fathom what was to happen to me and Kurt alone. Everything we do, we do as a family . . . so much, it's often embarrassing. Everyone came to watch me in the school science contest, even Grandfather and Grandmother. The 9 of us took up the whole front row at your ballet performance. Remember, before the Germans came, when we would go to the symphony? All of us except the baby, in our finest clothes. Mama will not even allow us to go to the Luxembourg Fair with our friends, we have to attend as a family instead. I blush even now to think of it . . . 10 people, 2 of them identical, 2 of them elderly, walking as a group through the Schueberfouer. We might as well be on display in one of the tents. With all this togetherness, what could Mama possibly mean by just "Anna un Kurt"?

I close my eyes now and imagine us there in bed that night. One of your feet was sticking out the bottom of the blanket. I could see the fresh red paint on your toenails despite the darkness. You sighed in your sleep and a pleasant feeling washed over me . . . you must have been having a nice dream.

This I will miss the most, Belle . . . the way we connect as twins in our sleep. It is as though our deepest minds are connected by an invisible yarn, the way we used to tie string between paper cups and whisper secret messages. With an ocean between us, will we still have the same dreams? Will we still wake in the middle of the night, trembling from a shared nightmare?

I do hope so. That string is all we have until the rest of you join me for a happy, safe life in America and all 10 of us once again do everything the way we're meant to. As a family.

I must stop here for a moment. I am becoming sick.

Dear Belle,

I spent most of yesterday terrifically ill. I was
not alone in the infirmary . . . many people were
in horrid condition due to the waves. At home,
the nice part of being ill was staying home from
school and having Mama all to yourself. And the
little treat Papa used to pick up on his way home
from the university "for the patient" . . . remember
when we both had chicken pox and Papa brought
us dolls with red spots on them? How sad and
lonely it is to be sick by yourself.

That night in our bed, the night of "Anna un
Kurt" . . . you with your happy dream . . . believe
me when I say that was my last happy night. I
woke up before you (as usual), and I never gave
you a full account of what happened that morning.
Oh Belle, it was dreadful. I went downstairs in my
nightgown and saw Mama looking weary. Papa
was home (no work to be found that day, again)
and said he needed to talk to me and Kurt. I said,
"Should I wake Belle too?" and Mama had a big
sob, and Papa rubbed her back and said, "Just

Kurt for now. Let Belle sleep." That's when I knew for sure it was about the argument . . . just Anna un Kurt . . . for what do you and I do apart?

Grandmother pulled the little ones out the door. (Of course Greta insisted she was <u>not</u> a little one and she should stay, but Grandmother gave her her sternest look, and they all left.) Nervous, I tapped on Kurt's door until he stirred, and we all (Mama, Papa, and I) went into his room. I sat at the desk, Papa leaned against the bureau, and Mama sat at the edge of the bed, where Kurt was still lying down, his hair a sight and a pillow line running down his cheek. You were still down the hall in our bed, sleeping peacefully. (The only time I can think that we met like this, without the whole family, was planning Mama's birthday surprise a few years ago. Remember how we giggled then, with the excitement of a secret? How different this was . . . even the air felt weighty.)

I understand your anger at being excluded. I thought you were furious at hearing the information after us, but now that I've been mulling it all these days, I realize that you felt lied to. You think Mama and Papa didn't give you all the information . . . that they gave more explanation about their decision to me and Kurt that morning, keeping you in the dark. But Belle, it's not true! I know only as much as you, and if I could change places with you then and most certainly now, I would in an instant!

Here is a record of our secret meeting, and you must believe this is everything.

The first thing Papa said was, "Luxembourg is no longer safe for Jews." (I already knew that plain, of course, but to hear it from <u>Papa</u>? Papa, who is filled with endless faith in good things . . . he never even takes an umbrella, he is so hopeful about nature!) Papa said he and Mama had secured papers for us to move to America. He said our cousins Max and Hannah Schoelstein will sponsor us.

I got excited (this seemed like good news) but Kurt said, "Max and Hannah? Who are they?"

Something odd happened then, Belle . . . I think Papa caught Mama's eye before answering. It was a strange look, but so quick I couldn't decipher it. I cannot say, even now, and there is no one here to help me analyze it. But it makes me anxious . . . these are the people I will live with until the rest of you arrive. Mama and Papa could not share much about them. Here is everything they said they know. (You know all of this already, but I am writing it here anyway, for I wish we were here together, reciting these facts in preparation for meeting them together.)

- Max is Papa's second cousin. They played together when they were children.

- Max moved to America long ago, before any of us were born.

- Mama and Papa have never met Max's wife, Hannah. They only remember her name from a wedding announcement years ago.

- Papa found their address and wrote to them about our situation. They were willing to sponsor us. (That must be good, yes?)

- They live in New York, in a place called Brooklyn. (I know your disappointment at this . . . not Georgia or Hollywood . . . Could there be even a trace of glamour in a place called <u>Brooklyn</u>?)

After learning this, I said, "But this is all good news. Why is Mama so sad? Why can't we tell Belle?"

So Papa talked about how difficult it is to

get out of Europe now, even with papers and sponsorship. It is not impossible, he said, but it is very dangerous. Mama added (of course) that it is expensive. The papers . . . the train to Lisbon . . . the boat to New York . . . She also said what she always says when discussing something expensive: "There are a lot of us."

I remember that Papa moved from the bureau and took my hand in his. His palm was warm and wet. He said, "We have been saving money. Grandmother and Grandfather too. But now that Rabbi Serebrenik is himself in America, there is only one man who is willing to take Jews along that route to Portugal, and his price is very sharp. More than a year's salary for each person, and as you know, I have not had a consistent salary in some time."

Mama said, "We think it's best to get some of our family out now, before things become worse. The rest of us will follow when we have saved more money."

"How many will go now?" Kurt asked. He was sitting up now, with his pillow propped against the wall.

Here, Papa closed his eyes for a long time. When he opened them again, they were fixed on the desk. He answered, "Two."

Kurt could not believe it (nor I). He said, "Two! Only two?"

Mama said, "Right <u>now</u>. The rest will follow," and Kurt asked, "So, who?"

It seems so obvious when I write it now, how the discussion went. Surely, I should have realized before this moment who was going. But I'm telling you truthfully, Belle, I did not know it until right then . . . about half of one second before Papa spoke it aloud.

"You two," he said.

Oh Belle, I was in terrific shock! The unfairness of it all. Why did any of us have to go at all? Why not you? Why not <u>us</u>, together? I felt so lonely then, Belle, without you in the room.

Kurt could not believe it. He said surely an adult would go.

Oh, Belle, if you could have seen Mama's face. It broke my heart in two, and then the pieces dropped down into my belly . . . plonk, plonk, like stones into water. Mama was in terrific pain as she said, "We can only afford to send two right now. We decided to send the two eldest children."

How absurd! I'm older than you by 9 minutes! How can 9 minutes determine that I must leave behind everything and everyone who matters, while you must stay?

Trying to sound resolute, I said, "Let someone else go in my place. I'll stay and help with the little ones."

Kurt said, "I don't want to go either. I'll wait until we can afford to go together."

I said, "Yes, I'll wait too, at least for Belle."

Mama looked as if we'd convinced her . . . as if this was all she needed to change her mind and let us stay! But Papa was firm. "We've made a decision. You two will go now, and the rest of us will follow as soon as we can."

I cried, "But I don't <u>want</u> to go!"

Now Papa was becoming angry, and you know what that means. He banged his fist on the desk, and his voice became quiet but hard. "Do you think Mama and I made this decision lightly? Do you think we want to split up our family? Do you think we want to send two of our children away? Do you think we want to leave anyone here to face Hitler?"

That's when you opened the door and said, "What's happening?" How can I describe my flood of feelings at that moment? Anger, fear, and . . .

guilt to be caught having this conversation without you. I suppose it was the first of many, many (how many?) things I will have to do without you until you arrive. (I can hear you protest that you must do everything without <u>me</u> too. But you are not alone, Belle. Not like I am.)

You know the rest, of course. And you now know that what Mama and Papa told you is really the same as what they said before you arrived, about why they chose who they chose. But it wasn't until you asked (through your rage, through your tears) when we would be leaving that Papa began to blink away tears himself.

He said, "Tomorrow night."

CHAPTER 8

The room went dark. I screamed and grabbed Madeline's arm. The lights flicked back on, and I heard laughter from the top of the stairs.

"Henry!" Madeline shouted. "Knock it off!"

I exhaled and released my grip on Madeline, relieved it was just her brother playing with the lights. My heartbeat was still fast, though. It had sped up when I'd learned the meaning of "Anna un Kurt."

Henry flicked the lights again. "I didn't even know you guys were down there," Henry said from the top of the steps. "You're so quiet. What are you even doing?"

"None of your business," Madeline called.

I heard the stairs creak, because of course Henry now had to make it his business.

"What are you doing?" he asked again. His blond

hair was all wild, like he'd been experimenting with electricity.

"Nothing," Madeline said.

Her little brother stared at us for a second, then walked over to the TV and turned it on.

Now it was Madeline's turn to say, "What are you doing?"

"Playing Xbox," he replied.

"No you're not," Madeline said. "We're down here."

"But you're not doing anything," Henry said, all fake innocence. He grabbed a controller and squeezed between Madeline and the arm of the sofa, even though there were tons of other places to sit. I took the diary from her and marked the page with the green ribbon. Then I held it to my chest protectively.

"Dad!" Madeline called.

The video game started, and Henry turned the volume up really loud.

"Dad!" Madeline shouted again.

No response. Madeline stood up from the couch—making sure to squish Henry as she did—and pounded up the stairs. I stuck my tongue out at him and followed.

"We were down there," she was telling her dad in the kitchen, "and Henry just barged in and started playing Xbox."

"Well, what were you two doing? Hello, Imani."

"Hi," I said.

Madeline glanced at me.

"Reading," I told Mr. Winter.

"Reading?" He almost laughed. "You can do that somewhere else, can't you?"

"But Dad—"

"The Xbox is only in the basement," he said. "But last I checked, a book can go anywhere."

Madeline gave the biggest eye roll I've ever seen. "Dad."

Video game sounds wafted from the basement. Henry shouted, "Yes!"

"What are you reading?" Mr. Winter asked casually.

"Nothing," Madeline snapped.

I put the diary behind my back. "Come on," I said. "Let's go to your room."

"This is so unfair," she grumbled. "You always take his side."

"Yes," Mr. Winter deadpanned. "Because Henry's my favorite child."

"Ha-ha," Madeline said as she stomped down the hall. I stomped too, in solidarity. Their eco-friendly bamboo floors were great for stomping. Nice and loud, but still soft on your feet.

Once in her room, Madeline slammed the door behind us, and I gave her some time to calm down.

"Sorry," she said finally.

I shook my head. "Whatever. Henry started it. And parents shouldn't joke about having favorites."

"I *know*, right?" She sighed and collapsed onto her bed. I sat down at the edge of the mattress and pulled the diary out from behind my back. "Keep reading?"

27 August 1941
t. July 1950

My dearest Belle,

Two more days have passed here on the Mouzinho,
though it is difficult to keep track. I have been
sleeping-sleeping-sleeping, all night and for long
stretches during the day as well. Is this what it is
like to be you in the morning? Sleeping so late, not
hearing Mina's squeals or Greta's loud voice or
Oliver pulling that silly toy duck along the floor? I
never understood how you could sleep so heavily,
but now, Belle, on this boat, we could be attacked
by pirates and I wouldn't wake! My sleep is so deep,
I have not had a single dream. This saddens me too,
for it is in dreams that our connection is strongest.

I can't stop thinking about what you said on my
last night at home. I didn't have the right words
to say to you then. It was all such a shock, and so
rushed. And you were so huffy, refusing to help
with the preparations. (Not that there was much to
prepare. I could bring so little . . . why, it took less
time than packing for a week in France!)

I was not trying to be aloof, Belle. I wanted
desperately to talk together all day, but how do

you begin when there is too much to say, and none of it will make one ounce of difference? Then bedtime . . . the two of us lying next to each other in heavy silence. Oh, the thoughts that were in my head. I was thinking many of the same things I continue to think every moment of the day now: How long will it take to save the money for the rest of you? What might happen in Luxembourg before Mama and Papa are able to save enough? I was also thinking: Why Kurt and me, truly?

Why? Yes, it sounds diplomatic that the two oldest would go first. But if it were so simple, there wouldn't have been an argument the night before. There is a reason they chose to get rid of Kurt and me. Here is my best explanation:

- They cannot send Mina or Oliver without one of us to take care of them.

- Papa's favorite is Greta (that is plain), so he wants to keep her.

- YOU are Mama's favorite. (Don't argue. You know it's true.)

- Kurt and I are the most withdrawn. If only I had been more helpful around the house . . . more willing to spend my afternoons playing with Oliver and Mina instead of trying to escape for moments of solitude . . . Maybe Mama and Papa believe I <u>wanted</u> to leave.

Kurt . . . did they want to send Kurt because he'd been trying to break away too? Since he started high school, he's turned inward . . . staying late at track and field, sleeping like the dead, ignoring his chores and us all. Do you remember when we were little, how we were close friends . . . you and Kurt and me? How we'd spend hours playing our favorite game, Super Hirsch? I smile to think of it . . . two of us would pretend to be starving, or crushed by an automobile, or hanging from a cliff, on the edge of death until . . . Super Hirsch to the rescue! Remember how we fought over who would get to be Super Hirsch? We hated taking turns because we all wanted to be the hero. How long ago that seems. Lately you and I joke that Kurt is becoming a machine . . . all muscle, no brains or heart. I feel a bit guilty about it now, because clearly it is not true. What happened with the passeur . . . either Kurt is a coward, or else (and this is the truth, I believe) he has more heart than we ever knew.

All of this was running through my mind that

night, Belle, and has not gone away. That I am the twin they no longer want.

I am still shocked to think that you believe the opposite, that since it is so dangerous at home, Mama and Papa were sending their two favorite children to America, to survive. You said . . . and it hurts me to remember or write it down . . . you said, "It's okay. I understand. What's the point in saving me? I'm not as smart as you. My future's not as promising. What would be the point of saving my life?" Your voice cracked as you spoke, the way my heart cracks to remember. You said, "It's not such a shame if I don't make it."

Dear sister, how could you <u>think</u> such a thing?

What did I say then? Nothing adequate. How I wish I knew the right thing to say at that moment. But I do now, and here it is: It's simply not true. You'd do <u>better</u> on your own. You'd view this journey as an adventure, not a nightmare. You're better at making friends, people like you more, you're so charming . . .

Oh, Belle, what a case of "l'esprit d'escalier," or in this case, not staircase wit but ship-across-the-ocean wit, for I finally know the <u>perfect</u> thing I could have said to make us both feel better. When you said it is not a big deal if you don't survive the war, I should have quipped, "It is <u>not</u> about our potential in life. After all, they are sending Kurt."

Of course it's not true, but think how we would have laughed! So full, we'd shake the mattress. Maybe then we would have done more talking, less lying in silence. Perhaps we could have planned one of those twin tricks you were always begging me to try. But we didn't plan or laugh or even talk. We were still silent when Oliver appeared in our room . . . his cheeks were so wet, and his hand was gripping Bier so hard I'm surprised the stuffing didn't pop out. You put on a good face and told him, "Anna's going to find movie producers, so I can become an actress when we get to America."

You are certainly the better actress. When I told Oliver he'd be on the boat right after mine, he only began crying harder. I'll always remember how lovely it was when Oliver got in bed with us, though. I tucked the sheet under him, so that the three of us were packed tight, a triple cocoon. That was a nice way to spend our last night together in Luxembourg . . . the best way, really.

Until tomorrow,
Anna

28 August 1941
t. July 1950

Belle,

Do you remember, that awful night, when Kurt
asked Papa if we could trust the passeur, and Papa
merely said he hoped so? Despite the nasty change
the passeur pulled at first, I now know the answer
to Kurt's question is yes. I can take comfort in that,
at least, as I think of you making the journey soon.
It is dangerous, yes, and scary, with lies and fake
papers and blind trust in strangers. But it seems I
was fortunate to get here as quickly and smoothly
as I did, and with cars and trains . . . some people
aboard the Mouzinho crossed the Pyrenees
mountains on foot! (I daren't record any details
beyond that. There are so many pieces and people
at risk, and I worry about this journal falling into
the wrong hands . . . some speak of German spies
even here, on the boat. That's why I am writing in
Luxembourgish . . . safer than French.)

Was your heart racing as the clock neared 8 that
day? My body trembled all through my goodbyes.
Oh, Belle, my goodbyes . . . they were terrifically
inadequate. Grandfather wrapped me in his bony

arms. His thin lips kissed the side of my head, and my nose was buried in the collar of his shirt, which smelled like his pipe. Grandmother . . . never one for kisses or emotion, as you well know . . . she clasped my hand with hers. Her skin was smooth but her grip was firm, and her hand was trembling. Oh, I was so anxious to get the difficult part over, I didn't linger long enough! I should have realized that I will never see them again. I am certain of it now. Grandfather's too frail to make this journey, and Grandmother wouldn't leave without him. Could Papa bear to leave them, do you think, if it comes to that? What a horrid situation to be in, choosing to abandon one's children or one's parents. . . .

Papa came while I was taking one last look at our room. He wrapped me in his arms and pressed his lips into my cheek. If only I could freeze that moment and stay in it until this war is over.

I whispered into Papa's ear, my voice breaking, "Can't I just stay here?" and I felt his throat go up and down as he swallowed. Then he moved his hands to my head and held it arms' length from his own. He said, "Be brave, Anna. You're going to be brilliant."

I tried to be brave. I said, "I'll see you soon," and he smiled sadly, forcing his chin up. "Very soon," he promised.

The 7 of us stepped out the front door and onto the dark sidewalk. I held Oliver's hand tightly. I wanted to walk close to you too, to link our arms together until we meet again, but Mama wouldn't allow it, since twins are too likely to draw attention. You were carrying Mina, a bit behind . . . I listened as you sang softly to keep her content.

I tried to commit to memory the street as we walked . . . so many shops and sights I'd seen every day and might never pass again. The bakery, where we'd treat ourselves to a pain au chocolat for breakfast before school. The button store, where I once spent 20 minutes searching the small baskets for a button to replace the one that had popped off my jacket, only to finally ask the shopkeeper and have him find an exact match right away. The narrow alleyway where Kurt and his friends used to play soccer, "no sisters allowed" . . .

At last we found the man with a long coat and brown hat. He nodded at Mama, and she stepped close to him and spoke quietly. My blood coursed with anger seeing him for the first time. How dare he separate our family with his steep fee?

You stepped close to me then and threaded your arm through mine. Your gaze was straight ahead, but I could feel your blood racing as quickly as mine.

Do you remember what he said? His brisk voice . . . so serious. He said, "Who, then?"

Mama said, "Two. Kurt and Anna."

You were the brave one, Belle . . . it was you who unlaced my arm from yours and gently pushed me forward. Oliver was still clutching my hand. I tried to catch Kurt's eye, but he was staring straight at the man, his face stoic.

Mama handed the man a paper bag with the top folded over. She took Mina from your arms and spoke to the passeur very strongly. I am so proud of how she spoke . . . very sure and direct. She said, "I have six children, and our family in New York is willing to sponsor them all. Please, would you consider taking more?"

But the man opened the paper bag and counted the money. He shook his head, and my stomach knotted. The passeur said, "This won't even cover two."

Mama whispered loudly for him to count it again. She said, "I'm sure it's correct. Enough for two."

"Things have changed," the man replied. "The Gestapo found Jewish children hiding on the train last week. They deported them. Killed the man helping them cross. A friend of mine." The passeur looked down for a moment here, paused.

I realized then (and know so much now) that even though he was taking advantage of our situation, charging such a steep fee, he was risking his own life too. Even so, and even after all he did for me, what happened next broke my heart.

He looked up and all signs of weakness were gone. "My fee has doubled," he said firmly. "This will only be enough for one."

I gasp now, again, as I write it. How stunned we all were, how upset. How he put a finger to his lips and stepped closer to the wall, out of view. How he spat, "One. Quickly. Or no one."

How Kurt said, "Anna will go."

I tried to protest . . . did I try hard enough? I was stiff from fear. Kurt was insistent. He took a step to me, gave me a hug and a kiss on the forehead.

I remember Mama . . . holding Mina close, to calm her and muffle her cries. When she lifted her head, her eyes were wet but resolute. "Anna," she said.

And so it was settled.

My goodbyes were a haze. I know I kissed everyone, exchanged words of love. I think Greta was crying. I know you held me the longest. I know Oliver gave me his Bier to take along. It all went too quickly. I was in such shock, I don't think I even cried.

But here I am now, safe on the boat. Recording the story, all alone. If only you were here with me, Belle. Then you would know how my tears are coming, so many that the ocean is nothing but a wet, blue blur.

Missing you with all my heart,
Anna

CHAPTER 9

I read those last words slowly, on the verge of tears myself. (Maybe I'm not so cold-hearted after all.) When Madeline finished the entry, she took a big breath and raised her head. Her face was dazed, and she was squinting and blinking, like she'd just come out of a dark movie theater. In fact, it was the opposite. When we'd moved to her room it was light out, but we'd been reading so long that it was now dark. It was silent too. Either Henry had turned the Xbox volume down or he'd stopped playing long ago. That whole argument felt like the distant past, and 1941 felt like the present. Weird.

The two of us looked at each other and breathed out deeply, so in unison that it made us laugh. Madeline went to turn on the light, and I rubbed my eyes.

"Wow," Madeline said, propping herself on a pillow next to me.

"Double wow," I said.

"It's weird," Madeline said. "Whenever we learn about the Holocaust—"

"Which is every year."

"Every year in Hebrew school and in regular school, so really twice a year. I guess they do say that some people left before being put in concentration camps. But I never thought of it like this."

"I never thought about it at all," I admitted. I especially never thought that one of those people was in my family. That this story was somehow part of my history. Even if that history is adopted.

So in a way, Anna *was* about to be adopted. She was twelve—the age I am *right now*—and crossing an ocean all by herself. Leaving behind her parents and grandparents and a twin sister. And Oliver. Little Oliver—my great-great-uncle—who she clearly loved so much.

I wonder if Oliver made Madeline think of Henry. I know he made me think of Jaime. I've always taken for granted that he'll grow up alongside me. We kind of used to be like Anna and Oliver. My parents have a photo on their bedroom wall: I'm seven, and Jaime's four, and we're next to each other with a glowing menorah in the background. There are six candles lit, so it must have been the sixth night of Chanukah. I know that I was seven, because in the picture my hair is in two puffy ponytails on the top of my head—the way I wore it almost every single day until third grade—and I'm holding up a box with a set of earrings, which meant the very next day, my mom would take me to get my ears pierced. And Jaime is wearing footie pajamas and grinning with gritted teeth, holding a toy fire truck above his head like a winner's trophy. Thinking of the picture made me smile. I forgot how much Jaime had been obsessed with fire trucks when he was little.

"Maybe I'll do my research project on people who left before being put in concentration camps," Madeline said. "With lies and fake papers and crossing the mountains on foot. I wonder if Mrs. Coleman would let me do that instead of Kristallnacht."

"That'd be really cool. Maybe I should switch mine to being about Luxembourg."

Madeline gasped, her public radio dreams ignited. "Imani! You could find Anna's old house! You could find out what happened to her family!"

"I'm hoping the answer to that is in here," I said, tapping the cover of the journal. We both looked at it for a few seconds, wondering what other secrets it held. Then my mind flicked to the way that I was keeping this whole thing a secret from the rest of my family. It made me feel uneasy.

To be fair, though, aren't *they* also keeping secrets about *my* past from me?

My phone buzzed. Neither of us needed to look to know it was my mom, telling me to come home for dinner. I sat up and reached for my sneakers.

"I know it's not really fair to ask," Madeline said, shifting in her spot on her bed, "but can you wait for me to read more? We can hang out after school tomorrow. I really want to know what happens next."

"I'll try," I said, knotting my laces. "But no guarantees."

CHAPTER 10

When I got home, the house smelled warm and spicy. Mom must have made chili.

"How's Madeline?" she called, but her voice wasn't coming from the kitchen, and it sounded kind of muffled.

"Good," I called back, looking around for her. I finally found her in the living room, crouched under the desk. "What are you doing?" I asked.

She stuck her head out and smiled at me. I stuck the diary behind my back.

"Filing," she replied, holding up a pile of papers.

"Oh," I said. I always put my feet on the filing cabinet when I'm using the computer. I'd never thought about it serving another purpose. But . . . "What are you filing?"

"Just some paperwork about Grandma Anna's

estate. You know, boring adult stuff." She and the papers disappeared back under the desk.

Paperwork about Grandma Anna's estate. Could that include Grandma Anna's adoption papers, the ones I'd hoped to find on her bookshelves? What other paperwork might be in that filing cabinet? *My* adoption records? If I found those, I could get the answers I was looking for without having to upset my parents at all. What's that thing people say? What you don't know can't hurt you.

"We're going to eat once I finish this," Mom said, her head still buried. "Why don't you go wash up."

Would my parents keep my adoption papers here, in our own family room? My legs were suddenly tingly, like I was preparing for a tennis match. I was going to look in that filing cabinet later. The answers I'd been craving might have been here all along, filed in my large metal footrest.

But before I searched for secrets they were keeping from me, I had an important one to hide from them: the diary. I took the stairs two at a time up to my room, then scanned it for a place to hide the journal. Maybe I could hide it in plain sight. (Kind of like putting my adoption paperwork in the family room filing cabinet. . . .) I stuck the diary in the middle of the stack of books on my nightstand, then stepped back and cocked my head. Too risky.

"Dinner!" my mom shouted.

I looked at my open closet. A row of shoeboxes lined the top. Perfect.

I rolled my desk chair over and took one down. The top was dusty, but I knew the journal would be safe inside. I stuck it in, slid the box under my bed, and stood up just in time for a loud knock on my bedroom door. I brushed the dust from my hands before turning the knob.

"Dinner," Jaime said.

"Thanks," I said, fighting this crazy urge to give him a bear hug. "I'll be right there."

I've often wondered if Jaime wants to know about his birth family as badly as I want to know about mine. Or what my life would be like without him; like, if he'd been adopted by a different family, or still lived with his birth parents in Guatemala. A few times, when I've been *really* mad at him, I've even wished my parents hadn't adopted him. But right now, watching his black hair and stocky body bounce down the steps on the way to eat chili with Mom and Dad, I'd have dared anyone to say he isn't really my brother.

No matter what I found in that filing cabinet— and I was going to find something, I just *knew* it— my brother and I would still be family.

CHAPTER 11

The stars aligned shortly after dinner. Dad and Jaime went outside to play catch, and Mom went up to her room for a bath. If I was serious about checking that filing cabinet, I had to do it now.

I went to the family room and crawled under the desk. I took a deep breath, gave myself a silent pep talk, wrapped my hand around the handle, and pulled. It wouldn't budge. I pulled it three more times, each progressively harder, before I finally realized, like an idiot, that it was locked. My heart started pounding. Maybe my adoption paperwork really *was* in here. Why else would this filing cabinet be locked?

What's more, I knew where the key had to be. I'd seen Mom put something away before dinner, something that went in a place with other keys. I glanced out the window again—Dad and Jaime were absorbed in their game—then walked to the kitchen and opened the spice cabinet. There, to the left of the basil and tarragon, was an old jelly jar with keys in it. It had spare keys to both cars, the key to Jaime's bike lock, the key to our neighbor's house that I used to feed their cat when they went away, and—now in my hand—the key to the filing cabinet.

As I walked back to the computer, my armpits started to sweat like they do at tennis matches, usually before my first serve. Was I really going to do this? Was I really going to snoop around my own house like some white-collar criminal? Then again, it is my own house, right? And I was doing it to spare my parents the pain of talking about my adoption openly. If you thought about it that way, I was, as Grandpa Fred would say, doing a mitzvah.

The key fit in the lock perfectly, and it turned with a definitive click. I pulled the handle again, and this time the door slid open, smooth and silent. The drawer was heavy with papers; I don't know how the cabinet could withstand the weight of what was inside. Squinting through the darkness under the desk and the messiness of my dad's handwriting on the labels, I skimmed the row of folders. Mortgage payments, health insurance, property taxes . . . Mom wasn't lying when she said it was full of boring adult stuff. Toward the back, though, the folders began to be more relevant. One said I & J—COLLEGE FUND, and another I & J—MEDICAL. I pulled out a stack from the very back and saw words that made the sweat spread to my hairline. IMANI—ADOPTION.

This is it, I thought. *Do I really want to know what's in here?*

The answer was apparently yes, because I pulled out the folder. But the answer was also, apparently, no, because I was relieved to find it was empty. Totally empty. Not one form or photocopy or note. I saw that there wasn't even an adoption folder for Jaime. At some point, my parents either threw everything away or decided this paperwork did not belong in our living room, locked or not.

I heard the door open. I jumped, hitting my head on the bottom of the desk.

"Ice cream truck!" Jaime announced. "I'm getting Dad's wallet."

I bolted from under the desk and sat in the chair. My head was throbbing, but I resisted rubbing it.

Jaime came running into the family room. "Come out and get something," he said breathlessly. "The ice cream man said this is his last time around until next summer."

"Um," I said. "I'm okay."

Jaime paused for a second, suspicious, but then shrugged and ran back outside. The ice cream truck music got louder and then softer as he opened and closed the front door.

I let out my breath and rubbed my head. My armpits were soaked. I dove back under the desk and stuffed the folders in the cabinet, then slid the drawer closed and locked it. I raced to the kitchen and returned the key to the spice cabinet. Then, not knowing what else to do, I ran up the stairs and into my room. I collapsed on my bed, panting like crazy. I felt like I'd just run suicide sprints up and down the tennis court.

I heard the front door open and close again. "Imani," my dad called. "Come here."

Oh no, I thought as I walked slowly downstairs. Had I left a manila folder on the floor? Had Jaime seen the open filing cabinet and told my dad?

But no. He'd just gotten me some ice cream after all.

"Chipwich," Dad said, holding it out. "Your favorite."

The relief that washed over me was followed instantly by guilt. I was spying on my dad, and he was out buying me ice cream. "Thanks, Dad," I said. "You're the best."

He pulled me toward him and kissed my forehead. He couldn't have cared less about the sweat.

31 August 1941
t. August 1950

Dear Belle,

Today, a roar erupted from the deck, and I went to see the cause. Everyone was hugging and crying and singing . . . and pointing to a speck in the distance. That speck is the Statue of Liberty. Tomorrow we will dock at New York Harbor! The excitement is so rich, it's like a strong wind blowing across the ship, and it's difficult to not be swept away.

I am not the only child traveling without parents. There are some in a group with a chaperone of some sort. If you were here, you would have become friends with them, I'm certain. You wouldn't have stayed so quiet and removed as I have. Every night and much of the day, I lie in my small bed and hug Oliver's bear tightly, like I'm the one who's 4. It still has Oliver's smell on it, so when I put it up to my nose, it's like I'm leaning down to wipe his face or loop the button of his jacket.

Oh Belle, Mama and Papa made the wrong decision, sending me. If only I had been quicker that night, and said Kurt should go. Then Oliver would still have Bier, and I would be with everyone else right now, instead of here, all by myself. What if Hannah and Max are horrid? Or what if they're too sweet, like Aunt Helen and her kisses? Or what if there <u>are</u> no Hannah and Max, and it was all a story Papa invented to send me away? What will I do then?

No matter what is happening in Luxembourg, it can't be worse than being here without any of you. If it were, I'd feel it in my dreams. I imagine the invisible thread that connects us getting longer . . . it's unrolling from a spool as long as the Atlantic Ocean, but connecting us still.

I am feeling better now, and braver about tomorrow. It is due largely to Frida, my one friend on the ship. She is only 7, and her blond hair bounces around her face in wide rings. We don't talk very much (my German is passable enough, so that is only partly the reason), but ever since the first few days, we seek each other out in the dining room and on the deck . . . we simply sit side by side and watch the water. (I know, I know . . . how dull. But you are not here, and it suits us both. So there.)

Frida's father is with her, but she might as well be alone, for he is so withdrawn and sullen. He sends her out of the room every morning to wander the ship alone. Every meal, she spreads a bit of butter on bread (the bread on board is square and white, with hardly any crust . . . odd, but I like the taste), then wraps it in a napkin and brings it back to her father. I saw him only once, when I walked with Frida to her room at night and he was lying across the bed in the dark. The light from the hall let me see that his body was there . . . his eyes were staring at the wall, but his mind was somewhere else. It is probably stuck in Vienna, where they lived. Frida told me that to escape the Nazis, her mother jumped out the window of their 5th-floor apartment, taking Frida's new baby brother with her. Oh Belle, can you imagine? I try to understand the terrific pain that Frida and her father are in, but I cannot even grasp it. I do know that it is worse than my own. A piece of me wants to stew in sadness like Frida's father, but another, stronger piece of me wants to shake his shoulders and throw a glass of cold water on his face.

I admire the way Frida continues on despite her pain . . . despite the way her father has given up. It has given me strength for whatever I face next. Yes, Mama and Papa sent me away, but they sent me away to a safer place, and I am not going to waste it by succumbing to fear and sorrow. I think of Papa, always saying, "Wien A seet, muss och B soen." He would joke that it meant, "If you say Anna, you must also say Belle," but that is no longer true, for here I am without you . . . now it simply means I must keep my promise. I told Papa I would be brave, and so I must. And you know what? I don't want to go home. I want all of you to join me <u>here</u>, in a new place, for a new, happier life without soldiers in the streets and gas masks under our beds and curfews for electricity and Hitler's horrid voice barking from speakers in the square.

Today is our last day, so I will not see Frida again after tomorrow. (She and her father will live in someplace called Chicago.) Tonight we sat together in our favorite place on the deck. The Statue of Liberty keeps getting closer . . . the skyline of Manhattan too. We could see it clearly in the evening sky. Frida had a great idea . . . for us to write to each other in America . . . in English! I copied down her address in the back of this journal, so I'll always have it.

But right before that, an amazing thing happened. You see, this whole journey, Frida's tooth has been loose. When we first met, she could only wiggle it with her fingers, and this morning it was so loose she could wiggle it with only her tongue. And right then, after promising to write to each other, Frida's tooth fell out! Right there on the deck, looking at Lady Liberty! I saw her reach up to her mouth and come out with a bloody little square of white tooth. Our emotions were so high already, this surprise put us over the edge. We both started laughing! The tooth dropped through a hole in the deck, and I exclaimed, "Oh Mamelikanner!" and Frida found that even funnier. Her laughter made me laugh harder. It was the first time I've laughed since I left, and oh did it feel good!

With hope and courage for my new start in New York City,
Anna

CHAPTER 12

Something landed on my arm. I flicked it away without looking, thinking it was a fly. But then something bounced off my face, and that didn't feel like a fly at all. I looked at the table where it landed and saw that it was . . . a piece of a protein bar?

I looked up and saw Parker, giggling, a half-chewed protein bar in her hand. She eats two of those nasty things for lunch, plus a green smoothie. "Finally!" she said between chews. "You two have been absorbed in that book all period."

It was true. Madeline and I had eaten our lunch in record time so we could read more of Anna's diary. I was hesitant to bring it to school, but Madeline begged, and swore nothing would happen to it. I covered it with paper, like we have to do with our textbooks, and then, before lunch, Madeline added a special waterproof cover on top of that. With those two layers, it was pretty safe from crumbs and spills, and—big bonus for keeping it secret—it looked just like any other book.

I'm glad I caved too, because Anna's story was the perfect lunchtime read. At first I thought it'd be hard to focus in the cafeteria, but it was amazing the way the outside noise had turned to static as soon as I started reading about Frida. (Frida! Would she make it to Chicago? If only I had her diary too.)

"What is that, anyway?" Parker asked.

"Yeah, what is it?" asked Magda, who was next to Parker. As usual. I've never seen Parker without Magda except at Hebrew school, seeing as Magda's Catholic. They braid each other's hair, borrow each other's clothes, and finish each other's smoothies when the other is feeling full.

"That book must be really good," Parker continued. "You guys were, like, zombies."

"OMG, is it *about* zombies?" said Magda. "Because then I want to read it too."

Madeline moved her reading glasses to the top of her head. I closed the diary and placed it carefully in the zippered portion of my messenger bag. Then I looked up and completely ignored their questions. "What's up?" I said.

Parker looked like she wanted to press on about

the diary, but Magda gave a playful raise of her shoulder. "So, Imani," she said. "How's Ethan?"

"Who?" Madeline asked.

"Ethan Bloom!" Magda cried.

Parker chewed her protein bar as she spoke. "He's been looking over here all through lunch. He's *so* obsessed with you, Imani."

I risked a quick glance in the direction of Ethan's table. He must've been reaching into his backpack or something, because all I could see was his sandy-colored hair. I don't know what I would've done if he'd been looking—waved? pretended to be looking at someone else?—but I was still kind of disappointed that he wasn't.

"Okay, he's doing something now," Parker said, "but I swear he's been looking over here every thirty seconds, just waiting for you to stop reading so he could come talk to you."

"Or lock eyes across the room," Magda said with a giggle. "There's nothing more romantic than locking eyes across a crowded cafeteria."

"Oh yeah," Madeline said, sarcastic. "Love in the time of tater tots."

I laughed. "That was good."

"Wasn't it? I just came up with it right now."

"Very clever."

"Thank you."

"He's looking again," Parker sang.

I didn't want to look, but how could I help it? Sure enough, Ethan's eyes were on us this time, but he was at the far end of the table next to ours, so if he wasn't reaching into his backpack, where else was he going to look? I summoned my courage to give a small wave. He glanced nervously behind him, then waved back.

"Awww," Magda said, her voice and shoulders going up, like she was meeting a puppy. "You two are so cute."

"Oh my God," Parker said. "Did I tell you he RSVPed yes to my bat mitzvah? You two can dance together!"

"Come on," I said, but my cheeks were totally warm.

Parker sat down opposite me, and Magda sat next to her, her legs straddling the cafeteria bench. "I wish my bat mitzvah was sooner," Parker said.

"I know *I* can't wait," Magda said. "It's going to be the third-best party of my life."

"Third?" Madeline asked.

"After her wedding and her quinceañera," Parker explained between bites of protein. "In whichever order."

Madeline nodded, doing a remarkable job of keeping a straight face. "Got it."

(If I hadn't been adopted, would I have a quincea-ñera instead of a bat mitzvah?)

"When's your B.M., Madeline?" Magda asked.

"Ew, don't say B.M.," said Parker. "It means, like, something else."

Magda giggled. "When is your bat mitzvah?" she asked Madeline again.

"Not till September. But I'm just having a small luncheon after, no party."

"I'm sure it'll be fun anyway," said Parker, ever the diplomat. She finished chewing her lunch and smiled for Magda, who studied her braces for protein particles.

"You're good," Magda told her. "What about you, Imani?"

"June fourteenth," I replied. "But I'm not having a party either. I'm getting a gift instead."

"Ooh, what are you getting?"

"I don't know yet," I said casually. There was no way I was getting into my "exotic" adoption mystery with Parker and Magda.

"You should ask for a big party!" Magda said.

I laughed.

"Her gift isn't for *you*," Madeline said. "Imani's going to ask for something meaningful." She elbowed me gently on this last word. It reminded me of my filing cabinet espionage last night, and my tortellini lunch turned over in my stomach. I felt so bad about what I'd done, I didn't want anyone to know, not even Madeline.

"You should ask for a smartphone, Imani," Parker said. "I need to send you snaps and emojis. You're, like, the only person in the whole seventh grade without one."

That is too true. Even Madeline has her mom's old Android. But my parents are completely overprotective about me being on the internet. I'm the only person I know who has a limit on "screen time," and they only let me join Facebook, like, five months ago, and by then no one was even using Facebook anymore. *No need to put yourself out in the world like that,* my mom likes to say. *Especially not in seventh grade.*

I don't see what the big deal is. Going online is nothing compared to Anna, who had to *really* go out in the world—across the ocean!—by herself, in seventh grade.

"I still think you should ask for a party," said Magda. "Or a date with Ethan Bloom."

"Are we seriously back to that?" Madeline asked with a sigh.

The bell rang right then, so Parker and Magda rushed back to their table to get their bags. Magda gave the top of my arm a squeeze on her way.

"Blah," Madeline said, moving her reading glasses into their case. "I wish they hadn't come over. We barely had time to read anything. My house after school?"

"Tennis," I reminded her.

"Oh yeah." We moved from the cafeteria into the hall, and Madeline had to talk loudly over the noise. "Can you wait to read more together, then?"

"Maybe," I said, but I don't think she heard me. She was walking backward down the hall to social studies, and I was moving backward the other way, to Spanish.

"Hasta la vista!" she called.

"Adios, amiga!" I spun around—and bumped *right* into Ethan. Our heads collided, skull to skull.

He straightened his glasses. "Ouch."

"Sorry!" I rubbed my forehead and hoped that if I was visibly sweaty, he'd think it was because I was in physical pain.

"Watch it, Williams," he said, and I laughed way too hard. He grinned. "What was in that bowl you brought for lunch?"

"Tortellini," I told him. "It's my favorite food."

"Just tortellini, or any cheesy pasta?"

"Tortellini."

"What about ravioli?"

"I'll eat it," I said, "but it's not as good. It's so flat. The pasta-cheese ratio is all off."

"How about lasagna?"

I shook my head.

"Manicotti."

I smiled.

"Stuffed shells!" he said, pointing triumphantly.

I laughed. "If you name any more types of pasta, I'm going to be late for class."

He lowered his hand. "What do you have now?"

"Spanish," I told him. "Second floor. You?"

"French."

We stood there for a second, not saying anything. His glasses were still kind of slanted from our collision, but it didn't look too dorky. People were moving past us, talking and pushing. It made me think of Anna, who'd soon be on the crowded streets of New York City.

"See you at tennis?" Ethan said.

"Yeah," I said. The boys' and girls' teams practice on separate courts, so the most we could do is wave to each other. My stomach sort of flip-flopped, though, at the thought of waving to each other.

"Okay," Ethan said. "Later."

I gave a small wave and went back to walking. Parker and Magda were about five feet away, against the wall, grinning. Apparently, they'd witnessed that whole thing. "Obsessed!" Parker mouthed. Magda's in my Spanish class, but I shook my head and hurried past them anyway, not wanting to talk about Ethan.

Determined to not *think* about Ethan either, I turned my thoughts to Anna. Was she going to love New York or hate it? Were her cousins going to be nice? Would she go to school in Brooklyn? She'd be the new girl from another country—would that make her more interesting or more of an outcast? At least she wouldn't look different on the outside, unlike me, being one of six non-white kids in my whole school. Then again, English wasn't her native language. That'd be sort of like when I'm in Spanish class, only all the time, not just for that forty minutes. I may look different, but at least I can talk to people. And, obviously, my adoptive home has been my home all my life.

As I climbed the stairs to the second floor, I imagined I was here for the first time, just off the boat from another country, walking into a strange new world.

Dear Belle,

I have just finished dinner and come back to my room . . . yes, I have a room all to myself now. We had roast chicken and potatoes, and there was so much of it, Hannah put the extras in the icebox for tomorrow! <u>Extra</u> food, can you imagine it? She says that on Sunday we will have a special dinner for my first weekend in New York. She has not said what it will be . . . she wants to keep it a surprise. Mamelikanner, what will I do if it is fish? You understand . . . is there a more repulsive food than fish? So oily, and it smells like sewage, and when served whole, that dead eye stares up at the ceiling from the platter. Ewww! Remember when Kurt used to make a show by putting a big piece of fish on his fork and LICKING it, just to make us cringe? I shudder to picture it. I would rather lick the bottom of my shoe!

Of course I will not say this to Hannah. I cannot tell you how kind she and Max have been . . . it would be horrid to appear ungrateful. So far I have been eating everything and making sure to say it is delicious even when it's not, like the strange beans we had my first night here. (And my, I was sick of beans. Are you still eating beans every night? I suppose you are, if Papa's friend is still giving him sacks for free.) Most of the food is delicious, however. Still, I take only one helping of everything. I don't want to be a burden, and I want them to have enough money to sponsor you and everyone else. So even if it is fish on Sunday, I will force down a whole serving, without so much as plugging my nose.

We are fortunate to have cousins so kind as Max and Hannah. They even came to New York Harbor to meet me and bring me to their apartment here in Brooklyn. I am glad they did, because until the moment the ship arrived in port, I had only thought about making it to America, and it never occurred to me to consider how I would get from New York Harbor to their address in Brooklyn. I had only begun thinking about this when I walked down the ramp and onto dry land. (After so long at sea, it is a strange sensation to be on land again! You'll see.) Behind a gate, a large group of people stood waiting, and what a relief to see one of them holding a paper with my name written across it, plain as day. I approached the man, and the woman standing next to him, who was looking very glamorous in a short fur jacket and a navy blue hat. She looked excited. As I got closer, she said, "Anna?"

I said, "Mrs. Schoelstein?" and her red lips broke into a smile, revealing the whitest teeth you have ever seen. She said, "Call me Hannah!" and threw her arms around me, and I was wrapped in soft fur. Oh Belle, just <u>wait</u> until you feel her coat. It's so <u>glamorous</u>! Simply touching it made me think of you, and I had to pull out of Hannah's embrace before I began to cry.

To my surprise, Hannah looked like she might cry herself. "Welcome," she said warmly.

I was missing you with extra passion and could not smile, which made me feel rotten because here was Hannah being so kind, and I was not. Hannah did not seem bothered, though. She was more bothered by Max, who was terrifically intent on folding up the paper with my name. Hannah poked his arm and spoke to him in Yiddish. (Yes, Yiddish! To think that all this time, Mama and Papa were so intent on us learning English and <u>not</u> Yiddish!) Finally, Max looked me in the eye. He seemed to be studying me. Perhaps he was trying to find resemblances to Papa. That is what I was trying to find in him . . . but I could not find any. I still cannot. They are cousins, but they are nothing alike. Here is why:

- Max is so short . . . shorter than Hannah, even when she removes her high heels . . . and his hair is almost gone. What's left of it is blond . . . another difference.

- Max does not wear glasses.

- His eyes are a deep brown, unlike our green-gray.

- Their noses. Papa's is rather small (do you agree?), but Max's is VERY large and full of indents, as though he pressed his face into a bucket of sand.

Papa is always charming around strangers, but Max would have remained silent if Hannah hadn't kept poking him. After the fifth or sixth poke, he finally nodded politely and said, in English, "Welcome, Anna."

Then we all set off onto a train called the "subway" to go to Brooklyn, 64th Street in

Bensonhurst (Hannah said that is the name for this part of Brooklyn). How nice it was to have them lead the way . . . to have an adult to take care of me again.

Belle, I have so much I want to record. About the apartment here (floral wallpaper . . . dark wood furniture that is very elegant . . . soft rugs), about Hannah's closet of fur coats, about Max's pair of uncles who eat dinner with us (both bald, both grumpy), about the streets and the buildings and the smells and the sounds. But as overcome as I am with everything, I am also overcome with sadness. How I wish you were all here to see and hear and smell everything with me! Even if Kurt had come along, then I would have someone to share this with. But for now, I will continue to pretend we are together by writing in this journal, until you arrive and we can truly share <u>everything</u> once again.

With much, much love,
Anna

4 September 1941

t. August 1950

Belle,

Today I received a letter from home! Hannah placed the envelope on my plate before lunch, and when I saw Mama's handwriting on it, I almost fainted. It would have been nice to read it privately, but I could not wait even a moment. I must have looked very conflicted, because Hannah laughed and said, "Go ahead! Open it!" Then she hurried away to ready the laundry for pickup, which was very kind of her.

I'm going to keep the letter someplace safe, so I will always have it. How lovely to read Mama's words, and now I can read them whenever I'd like. It's funny that Mama told me Oliver's drawing is of a ship . . . I would have known even if she had not. She mentions a letter from you, but it has not yet arrived. This one is dated 23 August, the day the Mouzinho set sail.

I must have read Mama's letter six times before I realized the laundry had been weighed and sent off and my lunch was in front of me. Hannah said that she was waiting to pour my seltzer until I was ready, otherwise it might have gone flat.

She said, "I hope they've received our message

that you arrived safely. They must miss you terribly."

I said, "They will come soon," but here is where I began to wonder, and my happiness about the letter began to spoil. I assumed Hannah would rush to agree and assure me it is so (I have only just met her, but it seems her optimism is in line with Papa's). But she didn't . . . not quite. She smiled, yes, but her lips stayed closed. And instead of saying "Of course they will!" she merely replied, "Oh, I do hope so."

There was a sadness in her smile, and it made me a bit cross. Who is Hannah to say if you are coming or not? What does she know about living in occupation, or Mama and Papa's plans, or living here while everyone who matters is there? Who is she to say, "Oh, I do hope so," because what does she know of hope? My desire for the rest of you to arrive is not merely hope. I am yearning . . . no, longing for . . . no, I NEED you to come . . . there is not a word in any language strong enough to describe it. Even if Hannah does "hope so," and she was not just saying this to be polite, it is nothing compared to the feeling that swallows me whole, as I write this, "hoping" that you will come.

Your sister,
Anna

CHAPTER 13

I was lying in bed on my stomach, my pillow pushed under my chest and the diary pressed onto my mattress. (Yes, I'd read more without Madeline. But waiting until tomorrow would've required some serious self-control.) When I looked up, I saw Jaime in my doorway.

"How long have you been standing there?" I asked, annoyed and embarrassed.

"Um," he said, making it obvious that he'd been there a long time. "Not that long. What's that book?"

I considered telling him the truth. All these secrets were starting to weigh on me, and maybe sharing this one would bring us together. Maybe it would even start a conversation about being adopted (which—surprise, surprise—Jaime and I had never talked about), and maybe the two of us could go to

Mom and Dad together to tell them we wanted to find our birth parents.

Or maybe that was the most selfish idea in history. Double-teaming my parents might make it easier for me, but it would only make it harder for them. What's the only thing more painful than one of your children suggesting you're not enough? *Both* of your children suggesting you're not enough.

I stuck my pillow over the open diary. "Just something for school," I said. "What do you want?"

"What subject?"

"History." I didn't even skip a beat.

"Oh." Jaime leaned against the doorframe. "Is it boring?"

"Can I help you with something?"

"Can you?" Jaime asked hopefully. "Math. I'd ask Mom or Dad, but they think I did my homework before watching TV."

I pushed myself up, sighed. I glanced at my pillow, then at his eager face. "Sure."

"Okay!" He disappeared for a second—just enough time for me to close the diary and put it back in its shoebox—then returned with his math workbook. "This page," he said, handing it over.

"*Units of measure,*" I read aloud. "*Number one. Which unit of measure is best for measuring the length of a car?*"

"I don't get it," Jaime said. "Which car?"

"Any car."

"But I didn't bring home my ruler."

"You don't have to actually measure anything," I told him, trying to be patient. "You just have to think about how you would if you had to. See, they even give you choices. *If* you were measuring a car, would you do it in inches or in feet?"

"Inches?" Jaime guessed.

"Jaime. An inch is, like, this big." I showed him with my fingers. "It'd take a lot of inches to measure a car."

"Okay, feet."

"Exactly. Circle *feet*."

He did, and I looked at number two. "See, this one would be inches, because it's the length of a tooth-brush. That's small enough for inches."

"Don't tell me the answers," he said as he circled it. "Just help me figure it out."

"Fine. Sorry."

We went through the rest of the page, picking the best units to measure a football field, a mountain, and a pair of glasses. Fourth-grade math was easy.

"Last one," I said. "The length of an ocean."

"Does that mean how deep it is?"

"No, how far across. Like if you wanted to measure the Atlantic Ocean all the way from here to Europe."

"Oh." My brother thought. "Yards?"

I shook my head. "Too small."

"Miles?"

I frowned at the choices. "Yeah, I guess." That had to be it. But miles didn't seem big enough—not nearly. In fact, it didn't seem like that should be a multiple-choice question at all.

Belle,

I have forgiven Hannah her closed-lip smile. She
won me over today. You see, I wrote a letter back
to Mama and wanted to mail it straight away.
Then I decided I would summon the courage to
ask Hannah if I could include a bar of Ivory soap
with it. There's a French-English dictionary in my
room (truly, they are so thoughtful), so I prepared
the words: "Please I send for my family soap?"
Hannah attempted to hide her confusion, but I
knew she didn't understand. She kept guessing
other words I might have meant. She guessed
soup (soup!) and stamps for the letter . . . It could
have been a comedy scene on the radio, if I'd been
in a better humor! I tried to explain about the
rationing, but to be plain I felt like such a fool, and
a burden on top of that. I had just about given up
when she suddenly ran to the bathroom and came
back with the soap. When I said yes, she put her
hand to her heart with such dramatics and cried,
"Why, of course we can send your family soap!"
The best part (the reason I am no longer angry

with her) is that she showed no pity about us needing soap. She simply said, "Let's pop over to the A&P."

Just wait until you see the A&P, Belle. What an enormous place! It has rows and <u>rows</u> of groceries, with fruit and even a butcher, right there inside the store. I followed Hannah as she gathered four boxes of soap, a tube of toothpaste, and a box marked "Dorothy Gray salon facial package" that she insisted Mama would appreciate. (I think she will but not how Hannah imagines. Maybe Mama can trade it for some extra food coupons, or sell it to help bring you here! I hope she thinks of it.) Hannah saw me eyeing a magazine with a picture of Vivien Leigh on the cover and said we could get that too. When I said it was for you, she looked delighted and said we should get something for everyone, so I chose magazines for each of you. Oh, I wish I could see your faces when you open this package!

I'm sorry I was upset with Hannah yesterday. It's unfair to expect that she understands how I'm feeling. To be plain, I don't understand what I'm feeling . . . I'm constantly overtaken by emotions, but I can't sort out what they are.

Max is a mystery still. He isn't rude to me, but he isn't kind either. Sometimes when he arrives home in the evening, he looks surprised to see me, like he forgot there's an extra person living in his apartment. Then the surprise fades, and he nods politely, like we're strangers passing on the street.

I can just see you roll your eyes at me for saying such things about Max. I can hear your voice: "Yes, Anna. You're one to complain that someone is quiet." I know, I know. It's not as though I am trying to start conversations with him either. Maybe he is just a quiet person, like I. Better Max be quiet than grumpy like his uncles. They are constantly muttering in Yiddish, complaining about who knows what. At least I only need to see them for supper. Max must work with them all day.

I will start school soon, I imagine, but for now, I spend the day at the apartment with Hannah. To think I used to crave silence and time to myself! Hannah plays the radio all day, but it still feels like silence compared to Mina crying and Greta arguing with Mama and Oliver playing. I imagine it is much the same there, without me. Nine in the house can't be much different from eight.

Oh Belle,

Today we had the special supper Hannah
had promised. It was not fish, thank goodness!
It was something entirely new and strange and
delicious . . . Chinese food! When Papa said the
food would be different here in New York, I
would not have guessed it would be food from
China! Oh, <u>wait</u> until you try it. It was exotic
and delightful. Crispy noodles with sweet orange
sauce . . . string beans with garlic and a salty
coating . . . beef with broccoli . . . long, slippery
noodles with savory brown sauce. And piles and
PILES of rice! We ate it at a Chinese restaurant,
where the cooks and the servers were all Chinese.
But imagine this, all the diners were Jewish!

I ate with terrific abandon. It was like there was
nothing in the world but noodles and rice. At one
point I stopped for air and looked up . . . everyone
was staring at me!

"Oy gevalt," said the uncle whose head is
shaped like an onion.

"Oy veyezmir," said the uncle whose head is shaped like an egg.

Hannah burst out laughing, and even Max broke into a hearty smile.

The uncles began mumbling to each other in Yiddish with their voices low and their bushy eyebrows high. Hannah didn't tell them to speak English, so I guess she didn't care for me to understand what they were saying. I doubt they know much English anyway.

But Cousin Max laughed and reached over to pat me on the shoulder. Then he said, in English, "Eat!"

Oh, I did!

CHAPTER 14

Not wanting to risk a protein bar interrupting our lunchtime diary-reading again, Madeline and I ate quickly and went to the school library. I was feeling a little guilty about reading by myself last night. I wasn't actually sure if I was going to tell her or not—maybe I'd just reread the part I read so she wouldn't know. But before I could decide which page to open to, Madeline opened her backpack and took out a folder.

"I did some research for you," she said.

I could see the librarian's ears prick up at the sound of the word *research*.

"On Luxembourg?" I asked. If I was going to do my Holocaust project on Luxembourg, I was eventually going to have to read something besides this diary.

"Not that," Madeline said. "Your other bat mitzvah project."

I looked at her blankly. "My Torah portion? My haftorah? Oh! Are you going to write my speech for me?"

Madeline knocked on my skull. "Your *gift*, O wise one." She opened the folder and took out a list of websites. She'd printed the whole thing out, knowing that a text with links would have done me and my dumbphone no good. "Adoption resources," she explained. "Organizations that will help you find your birth family." She slid it across the table to me. "But they all say that you need your parents' permission if you're under eighteen."

"I know." I mean, duh. If my parents' permission weren't required to find out more, I'd have, like, had brunch with my birth mom last week.

I skimmed Madeline's list of information. It was nice of her to put all this together for me. Or was it just practice groundwork for her journalistic investigation? Either way, it would definitely be convenient to have—if I ever worked up the nerve to talk to my parents, that is. I definitely didn't have the stomach to keep searching behind their backs. "Thanks," I said.

"You're just nervous about this, right?" Madeline asked. "It's not like you've changed your mind."

"Right," I said.

Then, "Well."

Finally: "I don't know."

"What's making you so nervous?" Madeline asked, and I could tell she was picturing us in some NPR recording studio, wearing headphones and speaking into microphones.

"Have you met my mom?" I said. "This will crush her."

"She can handle it, Imani," she said in her trademark practical tone. "She's a grown adult. And she adopted two children. She must know you're going to bring this up someday."

"I don't know," I said again. As crazy as it sounds, sometimes I wonder if my mom even *remembers* that I'm adopted. I once heard some moms with strollers in the park joking about how your hormones make you forget the pain of childbirth. Could my mom's loving-mom hormones have made her forget that she didn't physically give birth to me or Jaime? Even though we all look nothing alike?

"She'll love you no matter what," Madeline added, and her voice was so sincere, I rested my head on her shoulder.

"That's exactly the problem," I said with a sigh. I thought about Anna not wanting to appear ungrateful to her cousins. She *knew* her first family, and had a reasonable expectation to see them again. I don't even know who or where mine are, yet I still think about them all the time. It only makes me feel even guiltier. So guilty that I was willing to make Madeline mad at me, just to change the subject. "I have a confession to make: I read the diary without you last night."

"Imani!" She shrugged my head off her shoulder.

"I'm sorry," I said, smiling because my subject-changing worked. "It's just so tempting. And I can't promise I won't do it again."

Madeline frowned, but I could tell she knew she couldn't really protest. This was *my* great-grandmother's diary. She was just along for the ride.

"I told myself I'd just read one page, to see what the next entry would be about," I explained, "and then I got sucked in." I filled her in on Anna's new home, Hannah's kindness, Max's uncertainty, the grumpy uncles and the delicious Chinese food. "Do you want to read more now?" I asked. "Together?"

"Yes," she said graciously. Her hand hovered over the printout of adoption resources. "Do you want this stuff?"

"Yes, definitely, thank you." I folded the website list in quarters and stuck it in my bag.

"Do you want me to keep bugging you to talk to your parents?"

I looked at her hard, but my mind was picturing my dad handing me a Chipwich from the ice cream man, totally unaware that minutes before, I'd been trying to find information about my *other* dad. If Madeline hadn't been constantly on my case about this, maybe I wouldn't have done something so traitorous.

"No," I answered her. "I'm officially taking you off the case. I'm going to talk to my parents—honest—but I need to do it in my own time."

Her shoulders fell, but then her eyes flashed with hope. "You told me to not let you off the hook. Is this a test? Am I supposed to refuse to stop bugging you about it?"

"No," I said with a laugh. "You can really stop. I won't chicken out, I promise."

"Maybe you'll really do it just to prove that I can stop bugging you about it," Madeline said slyly.

Maybe she was right. Maybe I was reverse-psychology-ing myself into overcoming my fear. Or maybe, now that I knew that, I'd *reverse*-reverse-psychology myself into not doing it. Now I was confused. "Let's just read the diary."

Madeline rubbed her hands together, the hint of that sneaky smile still there. "Yes," she said, "let's read."

Wednesday, 10 September 1941

t. August 1950

Dear Belle,

I may have made my first American friend.
It happened yesterday, when I was feeling most
horrid and needed a pleasant distraction. You
would know why I was so distraught. (You are
a better sister than I.) Yesterday was Oliver's
birthday. He turned five. It hadn't even occurred to
me to send him a card or a gift, even though I have
been very aware of the date because of writing in
this journal and could have mailed a gift last week.
Suddenly it was the 9th of September, and he was
five, and by the time I realized, it was too late to
do anything but lie in bed with Bier pressed to my
nose, crying. My selfishness still turns my stomach.

I was terrifically upset this morning when I sat
down for breakfast, and Hannah could tell. She
suggested I go for a walk, and gave me money
to buy chicken thighs from the butcher. It was
sunny and warm. The streets were quiet except for
the old women who always sit in folding chairs
outside my building, gossiping about everyone who
enters or exits. Another group of old ladies were

playing cards at a folding table, and some women were pushing babies in prams. I started walking to the butcher, but when I was on the far side of 63rd Street, I heard a boy shout, "Strike three!" I was curious, but I just kept walking, and a moment later that same voice said, "Watch out!" and I looked up to see a small ball coming right at me. I put up my hands to block my face, and the ball fell right into them, a perfect catch.

I knew this boy was impressed because he said, "Yowza! Nice catch!" He was standing in a narrow alleyway, and wet clothes were hanging above him, pinned to a line stretching between the two houses on either side. He asked my name and I said it very quietly.

He shouted, "WHAT?" He was wearing a big leather glove on one hand (not for warmth . . . I learned it is a special glove for a sport called baseball) and waved with it to tell me to step into the alley. I took a small step closer and repeated my name a bit louder. He said his name was Freddy and held out his glove for me to toss the ball to him. I threw it very nicely, and he caught it in the baseball glove. Then he said, "Are you ill?" and at first I was insulted, because I thought

he meant my throw was very weak, but that
wasn't it . . . he wanted to know why I wasn't at
school. "It is because you're ill? Sick?" He held
his stomach and stuck out his tongue, as if to
demonstrate.

I said, "No. Are <u>you</u> ill?"

This was funny. He said, "You bet. I'm allergic
to spelling tests." Then he asked if I saw any
truancy officers on the street. I didn't know what
he meant, so I just said no. And he said, "Good.
I've been dying for a hot dog." He started walking
down the street. I wasn't sure if I should follow,
but then he waved his glove and said, "Come on,
Anna," using my name and everything.

We went down the street and around the corner
to a Jewish "deli." Freddy gave the man one coin (I
am not good at telling American coins from each
other) and told the man to put lots of ketchup on
his hot dog. He said, "Load it up." Then he said
to me, "You want a dog?" A dog is a frankfurter, I
realized. I said okay, even though I'd only just had
breakfast, and the man "load it up" the ketchup on
mine too.

Belle, I wish you could see what Freddy did with
his dog. First, he licked off all that ketchup. Some

of it stuck to his teeth and made them red. Then he ate the bread. He went bite by bite down the roll . . . he kept pushing the frankfurter out of the way until it was hanging from just a centimeter of bread, which he pinched between his fingers. Once the bread was all gone, he put the frankfurter itself in the pocket of his trousers! It wasn't wrapped in paper. It was just in there. He said, "Keeps it warm for later" . . . He tapped his head too, like he has such a big brain. Then he asked, "Are you going to eat yours?"

You would have said, "Not like that!" but I only said it in my mind. I ate my frankfurter all together (the Luxembourgish way, I suppose?) . . . end to end, with some bread, meat, and too much ketchup in every bite. It wasn't Chinese food, but it was good.

We talked as we walked back to 63rd St. Freddy had lots of questions, especially because he's never heard of Luxembourg. He was concerned when I told him where it is, until I assured him that we hate the Germans.

I must say that it was enjoyable spending time with Freddy, despite his horrid manners and the fact that he's only 11. (He swore it's true, but

I wish you could see a photograph, because he doesn't look nearly 11. He's very short . . . he only comes up to our shoulder.)

We tossed his baseball back and forth and against the wall in the alley. He tried to do some tricks with his yo-yo, but mine were more impressive. (I did the Eiffel Tower one you taught me. He was most impressed but of course he wouldn't admit it . . . he kept saying, "I know that one, I'm just out of practice.") He did so much talking that I didn't have to speak very much. But I understood everything he said, and when I did talk, he understood my English. I am proud of how far my English has come. I hope you are practicing at home.

Freddy thought it was neat that I've only been in Bensonhurst a couple of weeks. "I've lived here 11 years," he said proudly. "I'll show you around." Tomorrow we are supposed to meet again to play marbles and buy "shoe leather." (This shoe leather is very curious. It's a big roll of sticky candy that a man sells from a cart, cutting off pieces with a sharp knife.) And one day he wants to ride to the end of the subway line, to a place called Coney Island. He said we have to do that in the afternoon, once school is out, because there are always truancy officers waiting at Coney Island.

It was such an enjoyable morning that I almost forgot to stop at the kosher butcher for Hannah. I remembered just before I climbed the stairs to the apartment. Luckily, they still had chicken thighs. When Hannah asked if the walk improved my spirits, I replied honestly that it did. I'm smiling right now. That frankfurter is probably still collecting dust in Freddy's pocket!

With love from Bensonhurst,

Anna

Dear Belle,

Freddy's older brother found out about him "playing hooky" from school, so he hasn't been around in the mornings. It seems to me that Freddy really looks up to his older brother. His name is Milton, and he's 17. Milton has a very pretty girlfriend named Enid, and the two of them are always walking around arm in arm. Freddy says they are a "gruesome twosome." (My English vocabulary is growing every day!) Anyway, Milton has been making sure Freddy goes to school in the mornings, so I only saw him in the afternoon. We played something called "stoop ball" on the steps outside one of the houses nearby, and some other kids joined in. I wasn't very good at it, but I played anyway. Hannah is "thrilled" that I have been spending time with kids my age. She sends me out of the apartment to play every moment she can. It's too bad Freddy won't be there when I start school. He is still in the elementary school, but I will go to "junior high."

Here's something else. Last night, after dinner

with the uncles, Max took out a game called Chinese checkers. (Chinese food . . . Chinese checkers . . . I thought I was moving to America and not China!) This is Max's favorite game. He taught me to play, very patiently, and it's simple, really.

The board is shaped like a Jewish star, and it's covered in holes for marbles.

You start with your colored marbles in one point of the star, and you try to be first to move them all the way across the star to the point opposite yours, which Max called your "home."

A marble can move just one space on a turn, unless there's another marble in its way, in which case it can jump over.

The trick (I discovered this quickly) is to build a string across the star, so long that your marbles can jump all the way home, one after another.

I lost the first game, but I won the second.

When Hannah saw, she winked at me and gave Max a kiss on the top of his head. She said, "Anna is a worthy opponent. Does this mean I am relieved of my Chinese checkers duty?"

Max said, "It appears so," and Hannah practically danced her way out of the room. Max explained that she is not one for board games. He said, "She's a sport to play with me once in a while, but I could play Chinese checkers every night."

So I asked, "Do you want to play tomorrow?"

Max looked surprised and almost shocked when I said that. No wonder, it was probably the most words I've ever spoken in his presence. But I'm grateful he didn't say something stupid, like "It talks!" like Kurt's friend used to say when I opened my mouth around him and Kurt. (Pierre, of course . . . it's just as well his family moved to Vichy.) Max . . . who is kind and polite, unlike Pierre . . . just considered my question and said, "Yes."

So tonight, we played Chinese checkers again . . . two games. Without Hannah there, we sat in silence, putting all our attention on the marbles and holes and building a long string to home. It wasn't uncomfortable, though. It was pleasant. I hope we play again tomorrow.

Between Freddy and Cousin Max, it seems I have two new friends here in America. Today I even got a letter from Frida in Chicago, so that makes three. Four counting Hannah! They are no replacement for you and the rest of the family, of course, but they are something. Since this is my home now, I am happy to have something.

Love,
      Anna

CHAPTER 15

Madeline leaned conspiratorially into me. "Imani," she whispered. "Isn't your grandpa named Fred?"

I gasped. How had that occurred to Madeline and not to me? I was so glad we'd read this part together. "Yes!" I said. "Are you thinking what I'm thinking?" My body started to tingle.

"Do you think he's Freddy?" Madeline asked.

Yes! I wanted to scream. But then I came to my senses. "No. It can't be him. Grandma Anna was Grandpa Fred's *mother*. Not his wife."

"Oh," Madeline said, her shoulders sinking. "You're right."

Of course I was right. But it was still a major disappointment.

"What was Anna's husband's name?" Madeline asked. "Was he named Fred too?"

"I don't know," I realized. "I never met my great-grandpa. I think he died before I was born. But I doubt his name was Freddy, since Jews don't give their kids the same name as their parents like that."

"Oh. Right," Madeline said, clearly bummed. "They name after someone who died."

"Who are you named for?" I asked.

"My great-aunt Mildred," Madeline said. "What about you?"

"I don't know," I said. "My parents kept the name my birth mom gave me."

Wait, I thought. *My parents kept the name my birth mother gave me.* It wasn't like a lightbulb clicked on, but I could sense there was a switch nearby.

Madeline was still focused on Freddy. "Maybe Anna *did* marry Freddy, but he died before your grandpa was born. Like, while Anna was pregnant or something!"

I gave her a look to show how unlikely that was—if it were true, I'd probably know that story (though maybe not, seeing as I don't even know my great-grandfather's name). But Madeline must have thought my look meant that she was being insensitive, getting excited about my great-grandpa dying young, because she apologized.

"That's okay," I said. "Maybe my great-grandpa was named *Milton*." I raised my eyebrows twice.

"Scandalous!" Madeline said with an exaggerated gasp. "Milton and Enid are a gruesome twosome!"

I laughed, and Mr. Garonzik, the librarian, looked our way. "The bell is going to ring any second, girls," he said.

We both kept giggling as we packed up our bags. Until Madeline remembered that she had a test in social studies next period. "Quiz me," she said, handing over a list of famous explorers, the countries they represented, and the places they explored.

I skimmed the paper, full of names and places. "Vasco da Gama," I said, but in my head, I was thinking about my own name and history, and the words I'd spoken minutes before: *My parents kept the name my birth mother gave me.*

CHAPTER 16

Those words bounced around in my head all through school. They stuck with me while I walked home and the whole afternoon. I don't know *how* I know that my parents kept the name I was born with—I don't remember ever being told; it's just a fact of my existence, like my birthday being June 15.

But it had to be a good sign that my parents kept my name—Jaime's too; that was the name he was given in Guatemala. After all, if they wanted us to completely forget that we were born to different parents, they would have changed our names.

That wasn't the only thing, though. I wanted to know more about my ethnic background, right? I hadn't found the answer in the mirror, or in that old *Children of the World* book, or even in the filing cabinet under IMANI—ADOPTION. But maybe I'd been focusing on the wrong part of the label on that empty folder. Instead of looking up stuff about ADOPTION, maybe I could look up stuff about IMANI.

I went online first thing after dinner—the rest of my family was still in the kitchen, so I wasn't being *too* sneaky—and googled *people named imani*. I clicked to search for images. That's what I wanted to see first.

Suddenly, a whole screen of faces was looking at me. Girls and women, all shades of black and brown, with hair that was curlier or straighter than mine, and noses that were smaller or bigger, and teeth that were straighter or more crooked, and eyes that were lighter or darker or rounder or more angled. I scrolled and scrolled, staring at all these Imanis, their black and brown and almost familiar faces staring back at me. My birth mother might have looked something like the women on the computer screen. Or maybe she didn't, but she had *something* in common with them, at least. Enough to give me the name Imani without caring that it'd take teachers a few tries to say it correctly, without an invisible question mark at the end.

Back to Google. A regular search this time.

what kind of name is imani

The answer popped up in a neat little box at the top of the search results.

Given Name IMANI. USAGE: Eastern African, Swahili, African American. Means "faith" in Swahili, ultimately of Arabic origin.

I read the words hungrily, then again slowly, then once more out loud, in a whisper: "Eastern African, Swahili, African American."

My thumb tapped a drumbeat against the desk, quick and then slow. That didn't really answer much, did it? I already knew my birth mother was black. I'd always assumed she was African American, but was she actually from Eastern Africa? Were her ancestors? And what about "ultimately of Arabic origin"? Arabic is different from Swahili.

I tried not to get overwhelmed as I scrolled down the list of results. The word *faith* appeared a lot. That box said *imani* means "faith" in Swahili, and another result said that it was from the Arabic word for *faith, iman.* One site said it's a Muslim name for a girl who has a strong belief in Allah, which totally threw me. If I hadn't been adopted, would I be preparing for a Muslim coming-of-age ceremony instead of a bat mitzvah?

That made me remember something else: *Doesn't*

my Hebrew name, Emunah, mean "faith" too? I googled it. Sure enough, I was right. *Emunah* sounds a lot like *Imani*. What did *that* mean?

My breathing picked up in pace as I began to get frustrated. Who's to say my name held any answers at all? Most people just pick a baby name they like. It's not as if my birth mother sat there thinking, *I know! I'll pick a name that provides a concise historical summary of my daughter's genetic makeup.*

I googled *meaning of name madeline* as an experiment. The box at the top told me that *Madeline* comes from *Magdalene,* like Saint Mary Magdalene. My back slouched in the desk chair. *That* showed just how reliable a name is in terms of your race or religion. Madeline—my *Jewish* best friend—was obviously not named for some Christian saint. But Magda probably was, which meant a name *could* hold important clues, and maybe mine did too.

Some laughter drifted in from the kitchen. When it's my night to clean up dinner, I load the dishwasher so fast my dad stresses that I'll accidentally smash a plate. (I won't. I'm fast but in total control.) When it's Jaime's turn, like tonight, he runs the sponge over every inch of every dish, and it turns into social hour, with him and my parents hanging out and chatting like BFFs. Their laughter meant I could probably go over my allotted thirty minutes of screen time without being found out.

I took a deep breath and tried one more time, this time typing *imani faith*. Google suggested I add *Kwanzaa celebration*. My eyebrows rose. Kwanzaa?

A random memory bubbled up from deep inside my brain: In first or second grade, everyone was supposed to bring in an object from home for a schoolwide holiday party. I brought a Chanukah menorah that I'd made at Hebrew school using little tiles for a base and metal bolts to hold candles. I remember being really excited to show off my menorah, and to stuff myself full of holiday desserts. But when my class arrived in the cafeteria for the party, a teacher I didn't know assumed my menorah was for Kwanzaa, and she said she'd bring a group of her students to me to learn about my holiday. Too scared or shy to correct her—and totally freaked out at the prospect of talking to a bunch of older kids about a holiday I knew nothing about—I told my teacher I had a stomachache. I left my menorah with her and spent the rest of the party in the nurse's office, curled up on a row of small chairs.

Pushing that memory aside with a quick shake of my head, I pressed ENTER to see what *imani faith kwanzaa celebration* was all about.

Kwanzaa is an African-American holiday that celebrates the seven traditional values of African culture: Umoja (unity), Kujichagulia (self-determination), Ujima (collective work and responsibility), Ujamaa (cooperative economics), Nia (purpose), Kuuma (creativity), and Imani (faith). Each of the seven days of Kwanzaa is dedicated to one of the principles.

"What are you looking at, sweetie?"

I didn't panic that my mom was there, but I didn't *not* panic either. I guess the dishwashing party ended early tonight. "Um," I said. Just tell the truth, right? This could be a test to see how she might react to tougher questions, questions about my birth parents. "I was looking up my name," I told her. "Did you know that *imani* means 'faith' in Swahili?"

I watched Mom's face to see if her eyebrows would go up or down. It was like I was in science class, recording the color change of a piece of litmus paper. This result was better than I could have hoped: One eyebrow up!

"Really?" Mom said, sounding genuinely interested. "Your Hebrew name means 'faith' too. They must come from the same root."

"Yeah!" I said. "They probably do."

Mom kneeled down and squinted at the screen. "What's this?"

"Kwanzaa," I replied, without even a twitch of nerves. If this conversation continued going this well, I might have the courage to go all the way and bring up my controversial bat mitzvah gift request. It felt so much better in this moment than when I was underneath the desk, snooping and lying. Had I totally misjudged my mom? Maybe I'd been so nervous for nothing!

I said, "Did you know that imani—well, *faith*—is one of the seven principles of Kwanzaa?"

Mom read aloud from the screen: "*The Imani principle teaches us to have confidence in ourselves, our parents, teachers, leaders, and community.*" She paused, then looked at me and smiled. "Neat." Then she stood up, kissed my forehead, and started to walk away.

Have confidence in ourselves and our parents . . . "Hey, Mom," I called.

She turned back around.

Just say it, Imani. "For my bat mitzvah, I was wondering if maybe . . ."

Mom waited, both eyebrows up. Her face had brightened at the mention of my bat mitzvah, like all her pride and dreams and hopes and *imani* were wrapped up in her little girl continuing this Jewish family tradition. And sure, she was cool about me looking up the meaning of my name, but looking up the meaning of my name was totally different from looking for the mother who gave it to me, and bringing that up right now would sucker-punch all of the joy right out of *this* mom—the one who takes care of me every single day.

All of that confidence from a few seconds ago was gone. I couldn't ask to find my birth parents. Not right now, anyway.

"For your bat mitzvah, you were wondering . . ." Mom prompted.

"I was wondering if I could learn more about . . . Luxembourg," I finished. "Like, research it for my Holocaust project."

Mom looked happy before, but now she was a full-on hearts-for-eyes emoji. "Because of Grandma Anna?" she asked.

"Yeah," I said. "That's where she was from, right?"

"Yes, Luxembourg." Mom's hand was over her heart. No joke. "I think that's a wonderful idea, Imani. I know hardly anything about Luxembourg myself."

"Me neither," I said. I turned back to the computer and replaced the page about Kwanzaa with a search for Luxembourg. Mom came and tapped for me to slide over so we could share the chair.

Together, we found Luxembourg on a map of Europe. It was a small dot of a country squished between France, Belgium, and Germany. Then Mom took over the mouse to pull up some facts: the population (549,680 people), the size (998.6 square miles), the languages (Luxembourgish, German, and French).

"Here, I have an idea," I said. I went back to Google and clicked to see images. "Now we're talking." The pictures were like something straight out of a fairy tale. Stone castles on lush green hills. Winding streets lined with skinny yellow and pink houses. A long stone bridge with dramatic arches under it, crossing a glassy river.

"Breathtaking," Mom said.

It would have sounded cheesy if it weren't true. Who knew places actually look like this outside of Disney World? It was like the people who lived there should be permanently dressed for the Renaissance fair.

"How old was Grandma Anna when she left?" I asked, trying not to let on that I already knew the answer.

"About your age, I think. She came to America all by herself. Can you imagine that? Being your age and going to a new country all by yourself?"

I got a sudden pang of nervousness, like a pinprick

in my side. I could tell that Mom knew something about Grandma Anna's family, and I didn't want to know what it was. Not yet.

"She came to escape the Holocaust, you know," Mom said. "She got out just in time."

The pinprick got sharper, and I realized that deep down, I already knew the ending, and I didn't want Mom to confirm it. But it was too late. I'd opened the can of worms, and Mom was going to take the slimy things out.

"The rest of her family died in the camps."

I closed my eyes. There it was.

Mom took in a breath, and I waited for her to start crying. But when I opened my eyes, I saw that the breath was actually a gasp. She'd enlarged a photo of the Grand Duchess of Luxembourg and was marveling at her gown. "This dress is beautiful, don't you think? I love the color."

I couldn't believe it. A sappy commercial would make Mom sniffle, but the sad fate of Anna's family— her own family—barely registered a blip. I wondered about my *other* mother, the one I came so close to bringing up just a few minutes ago. Did that mother feel sad when she thought about me? Or did none of it even register anymore?

"I could see you wearing something like this for your bat mitzvah," Mom said.

The weight of everything I'd just learned was piling up, and I suddenly felt very tired, like Anna sleeping-sleeping-sleeping on the ship. The very last thing I wanted to do was look at clothes. Especially with my mom—shopping with her is the worst. I groaned.

Mom chuckled and patted my knee. "Okay. But we will have to go dress shopping eventually."

"I know," I said with a sigh.

Mom stood up, and the whole chair was once again mine. The spot where she'd been sitting was warm. "I'm glad you're researching our family history," she said.

I thought of the journal in my Converse All-Star box, hidden under my bed. How seventy-five years ago, Anna was starting a new life while the rest of her family was going to die in a concentration camp. And I thought about that blond girl I played in singles a couple weeks ago, the obnoxious one who said, "You might have this amazing history you don't know about."

"Me too," I told Mom.

Saturday, 13 September 1941

t. August 1950

Dear Belle,

It is Shabbat.

Our cousins observe the Sabbath, not like our family. On Friday nights before supper, Hannah lights candles and we drink wine and eat challah, saying prayers in Hebrew with Uncles Egg and Onion. Then on Saturday mornings, all the men walk to shul. I don't mean only Max and his uncles, but rather <u>all</u> the men in Bensonhurst. I watch them out the window, filing down the street in suits and hats, probably talking about business, even though it is supposed to be against the rules to do any sort of work on Shabbat. The women break the rules too. Today, Hannah drew the curtains and is using the Hoover on the floors!

She said, "I hope this doesn't offend you, Anna. Does your family observe the Sabbath very strictly?"

I assured her it is fine and said I used to go to the cinema. I searched for the words to describe that sometimes we'd see two films in a row, and Hannah laughed when she figured it out. Here is how you say it: double feature.

Hannah explained that the neighborhood is very religious, so we must "keep up appearances." She warned me not to tell the uncles, though I know better than to do that. I never speak to the uncles anyway.

Now we sit in the dark apartment with freshly cleaned carpets. Hannah has put on the radio (quietly, so the neighbors won't hear) and is looking through a magazine. I write in this journal and wonder how many neighbors are just "keeping up appearances." Are they pretending to observe Shabbat for <u>our</u> sake, when really we don't mind?

I wager God doesn't mind either. He has his hands full with everything going on in Europe. I hope he's not wasting his time with Jews who Hoover the floor on the day of rest.

CHAPTER 17

I closed my eyes and had a hard time opening them again. It was super late—almost midnight—and it must have started to rain. I could hear the soft tapping on the roof. I needed to go to bed. I shouldn't have been reading without Madeline again anyway.

Diary closed and lamp off, I lay there with my eyes closed, trying to fathom how despite everything, Anna still believed in God. She thought He had his hands full in Europe . . . she didn't even know how true that was. At this point, the rest of her family was still alive, or at least she thought so.

My eyes opened again, into the dark. Would Anna discover, in the course of this diary, that everybody died? My mind flashed to this tote bag Parker sometimes carries, with a quote in glittery letters on the side: "It's better to have loved and lost than never to have loved at all." (Parker loves that bag, so Madeline and I have this joke about her losing it.) But now I wondered about that quote for real. Anna loved her family for twelve years before she lost them. Would she agree that it was better to have loved and lost? Or maybe she'd have envied *me,* since I left my birth family without ever knowing what I was missing.

Maybe she did *envy me,* I realized, reminding myself, again, that Anna had been a real person. My great-grandmother. She knew me. She knew I was adopted. What did she think of that?

Maybe she'd left me her books on purpose. She knew I'd find the diary and hoped it'd help me find a way to talk to my parents about my past. After all, look how well things had gone tonight, when my mom and I talked about my name and Kwanzaa. I just needed to keep taking tiny steps, testing the water as I went.

Some words were already forming in my mind as I drifted off to sleep. Next-step words to gently let my parents know that I've always wondered about my roots.

Dear Belle,

What a day! I thought Hannah had so many fur
coats because she and Max are rich. But no . . .
it's because Max makes them! He is a furrier. But I
will start at the beginning and tell you everything.
(I can just see you on our bed, cross-legged and
leaning against the wall, begging me to do just
that. "Anna. Tell me everything!")

This morning while I was eating breakfast, the
telephone rang. Hannah said to me, "What do you
wager this is Max?" Then she picked up the phone
and winked at me because she was right, it was Max.

When she hung up, she laughed and said, "He
left his lunch in the icebox! He could eat out, but
then he'd be getting an earful about it all afternoon
from those cheapskate uncles."

The word "cheapskate" brought to mind a bad
memory. Remember how the shopkeeper at the toy
shop near school used to let me borrow boxes of
puzzles to do at home? I would put them together
quickly and return them with all of the pieces, then
he would seal the box again and sell it. But once

the Nazis invaded, he stopped letting me borrow them, saying (in German, though before the occupation he always spoke Luxembourgish) that I had to stop being a "Geizhals" Jew and buy them like everyone else. I never told you that before . . . I never told anyone. Oh Belle, the sting I felt when he said it! I left with my head low and my eyes burning. I wish to this day that I had stood up tall instead. (You would have, I know.) That's why I stopped going to his store, even before he put up the NO JEWS ALLOWED sign.

"Cheapskate" sounds sillier than "Geizhals," though. And I know Hannah didn't mean it hurtfully. . . . In fact, I think it is exactly right to describe those uncles!

Hannah decided that I would go with her to Manhattan to bring Max his lunch. She said, "The factory isn't far from Macy's, so I thought we might do some shopping too. We can get you some dresses for when you start to go to school."

I had been wondering when I will start school! The thought of it makes me both excited and anxious. There was no time to think about it then, though. We dressed quickly and off we went for my very first trip into Manhattan.

We took the subway (the Sea Beach Line) and it got more crowded with each stop. When we got off at 34th Street and emerged from Penn Station . . . oh my! I cannot say enough how tall the buildings are, and the street was filled with cars and taxis, and there were so many people, and they were all in a rush, hurry hurry hurry. The bustle was catching. Walking to 7th Avenue, it was as though Hannah had exchanged her high heels for roller skates. We wove our way through the sea of coats and hats, usually on people, but not always . . . a group of men hurried past pushing a rack of gentlemen's suits! Hannah explained that we were in the garment district, "the clothing capital of New York." Max's factory is in the fur district, which makes sense, and Hannah said just south of us was the flower district. She pointed and said, "Smells divine!"

New York is so <u>new</u>, Belle. There are no stones or arches, and not a single castle, not even in the countryside, I wager. Just steel and glass and skyscrapers with pointy tops. Compared to America, Luxembourg is positively <u>old</u>.

Hannah stopped at an enormous gray building that looked like all the others. She pressed a button at the entrance . . . there was a crackling noise, then a man's voice, probably Max's, said, "Schoelstein Furrier."

Hannah said both our names, smiling at the way they rhyme. The voice clicked off, then a loud buzz, and Hannah pulled open the large glass door. We took the elevator to the 15th floor and then down a long hallway, the ticking of Hannah's heels echoing as we went. We came to a door with a sign that said "Schoelstein—Furrier," and Hannah knocked a happy rhythm before opening it up.

I'm not sure what I expected to find, but this was not it. First came a small, carpeted room with a couch, a desk, and mirrors against the wall. This room was empty and quiet, though we could hear sounds coming from behind a door to the left, which Hannah opened next. Inside was the factory where they make the furs. It was messy and loud. There were some large machines in one corner of the large room. Near them were a long rack of fur coats on hangers. On the other side of the room were three long tables, with one man on each end, working with strips of fur. A third man was removing a large, wet fur from where it was nailed to a board. The nails dropped to the ground as he pulled them out, and this must be a common practice . . . the floor was covered with nails! Two women were at a table of their own, sewing. The uncle whose head is shaped like an onion was walking between the tables, looking over their shoulders and grumbling in Yiddish. The one whose head is shaped like an egg was seated at a desk, frowning over a ledger book. Cousin Max was standing in the corner behind a large table. He was arranging strips along the table by color, then stepping back to look at them and consider.

Max and Hannah are such an oddly matched pair. She went over to him right away and kissed the side of his head, but he didn't take his eyes off the fur. He only looked away when she placed his lunch sack in his hand. He did, finally, look up and give Hannah a small kiss on the cheek. I really do wonder how he and Papa are in the same family. Papa would never give such a reserved peck. He would wrap Mama up and plant a big kiss right on her lips! I always used to look away, but now I wish I hadn't.

Soon the door buzzer sounded because someone named Walter was downstairs. Hannah used a great saying, "We'll get out of your hair," but Uncle

Egg stood up and said, "Warten." He mumbled some more Yiddish, and Uncle Onion began nodding. You see, Walter is a buyer, and the uncles wanted Hannah to stay in case Walter requested to see what one of the coats looks like on a woman. So we stayed, and you won't believe what came next . . . just wait!

Max and Uncle Egg and Hannah and I went to the smaller, quieter room (the one with the couch and the mirror) to meet Walter. He shook hands with Max and his uncle. Max introduced Hannah, who seemed to be embracing her role as a model— she smiled like she had never been happier to meet someone. She looked truly ravishing.

Max showed Walter a short brown jacket. He gave some details about it, and Walter examined it while he listened, running his finger over the fur. Max asked him if he wanted to see what it looked like on. He said, "My wife can model it for you."

Walter smiled politely at Hannah, and then turned his head to look at . . . me! He said, with a perfect American accent, "How about this model?"

I thought I didn't understand his English . . . Me? Model?

Max didn't understand either. He said, "Anna?"

"Yes," Walter said, "if you don't mind."

Hannah squeezed my arm and said, "Oh, what a wonderful idea! Anna will look beautiful in this jacket."

Walter said, "I agree."

What could I say? No thank you? I think you have the wrong twin?

Max held the coat out, and I slid my arms into the sleeves. Goodness! First, it was so heavy, I had to make an effort to stand up straight and not let the coat pull me down. But it was so <u>warm</u> and so <u>soft</u>! I now understand how bears can hibernate. With a coat like that, you could just curl up and sleep for months.

It was big on me, but Walter paid that no mind. He asked me to step onto the pedestal by the mirrors and turn around. Facing the other way, I saw myself in the mirror and gasped. I looked like a movie star! Golly Belle, you would have <u>fainted</u>. In that moment, I closed my eyes and tried to transmit the sensation of being in this coat to you, all the way across the ocean. (I am doing it again now. Do you feel the warmth?)

When I opened my eyes, I saw Hannah behind me in the mirror. She was beaming. She said, "I forgot how wonderful it is, the feel of your first fur coat."

Walter liked that and kept repeating it to himself. "The feel of your first fur coat." He asked Max if he could make a coat that would better fit "this young woman." He was referring to <u>me</u>! Young woman!

Max said, "Of course." Walter said he wanted it just like the coat I had on, but the right size. He said he could convince the store owner to buy a few. For "teenagers," he said. He was talking quickly . . . figuring things out and getting excited, and Max kept saying "of course, of course." I don't know how much Uncle Egg understood, but he must have realized it was good news, because he was nodding like his head was on springs.

Max made sure it was okay with me, to be the model, and how could I say no? It was all very exciting.

Walter said a lovely English word that seemed to sum up the entire morning: "Splendid."

After he left, Max had me stand back on the pedestal to take my measurements. We decided that I won't start school until after the High Holidays. This way, I'll be more settled and my

English will be better—and I'll have time to go to the factory for fittings as the coat comes along. (Yom Kippur is at the beginning of October . . . perhaps by then, you will be here to go with me!) Hannah still wanted to stop at Macy's for dresses, however. I followed her around in something of a haze.

I simply can't believe it . . . me, a model. It's perfectly absurd! My stomach feels like it is back on the ship. If only you had come in my place . . . but I'm sure you can model when you arrive. We look exactly the same, after all! I am feeling dreamy and hopeful. If this is a success, and Walter buys lots and <u>lots</u> of coats, Max will make enough money to send for our <u>whole</u> family. <u>All</u> of you! Every single one!

CHAPTER 18

"Five minutes, girls," the librarian said, jarring me out of the past and back to school with Madeline. We'd taken the diary to the library again, and lunchtime was, apparently, over in five minutes.

I shook my head, rubbed my eyes. I always picture Anna's world in black-and-white—like episodes of *I Love Lucy*—so it was almost a shock to be once again surrounded by color. It also didn't help that I'd stayed up past midnight last night. I was yawning like crazy.

"Mr. Garonzik?" Madeline said. "Do you have any books about Luxembourg?"

"Luxembourg . . ." Mr. Garonzik said. He clicked his tongue as he thought.

"Specifically Luxembourg during the Holocaust."

That last word caught me off guard. Anna was finally starting to feel at home, and this last entry was so happy, I'd almost forgotten this was all happening during the Holocaust.

"Let me check." Mr. Garonzik went to the computer. When he came back, he was carrying three books. One about western Europe, and two about the Holocaust. "I don't have any books specifically about Luxembourg, but these are a good start," he said. "They have Luxembourg listed in the index, with at least a few pages to read. Do you want to check them out, Madeline?"

"No," Madeline said, "but Imani does."

"For my bat mitzvah," I told him.

He looked at me and started to laugh, then stopped when he realized I wasn't kidding.

"I'm Jewish," I said, almost daring him to contradict me. "And my great-grandmother's family was from Luxembourg. They died in the Holocaust."

"They did?" Madeline asked sadly.

"Yes," I told Madeline with a sigh. "All of them. My mom told me last night."

"Oh man," she muttered.

His face pink, Mr. Garonzik said he was sorry and told me to meet him at the circulation desk. The bell rang, signaling the end of lunch.

I flipped to the next page in the diary to mark it with the green ribbon before putting it away. But it was such a short entry, I read it quickly.

Saturday, 20 September 1941

t. August 1950

Oh Belle . . .

I have the most terrifying feeling that something bad has happened to you, to our family. I was napping and awoke with a gasp. My forehead is so sweaty that my hair is wet. I don't think I was dreaming, or if I was I don't remember it. Were you having a nightmare, Belle, all the way across the ocean? I hope that's all. That would be a comforting thought. After all, sharing our nightmares means the string connecting us might have frayed, but it has not snapped.

Why, then, am I not comforted? I am afraid.

I nudged Madeline with my elbow. "Read this," I said, placing the diary in her hands before walking, zombielike, to the circulation desk.

I thanked Mr. Garonzik as he slid the stack of books to me. The two Holocaust ones had classic photos on the cover: swastikas, cattle cars, prisoners with shaved heads and sunken chests. Stuff I'd seen six million times before. Only now, it was like I was looking at them for the very first time.

CHAPTER 19

Mrs. Coleman nearly fainted with happiness when I pulled the library books out of my backpack that afternoon.

"Imani's taking her research project very seriously," Madeline told her. "She had our school librarian help her find these books."

"Emunah!" Mrs. Coleman clasped her hands together, like some non-Jew praying. "And your bat mitzvah isn't even until June."

"Yeah," I said, trying to shrug it off. "I'm actually finding my topic pretty interesting."

Mrs. Coleman sighed a happy sigh. "You are melting my Hebrew-school-teacher heart. Everyone!" she announced. "Take a lesson from Emunah!"

Madeline grinned and pointed at me, in case anyone was unsure who to make fun of. I winced and batted her hand away. Everyone else was groaning, except for Ethan (*Eitan* here at Hebrew school), who clapped. That only made me duck my head more.

"All right," Mrs. Coleman said. "I will be calling you over one by one to hear how your haftorah portions are coming. You can practice while you wait or, like Emunah"—she smiled in my direction—"you can do research, using real books. Like Emunah."

Sheesh.

Madeline wanted to find a corner and pull out the diary. "That is research," she rationalized, "and it's a physical book."

But now I had a reputation to live up to, and I was actually pretty curious to know more about what was going on in Luxembourg that might have made Anna wake up in a cold sweat. "I don't think Mrs. Coleman could take it if I don't read one of these books," I said. "I just melted her Hebrew-school-teacher heart. I don't want it to freeze over."

Madeline pursed her lips. We could hear Mrs. Coleman correcting Ben Adler as he stumbled, slowly, through the first line of his haftorah. "Fair enough," Madeline said. "Can I borrow one of your books, then?"

I motioned to the pile in my best game-show host impression. Madeline selected the book with the biggest swastika on the cover. I shook my head. "I was going to use that one."

Madeline bought it for a second, which made me giggle. She elbowed my side and sat down with the book. I sat next to her and opened another. Remembering what Mr. Garonzik said, I went straight to the index and found Luxembourg. Two page numbers followed, and I flipped to the first of them. It took a minute to find any mention of Luxembourg on the page. No wonder; all it said was that Luxembourg offered refuge to Jews from other countries in the 1930s. The second page that referenced Luxembourg had a chart listing the approximate number of people who died from each country, and Luxembourg didn't even get its own line. Its death count was lumped in with that from Denmark, Estonia, Norway, and Danzig.

The other book was just as unhelpful. Didn't anybody care about Anna's homeland? I know it's a small country, but from these books, you wouldn't even know it existed, let alone that Jewish people lived there. If only Hitler hadn't known.

I was giving my stack of books the stink-eye when Mrs. Coleman called my name. I got the photocopy of my haftorah portion from my backpack and took it up to her desk.

"How's your research coming?" she asked excitedly.

"Not so well," I admitted. "None of the books I got have anything useful to say about Luxembourg."

"Luxembourg!" Mrs. Coleman was clearly surprised, but I could tell it was at my choice of topic rather than the fact that it was overlooked in history.

"It's a small country near France, Germany, and Belgium," I explained.

"Ah, yes. And what made you interested in Luxembourg?"

"My great-grandmother was from there. She moved to New York, but the rest of her family all died in the Holocaust."

Mrs. Coleman's expression softened. I pictured her heart collapsing into a puddle. "I know I insisted you all use books," she said, "but in this case, I'll permit you to try the internet. Legitimate websites only, of course. Do you have the list of websites I handed out with the assignment?"

"Oh," I said, hoping my face wasn't as blank as my brain when it came to remembering this handout. "I don't think so."

Mrs. Coleman opened a drawer in her desk and pulled out a paper I'd seen before. I'm pretty sure it was in the same folder as my haftorah portion. Whoops. She flipped this new copy over to reveal a list of "Suggested Resources," then ran down the list with her pen, drawing little stars next to a few of the websites.

"Yad Vashem . . ." she said, pointing at it with her pen. "U.S. Holocaust Memorial Museum . . . Holocaust Research Project . . . I'd start with those. Search for Luxembourg."

"Okay, cool," I said. "Can I do it now?" There's only one computer in the temple library, and ever since Mrs. Coleman caught Parker using it to look up cat memes, no one was allowed to touch it.

"As long as you stick to these sites," Mrs. Coleman said.

"I will. Thanks."

"You're welcome. Let me know what you find." She smiled and slid the paper to me. Then she looked at her class list and called out the next person in line. "Leah Mintz!"

It wasn't until I was waiting for the computer to boot up that I realized she'd forgotten to hear my haftorah. That was good, because I can't remember the last time I practiced it. I guess being a model researcher has its perks. I opened the browser and typed in the address of the first website Mrs. Coleman had starred.

"What are you doing?" Madeline asked in a low voice. She was kneeling down right by my chair, but I saw that almost everyone else was stealing glances my way from wherever they were.

"Mrs. Coleman said I could do research online. She loves me now."

"Seriously. Are you hanging out with her this weekend too?"

"Are you crazy?" I said. "She can't wait till the weekend. We're hanging out tonight."

Madeline laughed, and I tried to shush her without laughing too loudly myself. She went back to the table, and I turned back to the computer. "Come on, Luxembourg," I said under my breath as I typed it into the search box on the Yad Vashem site. "Jackpot," I whispered when the results popped up. Ten pages! Something here had to have answers. I clicked on the first link and found a neat summary of Luxembourg at the time of Anna's diary.

On May 10, 1940, the Germans invaded Luxembourg, meeting little resistance and being helped by local Volksdeutsche (ethnic Germans) . . . About a month after the installation of Simon's government, the Nuremberg Laws were introduced. More anti-Jewish decrees followed and the wearing of the Jewish Badge was ordered in September 1941. Around that time, Jews were placed in the Fuenfbrunnen transit camp, near Ulflingen. The camp was organized along ghetto lines, and later became the point from which deportation trains left for the East.

My eyes kept staring at *September 1941*. It shouldn't have surprised me that the timing of the diary and these events would line up—that was the whole point of this research, right?—but it still did. The word *camp* scared me too. A quick search for *Fuenfbrunnen transit camp* in another tab told me that it wasn't a concentration camp, but more like a temporary holding place, so that all the Jews were together and ready to be stuffed into cattle cars that would take them to a concentration camp. Good grief, the Nazis were organized. Was Anna's family headed there soon? How long would it take Anna to find out?

I was overcome with this awful sense of dread. It wasn't fair that I should be able to know this when Anna didn't. It was like that time Madeline and I had tried to watch a horror movie. *We* knew the killer was hiding behind the door, but no amount of shouting at the screen could stop the actors from opening it.

Jewish emigration was encouraged until the spring of 1941, and many Jews went to France and Portugal. On October 13, the Consistoire (Jewish Community) reported that 750 Jews were left in the country, and 80 percent were over the age of 50.

I knew who 9 of those 750 Jews were. It sounds stupid, but it only now struck me for the first time that the other 741 were real people too. As real as Belle and Oliver and Kurt. And they all had people who cared about them just as much.

I scrolled down, knowing I'd find what happened to them, and when.

The first and largest transport left for the Lodz ghetto on October 16, 1941, with 324 persons. Seven more transports followed, the last of which left on September 28, 1943. In total, 674 Luxembourg Jews were deported. Only 36 of those who were deported survived.

I pushed back in my chair and sat there in silence for a while. At some point, I don't know how long, I reluctantly emerged from my fog. I printed out the page, stuck it in my folder, and went back to Madeline's table. She closed her book the second she saw me take out the diary.

Friday, 26 September 1941
t. August 1950

Dear Belle,

Yom Kippur is on Wednesday, which means I
will begin school the following Monday! I must get
better at writing English, so I have made a decision
for the Jewish new year: Beginning with my next
entry, I will write only in English. I am feeling
confident speaking English, and I'm proficient at
reading it on signs and in newspapers and even
books that we borrow from the library. I will leave
blank pages first, to translate my earlier entries
from the Luxembourgish later, for more practice.
Then, when you arrive, I'll give you this journal
so you can read about all of my experiences in
English, and you can practice too. I am terrifically
pleased with this idea. New year, new friends, new
language! Signing off in Luxembourgish . . .

Love always,
Anna

Monday, 29 September 1941

Dear Belle,

Here I go . . . English! I will to make this entry
short . . . I should not be nervous but I am. My
fingers shake actually and my brain is soapy water
with nothing to write! I am being slow and careful
to make certain my words are correct and also my
verb tense. It can be easier then speaking because
I can take time to be correct without making slow
the conversation.

Here is something comes to mind. I am starting
to like Max. We have continue to play Chinese
checkers, many games after Rosh Hashanah dinner.
We are most silent during our games still, but we
do to talk a bit. He is starting to like me too, I can
tell.

You hope I come soon. You will like it here.

"Oh my God," Madeline said with a laugh. "And this is with her writing slowly and carefully to make sure she's doing things right."

"It's her first time writing in English," I said. "She's nervous. Cut her some slack."

"She needs some pretty big slack. I mean, 'You hope I come soon'?" Madeline laughed again.

"Maybe you say it that way in Luxembourg," I snapped defensively. Sure, Anna's English was a little rough. But Madeline didn't have to be so obnoxious about it. "English is Anna's—what?—third, fourth language? How many languages do you speak?"

Now it was Madeline's turn to get defensive. "Come on, Imani. I was just joking. Her English is fine."

"It's more than fine." I crossed my arms. "And she clearly got even better at it quickly. Look how perfect all the translations are." I didn't realize that my voice was rising until Mrs. Coleman said my name and put a finger to her lips. "Sorry," I told her. *But Madeline just made fun of my great-grandma,* I added silently. Even thinking it made me realize how lame I sounded.

Madeline put up her hands to surrender. "Okay, okay," she whispered. "I'm sorry I insulted Anna's English. Let's keep going."

"Are you sure you'll be able to understand her writing?" I whispered, fully aware that I was now the one being obnoxious.

Madeline crossed her arms. "I said I'm sorry. Can we please move on?"

Thursday, 2 October 1941

Dear Belle,

More to say today, I am hope I can to write
English fast enough. (I pretend to speak with you.
This makes the words come.)

My coat is almost ready. Max says it would to
be done quicker if no High Holidays, but it does
not much matter because Walter and the store
owner is not to come until next week. I went again
to the factory today to try on. Max is pleased with
how it looks. I imagine the uncles are too, as much
as they can be pleased with anything. (Not much.)
They should try to putting on one of the coats . . . I
feel so happy when to wear a fur coat. I feel terrific
guilt about this. I wear a mink coat while you wear
old clothings that Mama must mend and mend. I
remember this before and after I put on the coat.
While I wear it however . . . well, I can not think
of anything but how warm and soft it is, and how
dashing I am in the mirror.

Oh, listen to me! This pretty coat is in my head.
But Belle, it is such a pretty coat. The store owner
must agree. He simply must. Once he sees this
coat, he will buy it and order ten more, I just know

it. And then the uncles will agree to bring all of you to Bensonhurst, because <u>I</u> got the factory such a large orders. And we all live happily ever after. (I know. Now I have vanity like you and am optimist like Papa. But is that such a horrid way to be?)

Oh! I forgot to mention where for lunch we wents! I will write about its tommorrow because my mind is tired from write English. Not too bad however, isn't it? I will to keep practicing!

Dear Belle,

I dream in English last night. This journal in
English makes change in my brains . . .

Lunch yesterday we went to a place called the
Automat. What a restaurant! No waiters, just
machines, with rows and rows of buttons. Oliver
and Mina would be in heaven to pressing all those
buttons! All of the food is display in small glass
windows . . . small plates of noodles with cheese,
meat pies, sandwiches. . . . I will to spend hours
looking at all the choices but it was lunch "rush
hour" so it was very crowded.

Every one was very talking too, lots of argueings
about some thing called the "World Series." I
gather that its a game of baseball (big sport here in
America). From what I can tell, some people want
to win the Bronx Bombers and others want to win
the Bums, and everyone is very excited speaking
his opinions.

Back to the Automat. I selected a cheeses
sandwich. You put coins in the hole, push a button,
and a little door open with the cheeses sandwich
you just see, all ready to eat. Even more amazing

were Max selection. He choosed an apple, a cup of coffee, and a piece of chocolate cake! That were all. He said he was celebrating how nice my coat looks, and I should to celebrate too. He gived me another coin, so I got a piece of blueberry pie.

After lunch I rided the subway to Bensonhurst all by myself. I was nervous but I made it just fine to home. (I really made such a long trip from Europe all by myself only 1 month before? It seem like ages!)

All together, its were a very nice start to October. And look, I realize that I just called the Max and Hannah's apartment "home."

Dear Belle,

Freddy told me straight about the World Series!
I saw him after lunch. He was walking outside
his apartment building . . . back and forth, back
and forth . . . like a dog with chain to a tree. It
was quite the scene . . . I will to try to write it as it
happened. (Good for English practice!)

First I asked, "What's the matter?"

Freddy said, "What's the matter? What's the
matter? Its a subway series here in Brooklyn,
and I can't go to Ebbets Field because its stinken
Shabbat!"

Then think I would impress him with how
knowing I am, I said, "You like the Bombers or the
Bums?"

Freddy stopped and looked at me like I asked
if he like ice cream or brussel sprouts. He said,
"Please say you are joking."

I admit I don't very much know about the
World Series. Freddy taked this very seriously and
made me sit on the stoop for a lesson right then.
He is not a patient teacher, but yes . . . I cannot
describe in English . . . passionné. For Freddy it

was <u>most</u> important that I understand the World Series right away.

Here is what he taught:

The World Series is the biggest baseball game of the year.

It is a championship between the 2 best teams.

This year the 2 teams are both from right here, New York. The New York Yankees and . . . the <u>Brooklyn</u> Dodgers. Brooklyn! Right here where wes live. No wonder every one are so excited!

More exciting, its Brooklyn Dodgers first time at the World Series since 1920!

Brooklyn Dodgers won on Thursday, so actually they are tied with the Bronx Bombers (Yankees). Freddy said, "They are to go all the way."

"Go all the way" means win the World Series.

When we had this conversation, they was to play the next game in Ebbets Field (right in Brooklyn) in 10 minutes!

I asked to Freddy, "You have a ticket?"

He get very sarcastic, said, "Oh yeah. Front row. I'm going to bat too. I will hit the big sign and win a free suit."

I stared to him. I have no idea what this means.

He shouted, "No I don't have a ticket!" He said

it didn't matter because it is Shabbat and his mom watching to making sure he does not move from his stoop.

I looked up to his apartment window on the second floor and saw his mother there, yes watching every thing! She would not even let him open the radio. He said, "Its torture!"

I had an idea. "I'd wager Hannah let us put on the radio."

Freddy lifted his head and said, "She will?"

"I think so. Your mother will let you come in my apartment?"

I did not even finish the sentence before Freddy was away. I saw him a moment later in the window, begging his mother. She looked down for me, and I politely try to look like a good, Sabbath-observing girl. I saw her agree yes, and Freddy to gave her a big hug. He burst to the sidewalk again so quickly he jumped down the staircase. A moment later, his brother Milton followed.

Milton said, "I'm to come along, to make sure you only to shoot marbles, like Freddy promised." He did a thing with his eye . . . oh, what is the word in English? I can not think it now . . . but you know, when you close one eye quickly and smile like to share a secret.

Freddy said, "Let's go!" He set off to my apartment. Oh Belle, it was very funny, because he wanted to go at my apartment quickly but he knew his mother would suspect him if he went <u>too</u> quickly, so he did an odd walk-and-run, like the legs of his trousers glued together.

Max was asleep (what is the word . . . daytime sleep . . . Mëttesrascht) so Hannah agreed to change the radio station (she was listening to music). Freddy knew which station for listen to the World Series. The excitement was catching. Max woke up soon, and we all listened together. Dodgers to go all the way!

Love,

Anna

Belle,

Today I went at Freddy's apartment to listen to the baseball game with he and Milton. Enid was there too, and she knew more about the players than anyone! It was a very exciting game because the Dodgers <u>almost</u> won, but then a player named Mickey Owen <u>dropped the ball</u>, and that must be very bad, because every thing turn sour. I could not follow exactly, but Freddy and Milton and Enid all screamed and pulled a terrific lot at their hair, so I did too. When I walked the 2 blocks back in my apartment after, it was as though all Bensonhurst were sad, like the Dodgers died instead of losed a baseball game. I made a good, serious face, but secretly I glowed with happiness to be part of the World Series.

When you arrive, perhaps we can all to go at a baseball game.

With love,
Anna

CHAPTER 20

"Oh, Anna," Madeline whispered. "Your family will never go at a baseball game."

"It's killing me," I said. "She's so happy right now. She's got no clue."

"She's got some clue," Madeline pointed out. "Remember when she had that bad feeling? That dream or whatever."

"Do you think that was because her family was being transferred to that transit camp?" I took out the paper with the summary from Yad Vashem and skimmed it. "The dates kind of match up."

"I don't know." Madeline laid her elbow on the table and her head on her hand. "I mean, it's not like this is a sci-fi novel, and Anna's got supernatural powers. This all really happened."

"You're right," I said. "As usual."

"Of course. What would you do without me?"

I knew she was waiting for a clever comeback, but I wasn't in the mood. Anna's happiness was making me miserable.

Oh Belle, I am bursting with happy! The owner loved the coat, and he ordered 6 for his store! SIX! He was not friendly, he did not even said his name. But he did say, "It's beautiful, just like this young model." My cheeks got terrific hot, I tried to hide them in the collar of the coat. But oh! Can you imagine? I want to dance for joy!

The good news continues . . . I got a job at the factory! Here's how: When Walter and the store owner left, Max placed 5 dollar bills in my hand. "For modeling," he said. The uncles protested in Yiddish, and Max argued, calmly, right back. I'm glad he won the argument, because I <u>need</u> that money. You see, I was <u>planning</u> to ask Max for a job in the factory, to save money to bring all of you here. I was so very nervous to ask, but this money gave me courage. I didn't do it very gracefully or surely . . . but I did said to Max, "I want to work. I can sew, I will learn fast. I will work every day." Mamelikanner, it is good I was not asking for a job to give speeches. I did say the most important thing though, and I tried to say it loud enough so the uncles would hear, if they could understand. I said,

"I want to save money to help my family come."

Max looked sad for a moment, but then he resumed a normal look and rubbed his chin. First he said they will need me to model some more, and for me to help with the sizing of the 6 new coats . . . they will pay me for that time. Then he began talking to the uncles in Yiddish. They seemed to be coming to his side. Finally, Max gave the answer. "No sewing, but you can do odd jobs. Sweeping, running errands, answering the door . . ."

How perfect, n'est-ce pas? "I will come every day," I promised.

He added, "After school." (I was to begin school this week, but because Sukkot was yesterday and with the coat so important, I begin next week instead.)

Now it is set. One dollar each day. After school, I will take the subway for Manhattan to work at the factory, then come home with Max. It will be tired making, yes, but I will be helping, and saving money for you.

Uncle Egg opened a closet I have not noticed before, and he took out a broom. He held out it to me and said, "Nu?"

My job started right then! I used a big magnet to pick up nails from the floor (they call the magnet "the nail getter"), piled up the scraps of fur, and learned to work the door buzz. I can picture the big stack of Reichsmarks that Mama gave to the passeur. That was only enough for one, and the price is most surely more by now. I haven't a clue how many dollars or cents it takes to make one Reichsmark, but no doubt it will take a long time for me to save enough. I am happy, though, because I will be one dollar closer every day.

Oh Belle, another splendid day! To celebrate the coat, Hannah and Max took me to the cinema! Max wanted to see a picture called "Citizen Kane," but Hannah wanted something light and fun, so she pointed to "Fantasia" . . . she said is so good it have been showing at the Broadway for 1 whole <u>year</u>. They gave me the final decision, and I choosed "Fantasia." Maybe it is made for younger children (like Oliver or Greta . . . it has Mickey Mouse) but I thought it was wonderful.

Oh, I almost forgot. The World Series is over. The Dodgers lost. Freddy wears black every day. "I'm in mourning," he said. "This is the worst week of my life."

You would slap him. I wanted to, but I tightened my fists and just walked away.

CHAPTER 21

"Last but not least," Mrs. Coleman called, "Mayim Winter."

Madeline sighed and stood up. "Wish me luck."

"Good luck," I said dully.

She took her haftorah up to Mrs. Coleman's desk, leaving me alone with the diary and my unease, which had only grown from Freddy's thoughtlessness. I probably should have waited to read on, but the next entries looked short, and it was too hard to resist.

Belle,

Two letters I got today, one from Papa and one from you! Just the sight of your penmanship made my insides turn to mush. Your letter say that Jews are now required to wear yellow stars on there clothes for identifying. You wrote, "Not the accessory I would choose, but I can make it work." I must did read that sentence 500 times. It makes me smile even as it makes me hurt, I miss you so much, Belle. That sentence is simply <u>you</u>.

Apart from the stars, neither letter contains bad news, but they are both marked 10 September, a long time ago. I look at the newspaper each day, but there are never stories about Luxembourg. How I wish I could telephone! But if that is possible it must cost terrific much money, and there are no way the uncles would stand for it. At supper yesterday, we came to the subject of a lady Uncle Onion once knew. Hannah said that the lady wanted to marry him.

Uncle Onion look like that is silly idea. He said, "Why should I support some strange woman?"

Honestly!

Time for Chinese checkers.

Until later,

Anna

Oh Belle, I'm <u>fuming</u> with anger!

During our game, Max told me that he wanted to sponsor <u>our whole family</u> to come to America last <u>year</u>! They could have gived Mama and Papa jobs at the factory, but the uncles would not allow it. They said they could not afford the money! Max said, "That is probably true, but we would have found a way." The opinion of Max does not matter because the uncles own the factory, so their signature needs to be on the paperwork, and they would not sign.

How I <u>hate</u> those uncles! If we did have sponsorship last year, it would have been easier and <u>less</u> money to get out of Luxembourg. We would not have need to pay a passeur at all, and I could have made the crossing with everyone! I would be <u>talking</u> with you right now instead of writing in this stupid journal.

I <u>never</u> liked those uncles. Now I hate them through and through. I HATE them. I hate them hate them hate them HATE THEM!

I slapped the diary shut, hating those uncles along with Anna. Didn't they know that people's *lives* were at stake? That they were separating a girl from her whole family just to save a little money? Like Madeline said, this wasn't some sci-fi novel; these were real people whose lives were affected in a major way. My stomach churned as I realized that some of these real people were still alive. Grandpa Fred, Great-Aunt Janet . . . this was their mom's life story. And here I was keeping it a secret from them. I was as bad as the uncles.

Well, not nearly *that* bad, but still.

How could I ask to learn more about my biological family if I was keeping secrets about theirs? I had to tell them about the diary. Right away.

"Nailed it," Madeline sang, laying her haftorah portion on the table like a winning hand of cards. "Mrs. Coleman was so impressed, she said I can hang out with you two tonight."

My blood was rushing through my body. I had a plan. "I think it'll be just you and Mrs. Coleman. I need to bail."

"What! How come?"

"I'm going to talk to my mom tonight, and probably my grandpa too."

Madeline gasped. Leaned in. Widened her eyes. "About finding your family?"

"Maybe," I said, and it was really true, because my plan might be the perfect segue to my next-step words. "But first"—I tapped the diary—"I'm going to tell them about finding theirs."

CHAPTER 22

Mom handled the diary like it was made of egg-shells. She even asked Dad if he'd brought any rubber gloves home from the lab—she seriously thought her fingerprints would destroy the paper or something—but Dad and I convinced her that that wasn't necessary.

"This thing made it across the ocean," I told her, "and lasted seventy-five years on Grandma Anna's shelf. It's pretty solid."

Jaime, on the other hand, flipped through it with all the care he gave the Lands' End catalog when Mom decided he needed new shirts.

"It's not *indestructible*," I said, taking it back. "Sheesh, Jaime."

"It's technically mine too," he said. "Grandma Anna left her books to *all* of her great-grandchildren."

"Yeah, but you said you didn't care about the books in her room."

"Whoa, whoa," Dad said. "You sound like Mom and her siblings fighting over Grandma's silver."

Mom shot him a look, but he returned it with one of his own, and she backed down, since he was right.

"The point," I said, "is that this isn't any of ours. Or it's all of ours. I don't know. If anything, it's Grandpa Fred and Aunt Janet's."

"Imani's right," Mom said. She picked up the phone and dialed Grandpa Fred.

Five minutes later, we were all huddled in front of the computer, waiting for Grandpa Fred to Skype. The picture of the four of us filled the screen in the meantime, and I noticed how dark my skin looked next to my parents' and Jaime's. I see it every time the four of us are together, even reflected in a store window. It's a split-second reminder, in case I forgot: *Oh right. You're adopted.* Did anyone else in my family ever have that reaction?

The image of us four shrank and moved to the corner, replaced by Grandpa Fred. It was the first time I'd seen him since Grandma Anna's apartment, and he looked better, or was at least trying to look better. The rough stubble that had formed during shiva was shaved, and he was wearing a Hawaiian shirt. But some sadness still lingered. I could see it in the dark crescents under his eyes, which were only made darker in the shadow of his desk light. My heartbeat sped, not knowing if what he was about to learn would make things better or worse.

"Imani, my love," he said. "I hear you have something to show me."

I don't know what he was expecting—probably a tennis trophy or an amateur magic trick—but I know it wasn't what I held up. "I was going through Grandma Anna's books, and I found this," I told him. (All technically true. If he asked when this was, I'd be honest, but if he chose to think I found it while going through her books *today,* that was fine too.)

He moved his face close to his computer screen, giving us a close-up of his wrinkled brow and remaining hairs. "What is that?"

My mom started to sniffle. I glanced at the image of us in the corner of the screen and saw that she was dabbing her eyes with a tissue.

"It's Grandma Anna's diary," I said. "From 1941."

He bolted upright, like an acting student asked to demonstrate surprise.

"She wrote it when she was twelve," I continued, "and she first came to America." I opened it and held it up to the webcam so he could see the handwriting, maybe even read some of the words.

Grandpa gave a low whistle. "It's real?" he asked.

I pulled the diary away from the camera and nod-ded.

"Have you read it?"

I nodded again. "Some of it. I'm up to the begin-ning of October. She's really into the World Series."

"Wait," Jaime said. "Did you say 1941? Was it the 1941 World Series?"

I looked at him with surprise. "Yeah, why?"

Jaime's mouth dropped open. "No way. The sub-way series where Mickey Owen dropped the ball and Tommy Henrich hit a home run and the Dodg-ers lost?"

All our faces, from both parts of the screen, stared at Jaime with disbelief. "How'd you know that?" I asked.

"How do you *not* know that? That's a classic series! I can't believe Grandma Anna was there."

"She wasn't there," I said, still in shock about my brother's knowledge of baseball history. "She lis-tened to it on the radio with her friend Freddy."

Now it was Grandpa's turn to get excited. "Freddy!" he said. He rubbed his hands over his face and looked directly into the camera. "Freddy?"

"Yeah."

"I'm named for a Freddy!" he explained. "She always said he was her first friend when she came to America."

My jaw dropped. "That's Freddy! Her first friend. The same Freddy! He's in here!" Wait till I tell Madeline! We weren't completely off base. There *was* a connection between Freddy and my grandpa Fred. "Freddy seems really cool," I told him.

"My namesake," Grandpa said proudly. "He died in the Korean War."

No. Freddy—Freddy!—was going to die. Was there anyone Anna wasn't destined to lose? "Soon?" I asked.

"Huh?"

"I mean, like, was Freddy young when he died? When was the Korean War?"

I could see Grandpa thinking.

"Late 1940s?" my dad guessed. "Early 1950s?"

"Something like that," Grandpa agreed. "Freddy was pretty young. Probably twenty or so."

That didn't seem too young to me. At least Anna would have Freddy for another eight or nine years before he died. No chance she'd have to deal with *that* in the course of this diary, anyway.

"Imani's researching Luxembourg for her Holocaust project," Mom told Grandpa. "Since she found the diary and all."

Grandpa smiled, but I could see the sadness creeping back into his face. He was probably thinking of Grandma Anna. The diary was bringing her to life for me, but this was Grandpa's *mom*. He must have wished she were still alive for real.

"It doesn't seem like it should really belong to me," I said to Grandpa, hoping to get this over with before he started to cry. "Do you want me to mail it to you?"

Grandpa shook his head. "Grandma left all her books to you."

"To both of us," Jaime corrected, sticking his face right in front of the camera. "I want to read the part about the World Series."

"To both of you," Grandpa said with a chuckle. "Isabel too. That means it's yours."

"Are you sure?" I asked.

He didn't look sure, but he still said, "Yes."

That settled that, but it wasn't like I was suddenly feeling fine about the whole thing the way I'd hoped. I swallowed and reminded myself of my plan. *Now's the time to bring it up,* I thought, *just to test the water.*

"I would love to see the diary, though," Grandpa said, "if you're willing to lend it to me."

"Of course!" I said.

"Okay. But take your time reading. I'll wait my turn. And don't put it in the mail! It's way too valuable."

"Right," my mom said. As if she would've let me

mail it anyway. If Grandpa wanted it right away, she probably would have driven it to Florida herself. I could see it now: Mom at the wheel with the diary buckled into the passenger seat, locked in some sort of waterproof, crash-proof, tamper-proof case. Maybe she'd have rented an armored car.

"Grandpa?" I said, my armpits getting sweaty as I tiptoed toward my carefully crafted words. *You're probably worrying for nothing,* I told myself. *Remember how easygoing Mom was about looking up your name.*

"Yes?" Grandpa asked.

"Did you know Grandma Anna had a twin?"

He looked surprised but not shocked. "Yes," he replied. "But I don't know much about her. My mom didn't like to talk about her past. She changed the subject whenever I tried to ask."

Sounds familiar, I thought.

"It must've been painful for her," Mom said, "to remember."

"So," I said, my eyes on Grandpa and my heart beating in rapid thumps, "you've always wondered about where she came from?"

"Yeah," Grandpa said. "I've always wanted to know more." He smiled, even as he looked sadder.

Here I go! "I've always wanted to know more about my birth parents too." I forced the words out quickly, before I could take them back. And as nervous as I still was, I couldn't help but feel a little bit triumphant. Because, there. I'd done it. It was just a tiny step—a dip of a toe in a deep, dark lake. But I'd done it! Now what?

Grandpa looked lost in his memories, but I could see my mom flinch in the corner of the screen. She and my dad looked at each other. My words hung there like an airborne disease, with no one knowing whether or not to panic.

"Great seeing you, Fred," my dad said finally. "We'll keep the diary safe until you visit."

"Thank you, sir." Grandpa gave a small salute. "And thank you, Imani."

"Love you, Dad," my mom said. Her smile was fake, and her voice was empty, and my stomach tightened into a pit. Mom leaned over me and clicked to end the call. Then she straightened up and sniffed. I barely glanced at her, but I could tell her eyes were filling with tears.

"Mom—" I started. I didn't know what I was going to say, so I guess it was okay that she cut me off.

"I'm going to get ready for bed," she said. "It's been a long day."

Jaime, trying to pretend a bomb hadn't just gone off, asked my dad if he wanted to play catch. Dad's eyes flicked to me for a second, then, decidedly, to Jaime. "Let me put on a sweatshirt." He jogged up the steps, and I followed behind him, my legs like lead. Dad closed the door of his room, but I knew he was comforting Mom, and I'm pretty sure she was crying. Their words were muffled, but I think I heard her say something about not being prepared.

I sat down, heavily, on the top step and pressed my palms into my eyes. This was nothing like when Mom caught me looking up my name. How could I even think that it'd be the same?

"Imani," Jaime said nervously. "You made Mom cry."

"Everything makes Mom cry," I said, lifting my head and hoping my eye roll would mask my guilt.

"That's mean."

"But it's true." I was just making this better and better.

He stared at my face for a second, like he was trying to figure out if he knew who I was. He was probably wondering what kind of nasty, evil genes my birth parents had given me, and feeling confident his DNA came from a nicer set of people. People who knew all about the 1941 World Series. Then, looking like he might cry himself, he shook his head and went to his room to get his baseball mitt.

I lingered on the landing, debating knocking on

my parents' closed door. Then I heard the bathwater start running. Mom was making herself officially unavailable.

Dad came out in a sweatshirt. "Your mother . . ." he said, trailing off in such a way that I thought, for a crazy few seconds, that he was about to say something about my birth mother. But no. He was talking about Mom. "Just give her some time, Imani," he said. Then he jogged downstairs and out the door.

Some time? I thought. Like, she'll be better in the morning? Or should I wait another twelve years? My stomach turned over as I stared at the bedroom door. She'd probably stay in there all night, trying to set the world record for longest bath. Anything to avoid talking to her ungrateful daughter about her past.

So much for testing the water. If Mom got this upset when I dipped a toe, what would she do when I landed a cannonball?

Sunday, 12 October 1941

Belle,

What a day! I was "out of sorts" all week . . .
furious about the uncles, nervous about starting
school soon, worrying about you. . . . I told Freddy
I needed a clear head, and he said (this is funny),
"You need a ride on the Cyclone. That will whip
your head around so much, all your thoughts will
get Hoovered through your ears and go flying into
outer space."

In an odd way, that sounded appealing. So . . .
we went to Coney Island today! "We" was Freddy
and me, and Milton and Enid, and Hannah and
Max. And the most impossible thing: Uncles Egg
and Onion came too! (Coney Island is free if
you don't ride or buy anything, but still, can you
believe it?) We all put on nice clothes (well, not
Freddy) and rode the subway to the end of the
line. Freddy talked and talked about every ride
and game and food and in what order best to do
them.

There were so many wonderful, truly happy
moments today that I could barely list them all,
but I will tell some:

- Hannah wagered a nickel that her Steeplechase horse would win Max's horse, and it did!

- Eating a hot dog and fries from Nathan's. Uncle Egg said that it tasted terrible, and that it was too small. Freddy slurped the ketchup off first again, then ate the bun. He put the dog in his pocket for later of course . . . but he lost it on the parachute jump!

- The uncles rode the Human Roulette Wheel! Uncle Egg's hat fell off while spinning, and Uncle Onion tried to catch it but instead landed <u>on top of it</u> and flattened it like a pancake!

- We all took for a photo postcard. It was Hannah's idea. We could have weared silly costumes, but Max wouldn't hear of it (a relief because I didn't want the costumes either). The 8 of us stood together, even the uncles, and the photo was ready in just 10 minutes. Hannah said I could keep the postcard to remember the day. I can't stop looking at it and seeing myself with <u>this</u> people of 8. It makes me happy and sad at the same time. Before I left home, I did not know that feeling was possible.

- The very last thing we did was ride the Cyclone.

I needed the whole day to find my courage, and I almost didn't, but Freddy said, "You want your mind erased, remember?" So yes, I rode my first roller coaster!

ZOWEE, what a rush! Erase my mind indeed! We <u>whipped</u> around those curves like the track was on fire. It was so fast, so bumpy, it shook my <u>bones</u>. Freddy was next to me, and he pulled my hands up into the sky. I see now why you and Greta like the fast rides. Yes, the climb up is horrid . . . so long and slow . . . and then the car turns around a curve, and you see the dive coming and fear you aren't brave enough, but it's too late to get off. Then, ready or not, you start to drop. And my, does it feel <u>good</u> to scream.

CHAPTER 23

My mom left for work early the next morning, which was fine, because I couldn't decide if I was going to apologize or not. Dad and Jaime acted like nothing had happened last night. I was still feeling guilty. All morning, my body was doing the things it was supposed to do—shower, brush teeth, eat a pack of mini muffins for breakfast on the way to school—but, as my tennis coach would say, my head was not in the game.

I wished I could ride the Cyclone and have my thoughts Hoovered through my ears and into outer space. But no such luck. They stayed in my brain, screwing with my focus and making me do ridiculous things. I got chicken nuggets at lunch, totally forgetting until I bit into one that the cafeteria might as well bread their chicken nuggets with cardboard.

I accidentally volunteered to stand in front of the whole class and act out a scene with Magda—entirely in Spanish. And after school I changed into my tennis clothes, stretched, and filled my water bottle, only realizing when I got to the courts that there wasn't practice today.

"What is *up* with me today?" I shouted, pounding the net with my racquet.

"I don't know!" shouted some older kid who was walking by. His friends laughed and then ran away. Whatever.

I couldn't bring myself to go home yet, and I didn't feel like hanging out with Madeline either. I walked over to the edge of the court, sat down against the edge of the fence, and pulled out the diary.

Wednesday, October 15, 1941

Dear Belle,

I went to school today. Hannah was so excited and nervous, like it was <u>her</u> first day of school. She and Max presented me a nice leather book bag as a gift . . . this angered me at first. I thanked them of course, and I know they meant well, but I wish they'd spent that money on bringing my family instead of a leather bag. When I got to school, however, I was glad to have it, to be plain. Everyone else had a nice bag, and to carry my books or use my old bag would have drawn more attention to me. I just want to blend in and get by. Only one teacher ("homeroom") wanted I stand in front of the room for an introduction, so the rest of the day I was able to drift along without notice.

How strange to be at school and not have anyone know me, or mistake me for you. A girl in my math class invited me to sit at her lunch table, but I told her I was going home at lunch, which is what Hannah and I planned. My heart started beating quickly at the invitation, so I was glad to have an excuse. But then, walking to and from the apartment, I was sad and wished I accepted. You would have accepted without a care. You probably be spending the evening with that girl and her friends tonight, and by tomorrow every other girl in the seventh grade would beg to sit with you at lunch. I don't need that much popular, but it would be nice to make a friend beside Freddy (especially since he is still in elementary school . . . when he bothers to attend). I will try to channel you, the bold twin, and be braver and more fun. I told Hannah I will try eating lunch at school tomorrow. I don't need to listen to the next episode of "The Romance of Helen Trent." (This a radio "soap opera" she always likes at lunch time.)

After school, I took the subway to the factory. I used the nail getter on the floor and went to the stationer to buy more pens and ink. I helped Max arrange some pelts on the table as well. He is always staring at these things, arrange the strips of skins in different ways. When I help, I hand him pins in silence, much like the way we play Chinese checkers. Today he asked if school was okay, and I said yes, and that was all. He is so different from Hannah! She would want for me to perform a play of the whole morning while we ate lunch. I do hope Hannah gets to meet you soon. You would

be fast friends, so much that Hannah will probably
wish they sent the other twin from the first day.
I wonder if Mama and Papa believe they made a
mistake to send me. I remember the way Papa took
my shoulders in his hands before I left. He said,
"Be brave, Anna. You're going to be brilliant."

Tell Papa I'm trying. I'm trying my best.

Love,

Anna

Thursday, October 16, 1941

Ma très chère Belle,

Today I took your favorite class . . . French!
Hearing French was like jumping into a cold
lake . . . startling at first, but then you start
swimming, and it feels natural and refreshing. The
other students are just starting out, so their French
is very poor. Much, much worse than my English!
Mme. Veron called me to her desk after class.
She asked me where I was from, and she became
excited when I told her. She moved here from Paris
in 1936! She has never been to Luxembourg, but
she used to vacation in Marseille, close to where
we would go with Mama's family!

She said my French is very good (which it is, of
course, though I have not spoken in these many
months) so she will see about if I can transfer to
the 8th-grade class. It will still be easy for me, but
she thinks it might be "un peu plus interessant,
n'est-ce pas?" To be plain, I don't mind having 1
easy class, since I must concentrate so heavy in
English the rest of the day, but I daren't say so.
Mme. Veron had another idea as well, one that I
liked better.

She said she has a student who is struggling. She's in 8th grade, name Miriam. She scarcely got by last year, and then forgot everything over the summer, according to Mme. Veron. She said, "She's very sweet, though. You will like her. Perhaps the two of you can meet during lunch once or twice a week. You can help her with French, and she can help you with English."

I said I would like that, and I meant it. Before I left, Mme. Veron took me in her arms and kissed both my cheeks. She said, "The transition can be hard. It is still hard, even for me. And the news from home . . ." She closed her eyes and shook her head . . . she understands. "If you need someone to talk to, when the words won't come in English, you can always come to me."

Would you believe I started to cry? It was so sudden, I couldn't stop myself. Mme. Veron gave me a hug again, and even though I knew her less than one hour, it did not seem strange to be crying into her shoulder. When I stopped finally and pulled away, I saw that she was crying too.

"Hey," said a familiar voice. I turned around, which was really awkward, since I was so close to the fence. It was Ethan. He was wearing jeans and a jacket, because he's not an idiot.

"Hey," I said. I closed the diary and placed it in my backpack.

"Practicing on an off day? You're such a Williams."

I tried to think of something witty, but *thinking* clearly wasn't my thing today. Better to tell the truth. "I thought it was a Thursday. I'm stupid, I know."

Ethan walked onto the court. He took off his backpack and sat down next to me. Well, pretty close. We both leaned against the fence. "Once," he said, "I got up at six forty-five, showered, got dressed, ate breakfast, and walked halfway to school before I realized it was a Saturday."

I looked at him with my eyes wide, my mouth halfway open and halfway smiling. "No way."

"You're right, no way. I just wanted to make you feel better."

I punched his arm lightly. "Hey!"

"Oh!" Ethan said. "But I did stay up late last night to finish that essay for Mrs. Magill's class."

I cocked my head. "Why? That's not due till next week."

"Exactly." His voice cracked on the *ack* part, but he didn't even blush.

I grinned. "So, your form of being an idiot is being an extra-good student."

"And yours is being an extra-good tennis player."

"Right. That, and I'm having an identity crisis."

Ethan didn't have a response to that. To be fair, how could he? It must've sounded totally random and like way too much information. I was suddenly glad to have my tennis racquet in my lap. Fiddling with the strings gave my fingers something to do and my eyes someplace to look. I had to explain, but I didn't want to talk about the Skype call and my mom's record-setting bath. So I told him about the other thing consuming my mind, starting with, "My great-grandma died a few weeks ago."

"Oh," Ethan said. "I'm sorry."

"That's okay," I said quickly, "she was really old. But when we were at her apartment for shiva, I found this diary she wrote when she was our age. She had a whole bunch of siblings—a twin sister, even—but her parents sent her over to America by herself, to escape the Holocaust."

"Whoa."

"Yeah." The sun moved behind a cloud, and goose bumps rose on my bare arms. Some leaves blew across the court and flapped against the bottom of the net. "I've been reading her story, and just . . . I don't know. Thinking about it a lot."

"My great-grandpa was on the Kindertransport," Ethan offered.

I looked up from my racquet. "What's that?"

"It was this program that helped get kids away from the Nazis. No parents, just kids. They took a train to England—all these kids—and foster families took them in. My great-grandpa and his brother went." He'd been talking quickly, but then stopped. His cheeks got red. "I'm researching it for my bar mitzvah project," he explained.

As Anna would say, my insides turned to mush. If only he knew how cool I found it that he was into his great-grandfather's story; he didn't need to be embarrassed for my sake. "How old was your great-grandpa?" I asked.

"When he died?"

"When he left his parents."

"Oh. Nine, maybe? Ten?"

"Did he ever see them again?"

"His dad, yeah. His mom didn't survive. But apparently when he and his brother did finally see their dad again, things were really weird between them."

"How come?"

"It'd been a long time, I guess. They'd all changed."

I plucked at the strings of my racquet. That made sense. I assumed happy things would have come if

Anna had been able to reunite with her family, but she'd only been away for a couple of months. To see them after a few years, when they'd been in a concentration camp, that would be . . . well, different. If I did find my birth parents, and we reunited after all this time, what would that be like? It could go a million different directions.

"According to my grandma," Ethan continued, "he didn't get along with his foster family very well either. He moved to America to go to college and, like, never talked to them again."

"Wow," I said. "Why didn't he like them?"

"I don't know. But I watched this documentary about the Kindertransport, and it seems like it was pretty common. Some families didn't really want the kids; they just took them for the money the organization would pay."

"Seriously?"

"Yeah. Some had kids of their own who were jealous. And the Kindertransport kids had all sorts of stuff to deal with too. It was a new culture. They missed their parents."

"They didn't speak the language," I added. "They might have looked different."

Ethan nodded. I saw him glance at me, the shade of my skin, and then look away, squint through his glasses past the courts and into the trees. "Maybe my great-grandpa's foster family was fine, but he was angry and wouldn't have liked anyone. Who knows."

We sat there in silence for a while. I thought about Anna's day at Coney Island, and the photo postcard of her with Max, Hannah, and the others. When it came to adoptive families, Anna and I lucked out, I guess. A lump rose in my throat.

"Well," Ethan said finally.

"Yeah." I stood up. "I guess I'd better start my private tennis practice."

"With no ball," Ethan pointed out.

I laughed. Ethan laughed.

"Hey, what's your cell number?" he asked. He sounded like he was working very hard to make it seem like it'd only *just* occurred to him to ask, this very moment. I warned him that my phone is not smart, so he took out his: a flip phone that looked even older than mine. "Our parents went to the same store," he joked.

"In the same time machine," I added.

He grinned, added my number, and texted me so I'd have his. "Okay," he said awkwardly. "See you tomorrow."

I gave a wave that was sort of like a salute. Then I bent down quickly to gather my stuff and pretend I hadn't done that. (I mean, *really, Imani?* A salute?)

After he disappeared behind the school, I stood

there for a minute, enjoying the breeze and wondering how to smooth things over with my parents. I didn't have the guts to do it with words, but maybe I could do it with actions.

It's amazing how productive you can be when you have something to prove. By the time my parents came home from work, I'd done all my homework, including the essay for Mrs. Magill's class that was due next week. I'd also picked up all the clothes and junk from my bedroom floor, and—for the first time ever—"Hoovered" the carpet without being asked. It was a total coward's apology, for what I said last night and also for my snooping, which they didn't even know had happened, but it seemed to do the trick. My parents—cowards themselves, I guess—accepted it without any words, but with an act of forgiveness: tortellini for dinner.

Oh Belle,

I had again a terrible dream last night. I must have been screaming, because my throat hurts today. All day I was worried that something horrid had happened, and I think I'm right because I came home to find that all of the letters I've sent in the past month came back unopened . . . a terrific stack of them were placed on the desk in my room. Hannah tried to warn about it before I saw, and I could tell she was worried too, but nothing could have stopped the buckle of my knees, or the weight that seemed to push me down to the floor.

"Not at this address," the letters say. Why are you not at this address?

"Perhaps they moved," Hannah said stupidly. Not even she sounded convinced. I don't know why she bothered.

"They could be on their way here," she said.

Are you on your way here, Belle? But if you were, Papa would have found a way to telegram, or Mama would have written. I haven't received any letters in weeks and weeks . . .

"The war," Hannah said. "Surely all the mail is held up by the war."

The war. It is starting to sound like at home, with the war to blame for everything, all the time. Remember our joke . . . only not really a joke . . . that Mina's first word would be "Krich"? War.

Max said he will try to telegram tomorrow (but to what address, if you are not at home?), and Hannah spent all evening telephoning women from the synagogue to see if anyone has a way to get information. We are all afraid. Me most of all.

Thinking of you always,

Anna

Belle,

Still no information. I feel as though the string connecting you and me is stretched thin as a hair, but still intact. I close my eyes and imagine messages flowing across that string, winding their way across holes and objects, like a little marble in a game of Chinese checkers. That's what I need now . . . that is why I continue to write this diary as though you are here. I need my words in this journal to you, my twin, to be like a game piece, making its way across the stars to chart a path home. It has a long way to travel, and the string may zig and zag, but it will find its way somehow and let me know you are okay.

Are you okay?

Sunday, October 19, 1941

Where are you, Belle?

We still know nothing. Hannah is every day reading the uncles' copy of "The Jewish Daily Forward" and even listening to the Yiddish radio station instead of music, but we have no answers.

I have been trying to think of other things, <u>anything</u> but our family, but it's impossible. I played with Freddy and other neighbors in the street today, but my head was elsewhere. During a game called Johnny on a pony, I got crushed against a brick wall and I barely realized it, though now I've a terrific scrape on my elbow and my neck is sore. Then we played hide-and-seek. When it was my turn to count . . . and I opened my eyes to find everyone gone . . . I realized what a cruel game it is. I didn't look for anyone. I just ran back to the apartment and cried.

I wonder how long everyone stayed hiding. They probably think I played a trick on them, and they won't ever want to play with me again. Well, I don't care. I'd give up every person I know here for a single breath of news about you and Mama and Papa and Kurt and Greta and Oliver and Mina and Grandmother and Grandfather. <u>Where are you?</u>

CHAPTER 24

I stopped Madeline's hand from turning the page. "Madeline," I said. It was Friday night, and we were in her basement, reading the diary together again.

"There's something I forgot to tell you," I told her now.

Madeline looked at me over her reading glasses, expectant.

"It's bad news," I said. "Are you sure you want me to tell you?"

"Well, now you have to tell me."

"Freddy dies."

Madeline gasped, and her glasses slid down her nose. "What! When?"

"Not soon," I assured her. "He died fighting in the Korean War."

Madeline held up one finger. Then she did a quick search on her phone. "June 1950 to July 1953," she reported, showing me the screen. "So Freddy won't die for another, like, ten years."

I felt like I'd taken a tennis ball to the chest. When I first heard that same information, on the call with Grandpa Fred, ten years seemed like a long time—I've only been alive twelve, after all. But right now it struck me as impossibly short.

"How do you know?" Madeline asked.

"My grandpa told me. He's named for him, just like you thought."

"No way. Was Freddy his dad?"

"No," I said with a weak laugh. "He didn't really know much about Freddy at all. He just knows that he was named for his mom's first friend in America."

"That's so cool," Madeline said. "I wish *I* was named for my mom's first friend in America, instead of my great-aunt Mildred."

"Aw." I leaned my head on Madeline's shoulder. "I bet Mildred was really cool. Maybe she went by Millie."

"Nope. Mildred. My dad said she did some killer embroidery, though."

I laughed. "My middle name, Harper, is for my dad's grandma, Hildie. My mom sometimes makes her recipe for kugel."

"Hildie sounds awesome," Madeline said. "She and Mildred would've been best friends."

I nodded. "For sure. They were probably on the same roller derby team."

"When they weren't making kugel."

"Obviously."

We heard some footsteps on the stairs. Madeline's dad. "Hi, girls," he said. "There's Thai food upstairs. Come get some when you're hungry."

"Okay," said Madeline. "Hey, Dad?"

He stopped at the foot of the stairs. "Yeah?"

"Did Great-Aunt Mildred make kugel?"

"Yes!" he said. "Potato kugel."

Madeline and I looked at each other, our eyebrows up.

"It was awful," Mr. Winter continued. "She was a terrible cook. Her matzo balls were like bricks."

Madeline and I both cracked up.

"It's true!" he said with a grin. "You needed a steak knife to cut those things!"

I pictured two old ladies, Hildie and Mildred, hacking at matzo balls with a meat cleaver. The image only made me laugh harder.

Mr. Winter was on a roll now. "Don't even get me started on her brisket."

Madeline and I fell on top of each other, we were laughing so hard.

"You girls." He beamed and shook his head. "Come get some dinner soon, okay?" Then he left us to our laugh fest.

"Maybe that's why my Hebrew name is Mayim," Madeline said between deep breaths. "Millie's cooking was so bad, you had to wash it down with lots and lots of water."

I sighed a happy sigh. Maybe that was true. It was pretty random that Madeline's Hebrew name meant "water."

"*Imani* means 'faith' in Swahili," I told her. "I looked it up."

Madeline looked at me, surprised and eager for more. Then she remembered her promise not to bring up my birth parent search—I could see the restraint it was taking her to honor it. But she did.

"Come on, Faith Hildie Mandel," Madeline said, nudging me with her elbow. "Let's go eat pad thai."

Monday, October 20, 1941

Belle,

Today at the factory, Max told me why he is always arranging the pelts in different ways. It takes 35 skins to make a short jacket, and 60 or so to make a long coat. But Max knows there must be a way to make a coat using fewer pelts, if we just cut them right. It is like a puzzle that I will help solve.

Each skin costs $18, so if we can make a coat using 33 pelts for instance, or 30, we will save a lot of money. We could also sell each coat for less money then, so we'll "undercut the competition" and sell many more coats. I know the uncles would like that!

Uncle Egg kept looking up from his desk and peeking at me and Max by the table, not knowing if he should be grumpy or not. (What a decision! He is always grumpy.) It was like he wanted me to be cleaning or running errands to get his money worth, but he also knew it'd be more money if I could help Max figure out this puzzle. I know I shouldn't need to prove anything to those uncles, but part of me still hopes that if they see how helpful I can be, they will want to send for the rest of you, and very soon. I do want to help Max too.

Beside, the pelts is a good puzzle. At first it seems like it must be simple. But then you realize that while each pelt can be cut in many ways, they can't be cut just <u>any</u> way, or else the coat will look ugly. Are larger pieces better, or smaller? The colors must match up, as though the whole coat was made from one animal. We must avoid waste too. That is important.

Thank you, Max, for giving me this puzzle. It keeps my mind occupied more so than sweeping the floor.

Wednesday, October 22, 1941

Mamelikanner . . .

There is a FISH in the BATHTUB. A horse-
drawn cart came down 64th St. with a man selling
alive fish. Hannah heard the man ringing a bell and
ran out (in her dressing gown!) to buy. A FISH.
It is a kind called "pike." We filled the bathtub
with water, and the pike is swimming in there
right now, as I write. It will be fish for Shabbat
dinner. It will be dead by then . . . yowza, I hope
so . . . but I don't want to know how. Maybe the
uncles will kill it. (They complained that it is not a
carp, because carp is cheaper. I suppose we have a
luxury fish swimming in our bathtub.)

Oh, how I hate fish. It is making a terrific mess
of my stomach, and it is not yet near my fork.
This is truly the last thing I need, as I am already
so queasy with worry. I suppose on Friday night I
can say I'm not hungry because I'm worried. Then
I won't have to eat the fish. Unless I hear from you
or Mama or Papa by then . . . if it's good news I
will gobble up the whole pike as though it's chow
mein!

Thursday, October 23, 1941

Dear Belle,

I still know nothing about what matters. About you . . . about home. (For a moment I forgot the Luxembourgish word for home. How could I forget "doheem"? Doheem. Doheem.)

School helps for distraction, but not entirely. I sat with some girls at lunch one day. They were trying to be friendly, but I wasn't helping them very much. If only you were here . . . I could see they didn't want me to sit with them again, so I've been eating lunch in the apartment with Hannah instead.

Tomorrow I will have lunch with Miriam, the girl Mme. Veron said needs help with French. I do hope we get on. Then we can meet during lunch every day. I am tired of "The Romance of Helen Trent."

Lunch with Miriam was wonderful! We brought our lunch to Mme. Veron's room, so I did not have to sit in the cafeteria. You would be mad about her, Belle. She has masses of curled black hair. And a very excited humor always, like she just cannot wait to tell you secrets. And you will never guess what we talked most about . . . "The Romance of Helen Trent"!

Miriam adores that show, just like Hannah. She repeated the introduction, in a dramatic voice just like the man on the radio . . . "And now, the real-life drama of Helen Trent, who—when life mocks her, breaks her hopes, dashes her against the rocks of despair—fights back bravely, successfully!" She had me in stitches. She said, "Mme. Veron says you came here all by yourself from the war. You are a real-life Helen Trent!"

I put the back side of my hand to my forehead and said, "Yes, I also hope to prove that when a woman is 35 or over, romance is not over." (This is also in the beginning of the program.)

When is the last time I laughed with a girlfriend? I can't even remember . . . It felt warm and wonderful, I did not want our lunch to end. Maybe it is a good sign and there will be happy news from you tomorrow!

CHAPTER 25

The text message sound pulled me out of Anna's world. I wasn't even going to look at it. Madeline had left for a trip this morning, so her phone was off while she was on the plane. That meant the text was probably my mom telling me Jaime was stretching before his soccer match. I knew I'd get a whole bunch of messages throughout the morning, enough to re-create the whole game kick by kick. My dad probably brought his video camera too. He and Jaime would relive the match tonight with a bowl of popcorn. They'd want me to watch too. This is why it's usually easier to just *go* to Jaime's games. But it was super windy out, and I was feeling lazy. I'd decided to spend the morning lounging around in my pajamas and finding out if Anna managed to hear anything about her family.

My phone chimed again. Another text. I held my right hand in the crease of the diary and reached for my phone with my left. It wasn't from my parents at all. Both were from Ethan!

Hey Williams

U there?

I smiled. I closed the diary, making sure to mark my page with the green ribbon.

Yeah, I typed. *What's up?*

It took so long for Ethan to reply, I looked at the clock seven or eight times. Strangely, the time didn't change from 10:03.

Is ur brother playing soccer right now?

Yeah. Why?

Watching my sister on field 3. Come hang out.

No! I gasped and dropped my face into my pillow. Of all days for me to skip Jaime's game.

I'm at home! I typed, hoping I sounded disappointed, but not so disappointed that it'd be weird.

Ethan replied with a sad face, typed out because his phone is even older and less smart than mine. It made me grin.

I thought itd be boring, I explained, *and windy.*

It IS boring and windy, he said. *We coulda been bored and cold together.*

My stomach got genuine butterflies. I could imagine Parker and Magda shrieking behind me. I reread the whole exchange a few times, trying to think of the perfect response. The best I could come up with was a slanty-mouthed face and the words *Next time*.

Ethan didn't reply for a few minutes. Then he asked if I was going to Parker's bat mitzvah.

Yeah, I typed. *U?*

He replied with not one, not two, but *three* smiley faces. Three! Then he added, *See u there Williams!*

That exclamation point was better than a bowl of three-cheese tortellini. I sent him a grinning face and dropped my phone into my covers. Then I got up and shook out my arms and legs, which were kind of tingly.

I went to the bathroom and brushed my teeth. The wind was whistling against the window, and the trash bins were rolling around outside like drums, waiting for me to break into song. I spit out my toothpaste with a satisfying *pwew* and wiped my mouth on a towel. I didn't change out of my pj's, though. I got right back in bed and started reading the next entry.

Sunday, October 26, 1941

Belle,

My good humor from Friday has been buried by
worry again. The news from Europe is disgusting.
If I don't hear something soon from Mama or
Papa, I believe I will go mad.

Freddy and I rode the bus to downtown
Brooklyn today. This driver knows Freddy, so he
let us stand in the wheel well and ride for free.
We went to a store for magic tricks. Freddy kept
asking the boy working to demonstrate tricks,
but he didn't buy any, so it was as though we had
our own private magic show for free. Then we
went to a bakery where Freddy knows the owner,
and she gave to us both free doughnuts. It was
an enjoyable afternoon, and all for free, since we
made sure to catch a bus with the same driver on
the way back to Bensonhurst. But my mind is still
elsewhere.

Bier is starting to lose the smell of Oliver. Or
maybe I'm just forgetting what he smelled like.

Tuesday, October 28, 1941

Some news! Mme. Veron heard from someone
in Vienna that a train full of Jews left for "the east"
a few weeks ago. She said someone else got a letter
from Jews who were to be transported east from
Frankfurt. It could be that Luxembourgish Jews
were transported as well.

I can't make heads or tails of this. How I long to
see you, or just speak with you, or do anything to
contact you besides write in this dumb journal that
you can not read! Are you truly going east? Why?
You are supposed to move closer to me, not farther
away. Hannah has been on the telephone all
afternoon, but no one knows more. On Saturday
Max will see what he can learn from the other men
at shul. I have waited so long, and now I must wait
longer. How will I survive?

The wind shook the tree outside my window. I was no longer in the right mood to read about this. The whole situation was so unfair. If only the internet had existed in 1941. That would have made it so much easier for Anna to contact her family and find out what was going on. She wouldn't be at the whim of the post office during a war. She wouldn't have to just sit and wait and wonder.

Wait a second.

Anna didn't have the internet, but I do. So do my birth parents.

I had an idea.

CHAPTER 26

Downstairs, I threw together a bowl of cereal and brought it over to the computer. Outside, the wind was still going nuts, but inside, it had nothing on my heartbeat. The lousy feeling I had after snooping in the filing cabinet was still fresh in my memory, but I'd tried talking to my parents, and that'd felt even worse. This new idea might be a total bust, but it was safer to find that out while no one was home.

When Madeline had given me that list of adoption websites, they all looked really official, with URLs that ended with *.gov* and stuff like that. I knew those sites wouldn't tell me anything without permission from my adoptive parents, or at least the name of the adoption agency they used—two things I didn't have. But I did have something. Three things, actually: my birthdate, the city where I was born, and the internet. If my birth mother wanted to find *me*—or if any adult wanted to find a child they'd given up for adoption, just, you know, hypothetically—they'd use those same three things, right?

Here's what I typed into Google:

find daughter adopted philadelphia june 2002

Here's what came up: 604,000 results.

I slowly raised a spoonful of cereal to my mouth as I scanned the page. I decided to click on the third down, a link that said "Search and Reunion," and found myself on some kind of message board. There were thousands of posts (78,885, to be exact), all from people who were looking for someone or something.

Looking for half-brother born 1976 Rochester, NY
Girl born August 1982
Abandoned baby Dallas Texas 1960
Looking for my son born NJ 1984

As I scrolled more, I realized that some of the posts had different subjects:

I may have found my birth father
Meeting my birthmom today! What do I say?
HELP! Do they want to know me or not?

I kept scrolling, reading title after title and clicking to learn more about other people's searches. Some of these people were really old (their birthdays were from a *long* time ago), and some were looking for cousins or grandparents or siblings. Some knew nothing except which foreign country they were adopted from, and some knew a person's whole name (first, middle, and last) but still couldn't find them.

I chewed another bite of cereal, now warm and soggy, as I scrolled and read. It was as mesmerizing as the pictures of all the Imanis. Here were all these different people, all over the world, who were, in some small, important way, like me.

"Imani?"

I jumped so high, I banged my knee into the bottom of the desk. Tears came to my eyes, it hurt so badly.

My mom came running from the front door. "Ouch. Are you okay, sweetie?"

I meant to close the browser, but in my panic I only minimized it. And there wasn't time to do anything else. I limped over to the couch and rubbed my throbbing knee. I needed to keep Mom away from the computer.

"You scared me," I said.

"Sorry." She frowned and sat down on the edge of the couch, as I hoped she would. "I didn't want you to be scared when someone opened the door. That's why I shouted your name. But I guess I made it worse." She kissed the sore spot, like she used to do when I was a kid. "Better?"

"A little," I said. "Why are you home?"

Mom's eyes went up to a corner of the ceiling for a few seconds. "Oh!" she remembered. "To get Dad's video camera. He forgot it. And so did I, for a second there," she said with a chuckle. "Senior moment. While I'm remembering things," she continued, "do you have plans tomorrow?"

"I guess not."

"Good. You and I are going to go shopping."

My blood was racing and my knee was aching, but this still made me groan. "Why?"

"Parker's bat mitzvah's coming up, and that's just the first of many."

My body became a blob on the couch. Shopping with my mom is so embarrassing. She always gets the salespeople involved. When we went for new school clothes, she even called a salesgirl *inside* my fitting room to show her how big some pants were in the butt area. "Can't we just look online and I'll try them on here?"

"No, it's better to go to the mall," Mom said. "I'll be away for work most of next week, so this is our only time. I wouldn't know what size to get anyway. Your body's changing."

Great. Now my mom will probably tell the salespeople that my body is changing. Or she'll decide that this is a good time to talk about puberty. I needed to keep her away from the computer, but how desperate was I willing to get? Better to talk about dresses. "How many dresses do I need?"

"At least two or three. You can't wear the same thing to every party. And at some point we'll have to get one for your own bat mitzvah, of course."

I made a face.

"You can't wear jeans and a T-shirt on the bimah, Imani."

"Mo-om," I said with the tone of a verbal eye roll. Just because I don't want to spend the weekend dress shopping doesn't mean I plan to wear jeans and a T-shirt at my bat mitzvah.

"Okay." Mom stood up and patted my shoulder. Then she went to get Dad's video camera from—oh Mamelikanner—the desk.

Don't look closely at the screen, I willed.

"Do you want to come back to Jaime's game with me?" Mom asked. She was moving some stuff around on the desk, looking for the camera. "I'll wait while you get dressed."

My mind flashed to Ethan—we coulda been bored and cold together, he'd said—but it was too risky to leave my mom alone with the computer while I changed. "No thanks," I said.

"Yeah, stay home and relax," she agreed. "The wind is terrible. And it seems like it might rain. Maybe I should bring an umbrella. I'll just check the weather . . ." She opened the browser.

She opened the browser.

She saw the website that was there. Adoption search and reunion. And her whole body froze.

"Um," I said. Because what could I say? That this wasn't what it looked like? It was *exactly* what it looked like.

Mom stayed frozen in front of the screen, silent and stiff.

"Mom?"

Finally, she straightened. I couldn't see her face, because she didn't turn around. And I found that instead of feeling guilty, this time I felt angry. There were so many adoptees who wanted to know where they came from. Over 78,000 of them on one website alone. Clearly, it's normal to wonder. Why can't I?

"I was just—"

"That's enough screen time for today," Mom interrupted, shutting down the computer and this conversation. Because of course we weren't actually going to talk about anything. We were going to pretend that my body had lived in her belly for nine months, and that she was just upset about screen time. Never mind that the whole reason I was looking at stuff in secret was to avoid hurting her. Never mind that the only reason she even caught me was because I had to spend my measly amount of *screen time* on this family computer instead of having my own phone, like a normal seventh grader.

"Don't forget the video camera," I said coldly.

She took it. "Remember," she said, finally facing me, and forcing a fake smile, "tomorrow we're shopping for bat mitzvah dresses. Your bat mitzvah is in June."

That's all she said before she left, but I got the rest of the message loud and clear: *You're part of* this *family, Imani. End of story.*

Belle,

I am FURIOUS. I am positively fuming. I must write about what happened tonight. It began at dinner, when the uncles were talking about the conversation at shul. They looked at me with sad faces. They were speaking about Russia (in Yiddish, of course).

Hannah scolded them in Yiddish and told them to be quiet. I'd been eating in silence, but I looked up when she said, in English, "Things will be different for Anna's family."

Uncle Onion shook his head and began grumbling to Uncle Egg. They both seemed angry and sad. It seemed like they may have heard news for me at shul but were not sharing. So I said, "What? What will be different for my family?"

Hannah shook her head, but Max held up his hand. He said, "My uncles came from Russia about forty years ago," he explained to me, "to escape the pogroms."

Then Uncle Onion said (in English!), "Killing Jews. Always with killing the Jews."

Hannah tried to change the subject to how the

meat was a bit dry, but it didn't work. That word, "killing," hung over us all. Max cleared his throat and told me the uncles were teenagers when they came to America.

"Achtzehn," said Uncle Onion.

"Fünfzehn," said Uncle Egg.

18 and 15. Uncle Egg was only a bit older than Kurt.

"No money," said Uncle Onion.

"Nothing," said Uncle Egg.

"They came alone," Max told me. "Without their parents."

Uncle Onion said something in Yiddish. He wanted Max to translate. So Max said, "Like you. Only they didn't know anyone here. They had no place to live, no one to care for them."

Hannah put down her glass of wine so quickly that some of it spilled over the top, but she didn't even make a move to dab it. She said, "That's enough for now."

But Uncle Egg was still talking, and Uncle Onion was nodding along. If Hannah knew I can understand a little Yiddish, she would have done more to silence them, I'm sure. Because they were saying that they <u>never</u> saw their parents again.

That they were left all alone, hungry and poor, to make it on their own.

Can you believe it? They probably wanted me to feel grateful for having someone to care for me here. Maybe even feel grateful for having <u>them</u>. I am not grateful. I am furious! Shouldn't the uncles understand then, about saving <u>my</u> parents? They should be gathering every dollar they have hidden beneath their mattress to make sure my story ends differently. They might have been poor then, but they are <u>not</u> poor now. They <u>know</u> my suffering and still they cannot spare a <u>single penny</u>? They have <u>NO</u> excuse, unless they <u>want</u> me to suffer like they did.

My anger builds as I write this, just as it did at dinner. Months of worry and frustration and heartache piled inside me. Oh, I felt like a stick of dynamite that had finally been lit! I started to shout, "Let me see my parents again!" I shouted it so loud that everyone startled. Hannah reached her hand to me but I pulled my arm away and kept yelling. The uncles began to grumble in Yiddish, so I cursed at them in Luxembourgish (<u>my</u> private language!). Then I shouted, "How dare you! You have the money to save them! I don't want to be here alone!" I kept saying, "How dare you, how dare you!" and I threw my plate onto the floor, and it shattered.

Then I ran to my room, crying. Like something out of a soap opera, but I don't care. All my life I've let you be the one to throw tantrums for us both, but you're not here. YOU ARE NOT WITH ME! Who says I have to be the calm one? Who says I can't throw a fit?

I can see you—wherever you are—smiling and saying "Good for you!"

Belle,

I stayed in here for a long time, not knowing what to expect. Papa would have made me come back to the table, apologize, and clean up the plate by myself. I thought Max and Hannah might decide they don't want me anymore, if I am going to be so violent and ungrateful. But a little while ago there was a soft knock on the door . . . and it was Max.

He didn't say anything . . . he just sat down on the floor and set up the Chinese checkers set. We played in silence. When I cried, he offered a handkerchief, but no words. I played like it was an Olympics matchup, using both of our colors to make a long string, and had my marbles jump others one by one until they all landed home. Why not can life be like Chinese checkers?

After the game, Max said that he was glad to have me here with them. He said at first he was nervous because he worried he could not stand in for my family, and "what do I know of teenage girls from Luxembourg?"

It made me feel warm, what he said, but I could barely look at him, let alone reply.

Then he said, "There's more to the story." I
first thought he meant the story of why the uncles
won't pay for my family's passage. I was ready
to hear him say things aren't as easy as they
seem. Adults always say so, even when things are
plain as day. Thank goodness, that's not what he
said . . . he talked about the uncles again. He said,
"Their parents never made it out of Russia, but
<u>my</u> mother did. So my uncles lived with their sister
again, here in Brooklyn."

I have been sitting here by myself since then,
thinking. I feel so overwhelmed. I am still angry,
but I'm ashamed of my behavior tonight. It's not
fair to be angry at Max and Hannah. They've done
so much for me.

I can hear the radio playing softly, so Hannah
must still be awake. I will go say good night. I may
or may not apologize for my outburst, but I will
apologize for the plate.

CHAPTER 27

I f nothing else, I thought my mom's discovering the adoption site might make her less enthusiastic about our trip to the mall, but no such luck. She wanted to set out early, which meant she was already getting on my nerves by 10:30 in the morning. No matter how bored or rhetorical the salespeople's "Can I help you with anything?" my mom took them up on it. If they didn't ask, she'd call them over anyway and say, "My daughter needs a dress for a bat mitzvah next weekend." If she caught the flash of surprise on each salesperson's face when she referred to me as her daughter, she didn't show it.

I tried to wander off and look through the racks on my own while the workers pulled dresses I'd never wear, but Mom kept calling me over to hold stuff up in front of my body. We lucked out in the first store:

I found a shimmery gray dress that fit just right, and everyone agreed it looked good. I hoped that meant we were done, but Mom found it empowering. "Let's keep going," she said, looping her arm through mine. (Because everyone wants to walk through the mall arm in arm with their mom.)

In the second store, I tried on three things—one that I picked and two that they picked—but two didn't fit right and my mom said the third was "too mature."

In the third store, I agreed to try on a red dress with flowers printed on it. When I came out of the dressing room (my mom would've come in, if I hadn't flat-out refused) and stood in front of the mirror, my mom and the elderly saleswoman tugged at the sides.

"It's too short," Mom said, disappointed.

"That's how they're wearing them these days," the woman said. I tried to hide my frustration at having to hear fashion updates from someone who was, seriously, eighty years old.

"She's just so skinny," my mom told the old lady, as though I weren't right there. "She's not really filling it out in the bust area."

"Mom!" I cried.

Mom rolled her eyes, like *I* was the one who needed to grow up, even though *she* wanted to put me in a dress meant for a third grader.

We stopped for a soft pretzel, but Mom could tell it did nothing for my mood. "Should we take a break?" she suggested. "Walk around Brookstone, get some lunch before we hit Macy's?"

A break sounded good, but that would only prolong this day. Macy's was so big, we were sure to find something, and then we would be done. "No," I said. "Let's just power through."

I had higher-than-average hopes for Macy's for another reason: That's where Hannah took Anna for new dresses. (Not the same Macy's, obviously, but still.) But Hannah had style; I'm sure her selections were cool. My mom, on the other hand, went straight to the children's section, not junior's, so we were surrounded by moms with girls who came up to my waist. I could literally see the baby clothes from where we stood.

At least I wasn't likely to run into anyone I know there. Parker would never set foot in the children's section. Even so, I pretended to be invisible while my mom flipped through racks and held up various dresses, each one more babyish than the last. I tried to be polite as I turned them down, one after another. No thanks. Nah. Eh, not really.

"How about this one?" Mom said. It was yellow with a big blue bow on it. It'd look good on an infant. I shook my head politely.

She sighed. "Just try something on, Imani. It'll look different off the hanger."

"This stuff just looks kind of young."

"*You're* kind of young."

"No I'm not. I'll be a teenager in June."

"You're certainly acting like one today." She gave me a warning look, like she was about to count to three. "Please go try this on."

"This is kids' stuff. It won't even fit."

"We won't know until you try it on."

I gritted my teeth and grabbed the hanger from her. Stomped to the fitting room and threw the dress on. "It looks stupid!" I shouted through the closed door.

"Let me see," Mom said from right outside.

I opened the door, tired and over it. "See?" I tried to pull the door closed, but my mom held it.

"Come out to the big mirror so I can see it properly."

My mouth tight, I padded to the big mirror and stood on the stupid carpeted pedestal. My reflection scowled back at me. This dress was absurd. It probably came with a giant lollipop.

Mom gave a small smile. "I think it's cute."

I closed my eyes. "I wouldn't be caught dead in this."

"Imani," Mom said sharply.

"It's hideous! We're not buying it."

"Let's see what the salespeople think."

"Stop it!" I cried. "It doesn't matter what they think. *I'm* the one who has to wear it, so my opinion's the only one that counts."

"I'm your mother," Mom said, rubbing some fabric from the skirt between her fingers. "My opinion counts too."

"You're not my real mother," I fired back.

Mom froze, the fabric still between her fingers. Our faces were next to each other in the big mirror, hers pale and mine dark, both looking equally shocked. I saw her eyes start to fill.

"Don't cry," I muttered. "It's true."

She shook her head. Whispered, "How dare you."

I thought of Anna screaming those exact words at the uncles. They'd deserved it. Did I? "Mom—"

"First that adoption reunion site, behind my back, and now . . ." She held up a hand. "I can't deal with this right now."

My apology evaporated on my tongue. "Right *now*?" My words were like the pointy shards of a broken plate, aiming right where they'd hurt. "You can't deal with this *right now*? What about me? I've been *dealing with this* my entire life!"

She turned to face me, her eyes all red and dripping. Typical.

"Oh, Imani," she said. It sounded like an apology was coming next, and I didn't want to have to accept it. I stepped off the pedestal, still wearing the stupid yellow dress, and went back to the fitting room to change into my jeans.

It was understood that our shopping trip was over after that. The ride home was silent except for my mom's shaky breaths. When we got home, she went to her room and I went to mine. She was leaving for her business trip Tuesday morning. Until then, I'd just avoid her—and this whole situation—as best I could. Jaime called my name hesitantly into my door, but I ignored him until he went away.

I pulled out the diary from its place under my bed. I hoped Anna would have another outburst. I hoped those uncles would get what they deserved. I hoped she'd hear the worst of her news now so she could drown them—rightly, mercilessly—with blame.

Dear Belle,

I have not been writing because there is little to say. Another week has passed with no word from home. Mme. Veron is trying to find out more, as is everyone, but it is taking ages. Why? The war, the war, the war.

Ever since my outburst, it is uncomfortable to be around the uncles. I was tempted to stop working at the factory, but that would show weakness, and I want to be strong. So I have continued to go, despite how uncomfortable it can be. Perhaps the tension would ease if I apologize to them, but I refuse. I will apologize to them when <u>they</u> apologize to me for not sponsoring Mama and Papa.

No. I will apologize to them when they bring the last of you here.

Hannah and Max have not mentioned my behavior even once. I don't think I deserve to be here with such good people. Hannah has been extra kind to me . . . she has even offered to take me and Miriam bowling one day. Miriam says they have it at the Jewish Community House. It will be us 3 girls. I wish you could come too, to make 4.

Thursday, November 20, 1941

Dear Belle,

Today is an American holiday called "Thanksgiving." School is closed, and we are going to take the train to Hannah's mother's house in New Jersey to eat a big meal. I'm told it will be turkey. (Not fish, thank goodness!) The uncles wanted to keep the factory open, but Max convinced them to let the workers have the day off. They were not happy about it, though, because we have a big order to fill.

Miriam and I made a plan to go shopping together next Sunday. We eat lunch together most every day now, and we often hand a small note to each other when we pass in the hall between second and third period. (Sometimes her note is <u>very</u> small, just "Bonjour!" on a Beech-Nut gum wrapper!) How nice it is to have a friend at school, and a girlfriend close to my age! I wish I would see her this weekend, but she is spending the Thanksgiving holiday in Washington with her cousins.

Sunday, December 7, 1941

Belle,

The Japanese bombed America in a place
called Pearl Harbor! I was playing stickball with
Freddy and some others when all the mothers
began calling to their children to come inside. In
our apartment, Hannah and Max were sitting
right in front of the radio, intensely listening.
I felt scared—it reminded me of when the
Germans came marching into Luxembourg last
May, and the Grand Duchess fled. (Remember
how frightening it was when we picked up gas
masks at City Hall? We even needed one small
enough for Mina . . .) But Max showed me on
a map where Pearl Harbor is. It's in a place
called Hawaii, which is so far from Brooklyn,
I can hardly believe they are both part of the
United States. How different to be in such a large
country. The Germans occupied Luxembourg in a
few terrifying hours. The Japanese can not march
from Pearl Harbor to New York . . . they'd have
to swim an ocean first!

Freddy said Milton is going to enlist in the army
first thing tomorrow. He wants to sign up too.

I said, "I don't think they will take an 11-year old."

Freddy said, "I'll say I'm 16."

I could tell Freddy how much better it is to stay with your family, but I needn't bother. There's no way the U.S. Army will let him sign up. He still only comes up to my shoulder.

Thursday, December 11, 1941

Belle,

America is at war with Germany and Italy
now too. Milton is officially registered to fight.
(He said the line to register stretched two whole
city blocks!) He may leave before he finishes high
school. None of his family, or Enid, seems sad
to see him go. They're all just proud . . . except
Freddy. He is jealous. He spent much of yesterday
afternoon throwing his baseball against the wall,
catching it in his glove, and being angry. THWAM.
"Stupid army." THWAM. "Stupid Milton."
THWAM. "Stupid Milton gets to have all the fun
in the stupid army."

He's like you before I left, when you thought my
journey would be a big adventure. I suppose it <u>has</u>
turned out to be something of an adventure, but
still I yearn for news of you. And how I yearn for
<u>you</u> to be sharing the adventure with me.

Tuesday, December 23, 1941

Belle,

Nothing to write for many days, and then so
much in one day! The most important thing first:
According to people from shul, the Nazis have
been sending Jews on trains to Poland, and many
Luxembourgish Jews were sent to place called
Lodz. They said it is a "ghetto," a city only for
Jews. What does this mean, Belle? Do you have a
new home? Is it big enough for all of you? Are you
safe? One woman at shul thinks it is good to have
all the Jews in one place, away from the hateful
Germans. But how can it be good when they sent
you there, when they took you away from home?
And how can they make sure the Jews stay in the
ghetto and others stay out? SA officers . . . dogs . . .
a large wall? Still, I feel such relief to know
something of where you are.

A friend of Hannah's says she got a letter from
her cousins requesting (in some kind of code to
fool the censors) blankets, clothes, and food. This
has us all worried, of course. December in Poland
with no blankets! And food . . . can it possibly
be worse than the rations at home? But on the

very much bright side (I must be like Papa here, and try to be optimistic . . .) this friend <u>received a letter</u>, which means the people in the ghetto can send letters! Even better, the letter she received from Lodz was written in September, and it only now arrived. So if you or anyone else have written, there is hope that I will get a letter soon too!

The letter Hannah's friend received had a return address. I wrote a letter to every member of our family (from Grandfather down to Mina, and 2 for you and 2 for Oliver!) and mailed them in separate envelopes. Surely one of them has to arrive. I made sure to include my address here in Bensonhurst in all of them. Perhaps you had to leave so quickly, you could not take my address with you. (It makes me think of the story of Passover, how the Jews had to leave so quickly, they didn't have time for their bread to rise!)

Once we know where you are, we will send whatever you need. We will help you through the Polish winter while Max works his mightiest to bring more of you here! He has promised to do everything he can, as quickly as he can. That is the most exciting thing, and it gives me such great faith that it seems almost foolish to write about these other things, but I will.

Milton is set to deploy shortly after the new year. His family is planning a party before he leaves.

Freddy went to the war office to try again to register. He was again turned down. But they gave him a pamphlet about the "Junior Service Corps." They said they need responsible boys and girls to help here, on the "home front." Freddy is going to go to a Junior Service Corps meeting first thing in the new year. He can't wait. He said I should go with him, that they could probably use me because I can speak French. I think he's overestimating the sort of jobs you get in the Junior Service Corps.

Miriam invited me to her apartment over the weekend! I will go on Sunday. School is closed for the Christmas holiday starting tomorrow (funny because I doubt there is even one not Jewish person in my school) and we will spend more time together next week. Her cousins are coming from Washington, and she said she wants me to meet them, especially one who is 13 named David . . .

Uncle Egg has caught a terrific cold. Max is forcing him to stay home from the factory. Uncle

Onion is even staying home to help care for him. That means the factory will be much more pleasant for at least a few more days.

I've made some progress on the skins! I figured out a way to make a sleeve using one fewer skin than usual, and Max agrees it is a good way. Since every coat has two sleeves, that saves two pelts for every coat! With school closed, I will have lots of time to work in the factory, and I wager Max and I can solve the rest of the puzzle by the new year. If we can do so, we will surely make lots of money, and I will get a big bonus, which we can send to YOU in Lodz so you can leave <u>right away</u>. All of you!

I do hope you are well. My gut tells me that you are. I am feeling such optimism today! I have such great hope for 1942!

CHAPTER 28

My mom left for her business trip a day early. She claimed that her meeting on Tuesday had been moved up, so she had to fly out Monday, but she probably just wanted to get away from me. Whatever.

Dad seemed stressed about the whole thing. He knocked on my door before he left to drive Mom to the airport. I could see her behind him, in the hall with her rolling suitcase. "Can you at least say goodbye?" Dad asked. "I don't want her to leave with you two on such bad terms."

I came to the door and leaned on the frame.

"Bye, Mom," I said.

"Goodbye," she replied. "I love you, Imani."

I thought of Anna, the way she wished she could do her goodbyes over. The fact that she never saw her parents again. I thought of Milton and all the other men lined up around the block to go to war. I thought of Freddy, who was going to die fighting in Korea.

I was still mad at my mom—furious, really—but I walked over and gave her a hug. "I love you too."

Dear Belle,

Milton left for training today. His family hung a large white flag in their window with a blue star in the middle, to show their pride at having someone in the service. The flags have been popping up all over. There are so many servicemen on our street that Hannah is helping some other women sew an enormous flag to hang between our building and the next one, with a blue star for everyone on the block who is serving.

I went to Milton's goodbye party on Sunday. He looked very smart in his uniform, I must say. Enid clung to his arm all night, her bright red lips were in a proud smile. Freddy wore his Junior Service Corps helmet, and the armband that shows he's a "messenger." He's worn it every day since his training.

It was so frustrating, because when I asked him what a messenger does, he just kept saying, "I have to be ready at a moment's notice. For anything."

"Yes, but what do you <u>do</u>?"

He said a lot of other things about how important his job is before finally saying, "I convey messages from the air raid warden, in case the telephone system gets knocked out."

That does seem like an important job, I suppose. But he seems most excited about possibly being excused from school early if there's an urgent message to deliver. He bragged, "You're supposed to be 15 to be a messenger. And everyone else at the training was a Boy Scout."

I think the wardens allowed his enthusiasm to make up for his age. I doubt they believed he was 15. And there's <u>no</u> way Freddy passed for a Boy Scout!

Oh Belle. We turned 13 today.

I am exhausted, but my heart feels like it is being pulled in separate directions tonight, and I simply must write.

Max and Hannah surprised me three ways today. The first surprise was that they knew it was my birthday at all. I didn't tell them, but Hannah knew it from when we registered for school, and she remembered. How thoughtful! There was chocolate croissant on my breakfast plate this morning. She said, "You mentioned how you'd get a chocolate croissant with your sister before school some days. I thought you'd like it as a birthday treat!" I don't remember telling her this, but I must have done, and she made a note. How wonderful she is.

Second, when I got to the factory after school today, Hannah was there too! She said I was not going to work that afternoon, and neither was Max. We were all going to the theater! We saw a funny, silly play called "Arsenic and Old Lace." Hannah gave me a lovely gift of high-heel shoes, just like hers, only not quite as high. And Max suggested I wear the jacket they have been fitting me for. I thought it was supposed to go to a store, but no, it is for me! My very own fur coat . . . oh, I felt like Vivien Leigh herself, going to the theater in high heels and mink. I could have been on the cover of "Radio and Television Mirror"!

At dinner, Hannah ordered champagne, and made a toast to me. I remember every word that she said: "To Anna, who has filled our lives with so much joy these past few months. And to her family, who I have every hope will arrive in New York soon, to bring us even more joy."

It was all so wonderful except . . . this was the first birthday I have not shared with you. Do you remember when we were 8 or 9 and you paid a good portion of your saved francs to visit the fortune-teller at the fair? You refused to tell anyone (even me!) what that fortune-teller told you, but you boasted that it was worth every cent. Oh, how that infuriated me! Especially then, our lives were so entwined, I couldn't fathom doing <u>anything</u> without you . . . I was sure that whatever <u>your</u> future held, mine did too. I wonder now what you learned. Surely the fortune-teller did not say we would be separated by a war and an ocean.

You couldn't have kept that secret, could you?

What a strange turn our lives have taken. If a fortune-teller told me that I would spend my 13th birthday in New York with people named Max and Hannah, I would have demanded my money back. Yet here I am, and you are . . . where? Wherever you are, you are with the rest of our family, and for that I am jealous. I had a most lovely day, and yet I am jealous of <u>you</u>. How very selfish I am!

CHAPTER 29

Madeline pushed up from our positions side by side on my bedroom floor. She leaned back against my bed, moved her reading glasses to the top of her head, and placed her chin in her hand. I could tell by her silence that she was doing some heavy thinking, but I didn't know why.

"There's something about this that's weird," she said. "You see Hannah's toast, how she said, 'To Anna, and to her family'?"

"Yeah," I said. "So what?"

"*Her* family," Madeline repeated to herself, slowly. "Remember what Max told Anna about the uncles?" She flipped back a few pages, to Anna's meltdown at dinner, which I'd had her read today before we started this next part together. "The uncles said they came to America forty years ago," she said, pointing, "from Russia."

"Right."

"And their sister—"

"Max's mom," I said.

"—came later. From Russia."

"I guess," I said, still not sure where this was going.

"But didn't Max grow up with Anna's father?" Madeline asked. "In Luxembourg?"

My head dropped to the side. "Huh."

"Yeah. That's what Anna's dad told her, right?"

"Right." I leaned back against my bed, next to Madeline. That was kind of strange. There must have been an explanation for the timeline, but it was hard enough to get a mental image of Max's family tree, let alone dates and countries and connections to Anna's parents.

"Check this out!" Madeline said. She'd flipped back to the very beginning of the diary, the part Anna had written while still on the boat. She read aloud: "*Something odd happened then, Belle . . . I think Papa caught Mama's eye before answering. It was a strange look but so quick, I couldn't decipher it.*"

I leaned over her shoulder and picked up from the next sentence. "*I cannot say, even now, and there is no one here to help me analyze it.*"

Madeline's brown eyes caught fire behind her reading glasses. "She definitely saw a strange look, Imani. And it meant Max isn't really their cousin!"

"Slow down," I said. "Let's think about this." I didn't want to jump to any conclusions. Anna was in a good place. She still missed home, of course, but she was happy with Max and Hannah. If Madeline was right—if Anna's parents lied to her about Max being their cousin—it would ruin everything.

But Madeline was in investigative-journalist mode, ready to go live with her findings. "It explains everything! The stuff about Russia. All the ways Max is different from Anna's dad."

"She does say Max looks nothing like her father . . ." I granted.

"They're strangers," Madeline announced, almost giddy. "You should ask your grandpa. I bet he'll know. I bet you anything he'll say Anna's parents sent her across the world to live with *strangers*!"

"So what?" I said, my voice rising. "What's wrong with that? Everyone who's adopted lives with *strangers*."

Madeline's mouth closed. Her face turned bright pink. "I—I didn't mean—"

"Whatever." I stood up and moved onto my bed. I lay on my back and squeezed my eyes shut. I was not going to cry.

"Imani," Madeline said tentatively.

Was Madeline right? Did Anna's parents lie to her about being related to Max? Were they really cousins, or was Max just some guy who agreed to sponsor some kids so they could escape a bad situation? Did it even matter? Whether Max and Hannah were blood-related or not, they were still complete strangers when Anna started to live with them. They were still so nice to her. They were still giving her a home and a life. She probably would have died if they hadn't taken her in. What did it matter if they were or weren't her cousins?

And yet. It made all the difference, didn't it? If the people serving as your parents were blood-related or not. If you knew the truth about things or were kept in the dark.

"I'm sorry," Madeline said. She put a hesitant hand on my shoulder.

I opened my eyes. The tears that had been building came spilling out.

"I'm really sorry," Madeline said again. "That was a really stupid thing for me to say."

"It's okay," I managed.

Madeline sat on the edge of my bed and put her arm around me.

"I'm okay," I said, hugging her back. "Really."

We pulled apart, and a small smile played at her lips. "Do you want to play Chinese checkers?"

I laughed, making a tear zigzag down my face. If only I had a Chinese checkers set. There was probably some app Madeline could download, but that wouldn't be nearly the same.

Madeline looked at the time on her phone. "Should we keep reading? I think we're almost done."

I sighed. "I think I want to read the end by myself."

Madeline was quiet for a while. Then she said, "Text me later?"

I nodded. She got her shoes and closed my bedroom door behind her. I lay there for a long time, and I must have fallen asleep, because when I woke up, the room was dark and I could hear Jaime and Dad downstairs. In my post-nap haze, I gathered that they were talking to my mom on the phone, and I heard them each say goodbye. She must not have asked to speak to me. She hadn't even texted once since she left.

I rolled to the edge of my bed and saw the diary on the floor. I wanted to read the rest by myself? Well, I couldn't have been more alone.

Thursday, February 19, 1942

Oh Belle,

I received a letter from Kurt today.

I am willing it not to be true. If I don't write about it, maybe it will all be not true. I will wake up and it will have been just a nightmare . . . and you will be beside me, and we'll assure each other it wasn't real.

The postmark says Poland, so I was correct about that. He says I don't need to worry about you, but that is plainly a lie to fool the censors. Why else would he "remember with fondness" our times playing Super Hirsch? Super Hirsch, our invented hero, the only one who could save us from danger or death? The meaning is clear. If he needs Super Hirsch, wherever you are must be truly horrendous.

And the worst part of all . . .

I wish I had never received this letter. It would be better not to know.

Oliver . . . My Oliver. I left him first, and now he has left us all . . . How could this happen? I am like Frida's father on the boat . . . alive but dead inside. I am numb. I will be dead too if I concede it is true.

No, I will not believe it. It cannot be true.

CHAPTER 30

"No," I whispered. "Oliver can't have . . ."

I read the entry again, and my own issues seemed like tiny pieces of fluff. Why did I want to read the rest of this diary on my own?

I jumped out of bed and opened the door. My brother was in the hall, about to go into his room.

"Jaime!" I shouted.

He flinched. "Geez, Imani. You scared me."

"Sorry. Can you read something really quick? From Grandma Anna's diary?"

"Um. I guess?"

I shoved the open diary in his face. "Right here. Just this entry." I stood there while he read. My fingers drummed against my thigh impatiently.

"Who's Oliver?" Jaime asked when he was done.

"Her little brother," I said. "What do you think happened to him?"

"It sounds like he died."

"But maybe he didn't, right?"

"It sounds like he did."

I pulled the diary back from him. He didn't know. He hadn't been reading the whole thing. He didn't even know who Oliver was. Why'd I even ask him?

I went into my room and got my phone. But this was too urgent, too important, to talk about by text. I sent Madeline a quick message—*I'm coming over*—then slipped my phone into my back pocket, stuffed my feet into my sneakers, and ran downstairs.

Outside, I held the diary tightly in one hand. Madeline would definitely say Jaime was wrong. I sprinted the two blocks to her house.

Madeline opened the door as I ran up the front steps. "What's wrong?" she asked.

I opened the diary to the page I'd marked with the ribbon and rushed it into her hands. "Read this," I said. "Now."

Her eyebrows flew up. "Oh no." She disappeared inside for a second and returned wearing her reading glasses and a pair of flip-flops over her socks.

I shifted from foot to foot while she read. My hands were shivering in my pockets. My quick breaths formed clouds of fog as they came out of my mouth, then evaporated before my eyes.

When she finished reading, Madeline sat down slowly on her front steps. "Oliver," she said quietly. "He couldn't have . . ."

"He couldn't have, right?" I said desperately. "I needed you to read it, but I don't think it means that he . . . I don't believe it."

"Anna's upset," Madeline reasoned halfheartedly. "She's depressed. But not enough. She'd be much more upset if Kurt's letter said Oliver—"

"Don't say it!" I shouted.

Madeline frowned at me. "Oh, Imani."

I was like Anna. I flat-out refused to believe it, and so it could not be true. There was no way—no freaking way—that Oliver had died.

Sunday, March 8, 1942

Dear Belle,

I still feel sick with shame at how selfish I am.

My nightmares have returned, each night worse
than the last. My clothes are hanging loose on me
because I have not been hungry one bit, not even
for Chinese food. Mme. Veron invited me and
Miriam to eat lunch with her in the teachers' room,
and she prepared a French meal that brought back
memories of summers with Mama's family. But I
could not eat, and my baguette turned to stone.

I read Kurt's letter every night. It can't be
helping with my sleep, but I cannot stop myself.
Freddy's parents get the "Jewish Daily Forward,"
so Freddy brings me old papers and translates the
Yiddish. I don't know if he is being considerate or
just being a boy, but he doesn't try to comfort me
at all. He just sits there in his helmet and armband
and reads me the news from Europe.

Something truly awful is happening to you and
everyone else—whoever is left of you, wherever
you are. I am sure of it. Do we still have a twin
connection, Belle? It is becoming more difficult to
have faith. If you knew what a horrid sister I have

been (happily spending our birthday apart . . . oh I disgust myself) you would probably snip that string in two and leave the pieces to sink to the bottom of the Atlantic Ocean . . . until some German U-boat comes along and blows them to bits.

Belle,

I haven't been going to the factory lately, and I
haven't been playing Chinese checkers. But tonight,
Max convinced me to play, and during the game,
he told me that everything is changing. Many of
the workers have left to join the service, and now
the government has requested that the factory
make army fatigues instead of fur coats.

I was in shock when he told me. My little white
marble was suspended in my hand. I forgot where I
was going to move it.

Max said, "It's all right. No one is going to buy
a luxury like a fur coat during wartime anyway."

I suppose he's right, and I'm glad the factory can
play some part in helping defeat the Germans once
and for all. But all of the progress we made with
the pelts is not going to amount to anything now. I
have let you down again.

Why would I think that solving that puzzle
would help bring you here? There were so
many obstacles I refused to see. If all of Papa's
and Grandfather's savings could only afford to
send <u>one</u> of us, how could my meager salary at

the factory pay for <u>nine</u>? Even the millions I'm convinced are squirreled away in the uncles' apartment (hidden in shoes . . . in old cereal boxes . . . in mounds under the mattress . . .) even if I had every dollar of that, how would I get it to Mama and Papa? Mail a parcel full of coins? Ask Western Union to wire money to your ghetto? So much for being the thoughtful twin. So much for being 13. How childish my plan was. I am not only selfish, I am also stupid.

I was a dunce to think that any of you might join me here at all. Mama and Papa picked me to send away, probably because I am stupid. They didn't want me anymore. And now you are all together even farther away, in Poland. Except for Oliver.

I was stupid to write to you in this book. It did nothing to bring us closer. I do not have the heart to keep writing you notes you will never receive in a language you will never get to speak. The news about Oliver has changed everything. I am so hopeless against it all.

IT IS ALL SO UNFAIR. Why did those horrid uncles get to see their sister again, when it's clear I will never see mine?

CHAPTER 31

We'd moved inside, away from the cold, but my hand still trembled as I turned to the next page. It was blank.

"Oh no," Madeline breathed.

My heart started beating furiously. I turned another page. Blank. "I knew we were close. But not *this* close. That can't be all," I said. "It can't be. That can't be where this ends."

"It can't be." Madeline held out her hand for the journal. She started flipping pages, calm and confident. She flipped, becoming less calm and confident with every page, to the very end, where Frida's address in Chicago was written. Blank, blank, blank.

"Give it to me," I said. She did. I held the journal upside down, shook it. Now *I* was the one acting stupid—as if Anna had left some hidden entry that would only appear seventy-five years later, when her adopted great-granddaughter shook it loose from the spine. But I refused to concede that the journal would end there, that she'd give up hope now, on such a random day, on such a depressing thought. All the strings were just hanging there, disconnected.

"There's nothing," Madeline said with a sigh. "That's the end."

"Maybe there's another diary," I tried desperately. "One that picks up right after this."

"Maybe."

Madeline was just being nice. She was probably afraid to upset me again. But clearly there was no other diary. It wasn't like Anna had run out of space here. There were a decent number of pages to go; she chose to leave them blank. There wasn't some big change that would warrant a fresh journal, either. The new year had come and gone. Her birthday was over.

"There's just . . ." I spluttered. My hands were full-on shaking now. It took all my resolve not to throw the diary across the room. "It's not . . . Why didn't . . ." I closed my eyes, opened them again, placed the diary gently on the floor. Once it was safe from me, I gripped my hair and *screamed*.

Madeline made me sit down on the couch. "It was her real life, Imani," she said apologetically. "It's not some book we read in school with, like, symbols and themes. She didn't *have* to end with any closure."

I could have killed Madeline and her sensible reasoning. "I know," I said angrily.

"I hate it too," she insisted. "But Anna was writing for Belle, and she lost faith that Belle would ever read it. She said so herself. She was never writing for *us*. She wrote this long before you were even born."

"I *know*," I said again. But did I? Grandma Anna had left me her books. It was as though she wanted me to find this, to read it at this exact moment in my life. It felt like she had written it *precisely* for me.

I expected, when it ended, to be sad.

I hadn't expected to feel abandoned.

CHAPTER 32

Parker turned to a new page in her speech. "I'd like to thank the rabbi and the cantor for helping me prepare for this special day. Mrs. Coleman, thank you for inspiring me and everyone in my class to learn about our Jewish heritage."

In the seat next to me, Madeline snorted. "I'd like to thank the Academy," she whispered in a breathy falsetto.

I giggled and elbowed the side of her dress. It was kind of cool to see Parker up there on the bimah. She'd been jumpy with nerves when she first walked out. She'd even bumped into the side of the podium, and the microphone picked up her "oops" for everyone to hear. But she'd relaxed as the service went on, and now, nearing the very end, she was smiling as brightly as the rhinestones on her dress. Her braces had been removed for just this week, and she'd clearly spent some time in a tanning bed, but her grin was one hundred percent natural. Her professional photographer must've thought so too—he was taking photo after photo.

"And finally, thank you to my parents and my sisters for being so supportive. I love you."

From the aisle seat of our row, Magda whooped and shouted "Go Parker!" which elicited as many laughs as it did dirty looks. Parker giggled and blew Magda a kiss. Rabbi Seider led Parker back to her seat, then led everyone in singing "Ein Keloheinu."

My thoughts flashed to Anna, how she turned thirteen with no mention of a bat mitzvah. Was that just reserved for boys back then? Then I did what I did anytime this week when I found myself thinking of Anna: I forced the thoughts out of my head. My anger had cooled from a boil to a simmer, but I was still frustrated at how abruptly she'd left things, how many questions she'd left unanswered.

Nothing was settled with my mom, either. We didn't talk once while she was away, and when she got back yesterday, she looked like she'd spent the entire week crying. I wanted to apologize, but that would mean reminding her of what I said, and that'd only make things worse. Besides, apologizing at this point seemed like too little too late—it'd be like

Max's uncles offering a dollar or two to help Anna's family after she got the letter from Kurt.

So Mom and I only talked about surface things, like the logistics of attending Parker's bat mitzvah, and Grandpa Fred's arrival. He was coming to visit this week, and I was looking forward to turning the diary over to him. It was still in the box under my bed, but I kept taking it out and getting angry all over again. I couldn't help myself, like Anna with the newspaper or Kurt's letter.

There I was again, thinking of Anna. I shook my head and brought myself back to Parker's bat mitzvah, which was now over.

"That was *long*," Madeline said. She was standing up, stretching her arms. She gave a big yawn.

"Madeline!" I glanced at the bimah and was glad to see that everyone was too busy congratulating Parker to notice. "Do you want me to yawn during *your* bat mitzvah?"

"During it? No way. But after?" She gave an even bigger yawn than before.

"You'd better perk up," I said as we walked out of the sanctuary. "We've got a giant party to go to. You've got to dance all night."

"Afternoon," Madeline corrected, "but don't worry. I'm a slave to the beat."

I burst out laughing. I've never seen Madeline

dance in her life. If a dance contest breaks out at a slumber party, she makes herself the judge. She even brought a doctor's note to get out of square dancing in gym.

Parker made her way over to us. Magda was on one side of her and the photographer was on the other.

"Imani!" Parker screeched, as though she didn't know I'd be here. "Madeline! You are so sweet to come!" She gave us each a kiss on the cheek, something I'd never seen anyone our age do before. Maybe becoming a bat mitzvah really does make you an adult.

"You did such a good job," I said, trying to act casual despite the click of the photographer's camera. He was circling us, taking pictures from every angle, and it made it hard to know where to look. Photographers always do this when I'm around. They like to document "diversity."

"Was it very boring?" Parker asked.

"Not at all!" I said it quickly before Madeline could jump in with something more truthful.

"It was long," Madeline admitted. "What's it like up there?"

"Oh, I don't know. It's all, like, this big blur." Parker sighed, beamed. Some older people came over to congratulate her, and she lapped up the praise. "See you at the party!" she called over her shoulder before being moved along by the crowd. The photographer took a couple more pictures of me before following her.

A woman in a black pantsuit appeared in his place. She had a clipboard in her hands, a walkie-talkie on her belt, and a forced smile on her face. "Do you need a ride to the party?" she asked.

"Um, yes," Madeline said.

"Names?"

We gave her our names, and she found us on her clipboard. "You're on bus A," she said to Madeline. "You're on bus B," she said to me.

I said, "There are two buses?"

Madeline said, "We're not together?"

The woman said, "No switching. Line up outside. Buses leave in five."

Madeline waved dramatically as she boarded bus A with everyone else from our school. I stood in line for bus B with a bunch of strangers who all knew each other—they must have been Parker's friends from sleepaway camp.

"How do you know Parker?" the boy in front of me asked.

"We go to school together. And Hebrew school."

The boy got bug-eyed, like he was in a cartoon. "You're Jewish?"

I sighed. "Yeah."

"No way," he said.

"What?" said the girl in front of him.

"She says she's Jewish," the boy said, pointing at me.

"You can be black and Jewish?" the girl asked.

One of her friends gasped, elbowed her to shut up.

"What?" the first girl said defensively. "I didn't know you could be black and Jewish."

"Are you, like, half Jewish?" the boy asked.

Another girl joined in. "Oh wait, are you from Ethiopia? There are black Jews in Ethiopia."

"I'm adopted," I said dully, and watched the pieces click together. My mind flicked to the Torah portion I'd been practicing for my own bat mitzvah. In it, Moses takes a census of all the Israelites who were wandering the desert, to see who they were descendants of. That was where this conversation was headed for sure: a census of one. Only the camp friends were going to ask in the way everyone asked: What are you really?

Was it too late to pretend I didn't speak English? My bare brown legs shivered under my coat, and I looked at bus A with longing. Why on earth did Parker put me on bus B all by myself?

"Hey, Imani."

Ethan! I could've jumped into his arms. Or Parker's. She didn't put me on bus B to be alone; she put me on bus B to be alone with Ethan. And luckily, as soon as he arrived and started talking to me like I was a person rather than a specimen in some world heritage survey, the camp friends lost interest.

"I like your dress," Ethan said.

It was the gray shimmery one that my mom bought me before I stabbed her in the heart. But right now, it was totally covered by my coat.

"I, um, saw it inside," he explained. His face was pink, but that could have been from the cold.

"Right," I said. "Thanks. I like your . . . um . . ." I scanned him. "Purple yarmulke."

Ethan laughed and took it off. "Souvenir," he said, putting it in his pocket.

The line started moving into the bus, and all the camp friends raced to the back. I sat down in the second row, and Ethan slid in next to me, even though there were plenty of empty seats. Even though my row had a wheel well. I imagined Parker and Magda in the seat behind us, saying *awwww*.

"Did this make you excited for your bat mitzvah?" Ethan asked.

"Kind of," I said. "You?"

Ethan shook his head. "It stressed me out. I'm nowhere near ready. My haftorah's really long."

"The speech," I added.

"And the Holocaust project. Are you still using your great-grandma's diary?"

"Ugh, don't ask." I slumped back in the seat and wedged my bent legs on the back of the row in front of us. The skirt of my dress collapsed around my thighs, and I quickly pushed it back and secured it under my knees.

"Okay," he said. "I won't ask."

The bus pulled out of the temple parking lot and turned onto the road. One of the boys in the back shouted, "Party!" and the other camp friends cheered. Ethan sat quietly. I remembered what he told me about his great-grandfather being in the Kindertransport.

"So, I finished reading the diary," I told him, "and it was a total letdown."

"What do you mean?"

"It just *ended*. There's no closure. No resolution."

Ethan's eyes were narrowed. I could see that he was trying very hard to follow me, to be angry along with me, but he didn't get it. How could he? It'd been a week since I'd finished reading, and *I* still didn't get it.

"I thought she'd find out that her whole family died, and, you know, deal with it." I was trying to put into words exactly what it was that made me so upset with Anna. "And Madeline has this theory— she read it too—that the cousins my grandma went to live with were not actually her cousins at all. But

Anna doesn't write about that. I don't know if she found it out later, or if Madeline's wrong. And it doesn't even matter, right? Because she was living with people who loved her, so who cares if they had the same DNA or whatever. But I still just want to know."

"You were hoping for answers," Ethan said, nodding slowly.

"Yes!" That was it. I *was* looking for answers. "It's like . . ."

My eyes searched around and settled on a hole someone had made in the seat in front of me. It was the size of my thumb, and it was empty and dark except for some crumbly yellow foam and a few loose threads around the edges. For some reason, staring at that random hole made everything fit together in my head.

"There's so much I don't know about *my* history, you know? So when I found this diary, it was like I could fill in those gaps with information about my family's history."

Ethan nodded. "But it didn't do that."

"Exactly. Because it just *ends,* and Anna doesn't know any more than I do. There are still so many . . . blanks."

Ethan didn't say anything. I thought about when my brother was little, and he'd get all worked up about something, and Mom and Dad would tell him to use his words. I smiled a little, remembering Jaime, tiny, struggling to find the right words through his sobs. Once he'd done it, Dad could usually fix the problem, which was always dumb, like Jaime wanted a different color sippy cup. I guess what I was facing wasn't as simple as switching a blue cup for a red one, but putting it into words still felt like a step forward.

"This was your great-grandma's real diary, right?" Ethan said finally.

"Yeah." I thought he was going to say the same thing Madeline had said, about how it isn't some book that needs to have a satisfying ending. But he didn't.

"She was a real person, so this diary's not the only information that exists about her."

He looked at me with his green eyes, his eyebrows arched just slightly over his glasses, like he wasn't sure if what he said was totally obvious or completely brilliant. The amazing part: It was both.

"You're right," I said.

"You could ask other people in your family about her. They might know if her cousins were really her cousins."

I'd been determined to *not* ask Grandpa Fred—to just turn over the diary and forget all about it—mostly because of how smug Madeline sounded when she insisted Grandpa Fred would confirm her theory about Anna being adopted by strangers. But now that I'd read the whole diary, and some time had passed, it sounded a lot more reasonable. Grandpa Fred *did* know that Grandma Anna had been a twin, and he knew that Freddy was her first friend. He probably knew other things too.

"Maybe she left other stuff behind," Ethan continued. "Another diary from later, or old photos. . . ."

"The bear!" I shouted it so loud that the camp friends stopped talking, then laughed, but I didn't care. The ratty old teddy bear that had always been on the shelf above her bed, the one she left to my cousin Isabel—that must have been Oliver's bear!

"The baseball glove, the marbles . . . the fur coats!" This I said at a more reasonable volume, but I still said it out loud. Those things Jaime inherited—were they originally Freddy's? And all those fur coats my mom and her siblings were fighting over, who ended up getting them? One could be the coat she got for her thirteenth birthday.

"Maybe other things too!" Ethan said. He was getting excited along with me, even though he didn't have any clue what I was talking about. It was so cute, and I was so happy, and without even thinking,

I took his face in my hands and kissed him, right on the mouth.

When I pulled away, we were both in shock. We stared at each other, our mouths still partly open. "Sorry," I said.

"It's okay!" Ethan's eyes were dancing. He rushed forward and kissed me again, quickly, then pulled away just as quickly and turned to face the aisle. I turned to look out the window. I could see the reflection of myself, my grin.

The bus pulled into the parking lot. Ethan and I didn't look at each other as we filed off and into the dance hall, where we were barraged by flashing lights, thumping music, and a life-size cardboard cutout of Parker.

I didn't think of Anna once the entire afternoon.

CHAPTER 33

When Grandpa Fred arrived on Wednesday night, he was looking better. His face was kind of thin, and his pants were bunched up around his belt, but his eyes were happy, and he greeted me and Jaime by asking us to pick a card, any card. After dinner (and after making my card magically switch suits with Jaime's), he settled onto the couch with a big bag of pistachio nuts. I sat next to him with an empty bowl for the shells.

"Do you want me to bring you the diary?" I asked.

"Not right now," he said. "I've got nuts to crack."

I've never seen anyone open pistachios as quickly as Grandpa Fred. He often has two going at once— one in his hands and one in his teeth. Since he was at the beginning of the bag, each shell made a little *pling* as it dropped into the bowl.

"I have to warn you," I said, "the diary doesn't have such a happy ending."

Grandpa Fred nodded, his focus on his fingers. *Pling.*

"It doesn't really have an *unhappy* ending, I guess. Well, it kind of does. I don't know. It's just very abrupt."

Pling, pling. Grandpa Fred offered me a de-shelled pistachio and I popped it into my mouth.

"How old was she when she stopped writing?" Grandpa asked.

"Thirteen."

Pling.

"I still think you should read it," I said. "I just wanted you to know, so you won't be disappointed at the end."

Grandpa Fred stayed focused on the nuts. "I don't think I'll be disappointed," he said. *Pling.*

"Why not?"

"Because I know the end of the diary was not the end of the story. My mom lived another—what?— seventy-five years."

"Were they happy years?" I asked. It sounded silly, but I wanted to know.

"Most of them, yes," Grandpa said. "Very happy."

He went back to the pistachios. Shells covered the bottom of my bowl now, so the pile grew without a sound.

"Did you know Max and Hannah, the people who took her in in Brooklyn?"

This took Grandpa by surprise. His eyes moved from the nuts to me. "You mean my grandparents?" he asked. "Of course."

His grandparents? It took me a minute, but then I couldn't help but smile. Max and Hannah raised Anna like their daughter, so of course they would have been grandparents to Grandpa Fred and Great-Aunt Janet. Now I was getting excited for Grandpa to read the diary. How cool would it be to read about your grandparents when they were younger, and in such detail?

"Did you know Max's uncles?" I asked Grandpa. "The ones who owned the fur factory?"

"That would be Saul and Hymie," Grandpa said.

Saul and Hymie! I'd almost forgotten they had real names—not just Egg and Onion!

"They died when I was a baby. But I've heard lots of stories. They were quite the characters."

"*Quite* the characters," I agreed. "Wait till you read about them."

I balanced the bowl on my legs and began working at a few pistachios myself. There was so much Grandpa and I could talk about, once he'd read the diary. But for now, there was just one thing I had to ask. "Max was Anna's dad's cousin, right?"

Grandpa wrinkled his brow. "I don't think so, no. If I remember correctly . . ." Grandpa thought a moment. He cracked a pistachio between his teeth and chewed it.

If you remember correctly . . . I thought, trying to mentally urge him on.

"Grandpa Max's father was from Luxembourg," Grandpa said finally. "That's right. He was from Luxembourg, but he was living in New York. That's where he met Max's mother. She was from Russia, but she came over to be with her brothers—Saul and Hymie—around the turn of the century. Max was born in New York."

So Madeline was right; Anna's parents were lying when they said Max had grown up in Luxembourg with her father. But Max's father was from Luxembourg originally . . . "Was Max's father related to Anna's family?"

"No," Grandpa said. "In fact"—he raised a finger, sure of the story now—"Max and Hannah took in my mother after they got a letter from her parents. That's it. But the letter was addressed to Max's father, Daniel was his name. Someone in Luxembourg had known Daniel, maybe Grandma Anna's grandparents, or maybe a friend of the family. Whoever it was, they remembered that Daniel had moved to America all those years before. They were reaching out to anyone and everyone who might be able to help them get out of Europe, you see. But Daniel wasn't there to get the letter, because he died when Max was a baby. Max barely knew him himself."

I imagined a family tree in my head as Grandpa talked, with each of these pieces falling into place. Of course it wasn't technically a *family* tree, since Anna and Max weren't related after all, but it still felt like one. "Her parents lied to her," I told Grandpa. "They told her Max was her father's cousin. Why do you think they did that?"

Grandpa frowned as he chewed another pistachio. "I don't know," he admitted. "Maybe the government would only let people immigrate if they were sponsored by family. Or maybe they thought it would put her at ease and make her less scared to go."

I cracked a pistachio of my own and chewed it slowly. The truth wasn't upsetting after all; it was amazing. He and Hannah were suddenly even kinder than Anna realized. They got a letter from a complete stranger, half a world away, addressed to a dead man. Based on that alone, they were willing to become parents to as many as *six* children who needed a new home. If they hadn't done it, my grandpa wouldn't exist. Neither would my mom. I probably still would, but who knows where I'd be. Certainly not here, sitting on this couch, eating pistachio nuts and piecing together this very story.

How did Grandpa even know all this? Did Grandma Anna tell him? When did she find out the truth? How did she feel about it? "I'm going to ask you, like, ten million questions," I warned Grandpa, "once you've had a chance to read."

"Ten million questions!" Grandpa said. "That sounds time-consuming."

I giggled. "It probably will be."

"Are they all about my mother?"

"Yeah, is that okay?"

Grandpa folded over the top of the pistachio bag and placed it neatly on the side table. He took the bowl of shells and placed it there too. "How about this," he said, brushing off his hands. "I'm going to New York on Saturday, to finish going through my mom's stuff and get the apartment ready to sell. If your parents say it's okay, you can come help me. I'd love a weekend together, just you and me. And while we work, I can answer all the questions you want."

"Is there still a lot of stuff in the apartment?" I asked.

Grandpa blew air through his lips. "Too much. Who knows what we'll find."

I could hardly believe my luck. Ethan was right. Who knew what we'd find!

"I take it that's a deal?" Grandpa said.

"Deal."

We shook our salty hands. My heart was full of hope, just like Anna's was at the start of 1942. What Grandpa said had to be true—the diary wasn't the end. If anything, it might be the beginning.

CHAPTER 34

Grandpa and I left early Saturday morning and made it to Brooklyn by eleven. We parked near Grandma Anna's apartment (which is not, to my disappointment, the same one she lived in at the time of the diary; Grandpa said we weren't anywhere near Bensonhurst). We ate some bagels at a place around the corner, and then headed back to start working. It had only been six weeks since the shiva, but so much had changed since then, it seemed like a completely different lifetime.

"Yikes," I said when Grandpa opened the door. "There really is a lot of stuff. You couldn't go through all this alone."

"No," Grandpa said, patting my shoulder. "I couldn't."

Grandpa started with the big stuff: taking the plastic off the couches, stripping the beds, cleaning the furniture. I started exactly where I'd left off the last time I was here: the books. The stack I'd designated for donation was still there in the bedroom, and I went quickly through all of them, to make sure there wasn't another diary in the pile. There wasn't. The dressers didn't have any treasures inside either, just clothes and mothballs. I was about to open the closet and look at the fur coats when Grandpa called from the other room.

"Imani," he said. "You might want to see these."

He was holding a stack of photos in frames. The top one was my school picture from fifth grade, when my mom made me wear the ugliest shirt ever made. "This used to be on the shelf over there, right?"

"Yes," Grandpa said. "Janet took them all down after shiva, but we never decided who'd get which."

I started taking the frames off the pile one by one. Photos of me, Jaime, my cousin Isabel. My parents' wedding.

"I love this one," I said with a laugh. It was a shot of Aunt Jess, when she was just three or four, riding a big-wheel tricycle that was covered in stickers, just like the motorcycle she'd ridden to Grandma Anna's funeral. In the background, on the steps of the house, you could see my mom with a Popsicle in her hand

and a smug look on her face, and Uncle Dan pointing at her, crying.

"Some things never change," Grandpa said with a chuckle.

The pictures got older as the stack went on. Grandpa Fred's bar mitzvah. Great-Aunt Janet as a baby. Grandma Anna's wedding. And then there was a photo I'd seen a hundred times—it used to sit on top of the bookshelf in the living room—but had never given a second thought. It was of a young girl sitting at a table, across from a man. The girl (Anna, I realized now) was smiling very faintly. A pretty woman my mom's age knelt beside her, staring right at the camera with a broad grin.

I gasped. "Is that Hannah?"

"Yep," Grandpa said. "That looks like her."

Hannah! Anna wasn't lying; she was gorgeous. Curled hair pinned up, perfect teeth, and lips so defined that they almost looked red, even though this photo was black-and-white.

And the man in the picture had to be Max! I could only see his profile, but he looked different than he did in my head. Older, and balder. *Look over here, Max,* I thought illogically. But he was paying no attention to the camera. Instead he was staring thoughtfully at the table, where there was—I squinted to make sure—a Chinese checkers set.

I didn't know whether to click my heels or to cry. I wished Madeline were here; she would freak. If Anna's diary were a book, this photo would be the cover.

"Grandpa Max loved Chinese checkers," Grandpa Fred told me. "I used to play with him after school. Do you want to keep this picture?"

I swallowed, nodded. Grandpa smiled and handed it to me. This trip felt worthwhile already.

I kept staring at the picture as I walked back to Grandma Anna's room. I laid it carefully on the bed and stared at it a while longer. Then I slowly opened the closet and found the fur coats.

"Three coats," Grandpa said, appearing behind me. "Janet took one, I think. I'll take the others back to your house. I know why fur went out of style. But it is beautiful, isn't it?"

That was for sure. I reached out and touched the sleeve of one jacket. It was so brown, so smooth and soft. I wondered how many skins it took to make these. Had Anna ever solved the puzzle and helped the factory save money?

"Did Grandma Anna work at the factory when she was an adult?" I asked.

"No," Grandpa said. "Max took over after his uncles died—they were too cheap to retire, you know. One died at his desk, looking at sales figures."

He chuckled. "But fur started to go out of fashion. Max kept at it, made a nice living. My mom helped out with the books and things, and then she became an accountant. It was rare for women to work in those days, but she did well for herself. Met my dad one day on her lunch break, at the automat." He started to explain what that was, but I told him I already knew.

"My mom always did our taxes," Grandpa continued. "She loved it. If there was a mistake, she would spend hours poring over the numbers until she found it. It was like a puzzle to her."

"She always loved puzzles," I said.

"Yes, she did," Grandpa said with a sad smile. After a few seconds, he took out one of the coats. It was very big and very long. He put it on. It fit, but it was clearly meant for a woman. "How do I look?" he said, spinning.

I laughed. Grandpa did another twirl, then took it off and put it back into the closet. Then he pulled out another. "Oh, would you look at that. My mom tried to get Janet to wear this one when she was a teenager, but she refused. It sat in storage for years. I can't believe it's here."

This was the coat Max and Hannah gave Anna for her thirteenth birthday. I knew it, as sure as I know my right hand from my left.

I remembered the first day Anna went to the factory, that buyer asking her to model the coat. How transformed Anna felt. The way Hannah sighed. *The feel of your first fur coat.*

"It's probably just about your size," Grandpa said. "Want to try it on?"

I inhaled slowly. The answer, of course, was yes. Remembering the way Anna felt the silk on her bare arms, I removed my sweatshirt, leaving only a thin layering tee. Grandpa held the coat open, and I slid it on.

The coat was so warm and heavy, it reminded me of when I used to give Jaime piggy-back rides. The silk was cool and smooth on the inside. The fur was soft and lush. Grandpa closed the closet so I could see myself in the mirrored door. I spun slowly, the way Anna did for the buyer.

"Gorgeous," Grandpa said quietly, his eyes shining. "If only my mother could see you now."

We worked all afternoon, finally stopping for the day at six o'clock. At dinner, Grandpa cracked me up with funny stories he'd heard about Max's uncles, and a few classic memories about my mom and her siblings when they were kids. He even told a few stories about me and Jaime, which I relished even though I'd heard them ten million times before. Hard to believe I was really the little kid in those stories. I thought about Anna reading her diary in 1950, translating it all into English. That was eight years later, when she was twenty or twenty-one. Did she still feel like the same girl who'd written it?

Grandpa put his arm through mine as we walked back to the apartment. At home I would have slipped away, embarrassed to be out with my grandfather, but tonight I didn't. It was cold out, but I felt warm and fuzzy, like I had the best family in the world.

"It's okay to wonder about your past, you know," Grandpa said as we neared the apartment.

I felt a ball forming in my stomach, threatening to harden every soft feeling from today.

"It's hard for your mom because she loves you so much," Grandpa continued. "But that doesn't mean you can't be honest with her."

I didn't say anything because I didn't know what to say. Grandpa squeezed my hand tighter in his. When he let go, I felt something firm in my palm. It was a quarter. I looked at Grandpa. "How'd you do that?"

He shrugged. "Magic."

CHAPTER 35

I'd brought my sleeping bag, assuming I'd sleep on the floor of the living room, but Grandpa insisted I take Grandma Anna's bed. It was weird, lying there. I exchanged a few texts with Madeline and Ethan, read a little from the book I'd brought, but it was hard to concentrate. I knew I'd have to talk to my mom when I got home, but for now, I wanted to focus on Anna. Today was productive for sure, but I had an itchy sense that there was still more to know. To find.

I thought about the connection Anna described between herself and Belle, like a string tied between paper cups. It was as though the diary had formed a new connection, a thread running between Anna and me, and here in this room, that connection was so electric, it could be an actual telephone wire. It could've been creepy—Grandma Anna was dead, after all—but it wasn't. It was cool.

I closed my eyes. Anna always felt her connection with Belle strongest when she slept. When I fell asleep, would my dreams fill in every remaining blank? It could happen. For weeks I'd slept with Anna's diary in a shoebox under my bed, and now here I was, lying in *her* bed.

My eyes snapped open. That was it. The answers were here—I could *feel* it—but they weren't in Grandma Anna's bed. They were under it.

CHAPTER 36

Y ou seriously found this under her bed?"

"I swear. Remember how she kept letters from home under her bed? She did the same as an adult!"

"A shoebox." Madeline ran her fingers over the smooth cardboard. "Just like you used for her diary."

"Crazy, right?"

Madeline stared at me, her head shaking slightly. "It almost makes one believe in the paranormal."

"Almost," I said with a grin. I'd waited the whole four-hour car ride from New York to show Madeline the contents of this box, and I couldn't wait a second longer. "Open it!"

She gasped when she lifted the lid, just like I did. Looking at the contents made my skin tingle now, just like it had when I'd opened it for the first time.

"Letters," I said. "Ticket stubs, photos, playbills."

"No way," Madeline whispered. She picked up an envelope, ran her finger over the childish handwriting. It was addressed to Anna Hirsch, Sixty-fifth Street in Brooklyn, New York. What was more amazing was the return address, an apartment in Chicago. And the name: Frida Gottlieb.

"Frida," Madeline said, her voice full of wonder. She carefully took out the letter and unfolded it.

"It's in German," I said.

Madeline stared at it, like if she looked long enough, she'd be able to translate it. I was too excited to let her go at her own pace. I'd stayed awake for two hours going through this box Saturday night, and then spent another hour sharing it with Grandpa the next day. I couldn't wait any longer before showing Madeline the most amazing items.

I rummaged through the box, found one of them: a picture of a boat, drawn in pencil by someone very young. "I think Oliver drew this," I said.

"Oh my God," Madeline said. "You've got to be right." She took it from me slowly, but I kept going.

"Her ticket from *Fantasia* is in here. And one from a Dodgers game in 1943. Oh, and there's a bowling scorecard. Hannah beat her and Miriam by, like, a hundred points!"

"Are you kidding?"

"Nope. And get this." I fished around the box until I found the best thing of all.

It took Madeline a second, but then her eyes nearly popped out of her skull. "The photo postcard from Coney Island!" She grabbed it from me.

"They're all there," I said. "Max, Hannah, the uncles, Freddy."

"Their heads really do look like an egg and an onion!" Madeline said with a laugh.

"This must be the hat that blew off on the human roulette wheel," I said, pointing.

"Who's that?" Madeline asked.

"Freddy's brother, Milton."

"And his girlfriend!"

"Enid."

"This is incredible."

"Oh," I said, "look at this. This must be the letter my grandpa talked about. The one from Anna's parents to Max's father."

Madeline looked at it with wonder. "What language is this?"

"Yiddish. My grandpa told me, but he couldn't read it."

She nodded slowly, taking it all in. "Is there anything from later?" Madeline asked. "Like, shortly after the diary ends?"

I knew what she meant, and I'd looked for it

too. Some document that gave closure, like a notice from the Luxembourg government that her parents' bodies had been found in the ruins of Auschwitz or something. But there was nothing so definitive. I couldn't even find the letter from Kurt, the one that said that Oliver had died. I decided it was a good thing she hadn't saved it. I told myself that it may have taken years, but she eventually tore it up and tried to move on.

"There's this," I said, holding up a crumpled envelope. The return address was from Poland, and the envelope was dirty and worn, like it had been run over by a Jeep, if they had those back then. The letter inside was dated 18 August 1941, but the postmark on the envelope was from a smudged-out month in 1942. The diary ended in March; who knew how many more months Anna had to wait before she received this piece of mail. The letter wasn't very long—just the front of one sheet of stationery and a few lines on the back—but I could sense its importance. The handwriting was a beautiful cursive, compact yet flowy, and it was written in French.

Madeline flipped it over to look at the signature. Her face took on a cross between excitement and sadness when she saw. "It's from her mother," she whispered.

I nodded and told her, "Anna wrote back." I reached into the very bottom of the shoebox, where I'd put this last thing to keep it safe. It was an envelope, thick with what must have been a very long letter. The envelope was addressed in Anna's careful hand, to be sent to the same address in Poland from which her mother's letter had been mailed. But it was still sealed. No one had ever opened it. A stamp on the front declared in big, bold ink: RETURN TO SENDER. RECIPIENT UNKNOWN.

CHAPTER 37

Madeline wanted to type Anna's mother's letter into Google to get it translated on the spot, but I shot her down. I'd once used an online translation site to help me write a paragraph for Spanish class, and my teacher gave me a 62. This letter was *way* too important for a translation that was 62 percent of the way there. "Besides," I said to Madeline, "this is the last letter Anna ever received from her mother. That's a very personal thing." *The most personal thing in the world,* I thought. If my birth mother had written me a letter like this, there's no way I'd want its contents typed into Google, even seventy-five years from now. "Having it translated by a machine just feels . . . wrong."

"Okay," she said. "But who do we know who knows French?"

I tried not to smile as I answered. "Ethan."

"Imani. No offense, because I know you guys have a . . . thing going on. But, Ethan? You don't trust Google, but you trust a seventh grader who started learning French in September?"

"No, not Ethan himself," I assured her. "I was thinking he could ask his teacher."

Madeline's shoulders went down as she gave in. "I guess that could work. Text him."

Ethan came through for me once again. He suggested giving the letter to the student teacher in his French class, and once I met her, I knew she was the perfect person for this project. She was small and well-dressed, with her nails painted orange. Her English was fluent, but she had a thick French accent, which made sense because she grew up in France and only moved to America for college. Ethan took me to meet her during lunch, and she was eating a salad and a big, crusty piece of baguette. In other words, she was *French* through and through. I could just tell she would approach the contents of the letter with care and, well, *humanness*—the total opposite of a computer algorithm.

And get this: Her name was Mme. Veronique. So similar to Mme. Veron, Anna's French teacher in Brooklyn! That was a sign so clear, no one could deny it, even Madeline, who didn't believe in signs.

I brought the letter to school the next day, and Mme. Veronique allowed me to come with her into the teachers' lounge while she photocopied it, so that I didn't have to let it out of my sight. She carefully folded the original back into its envelope and gave it to me.

"I will translate for you tonight, yes?"

"That would be awesome," I said. "I mean, if you have time." I don't know why I was so nervous. "Just as soon as you can, I guess."

"I can see it is special, this letter," Mme. Veronique said with a smile.

"Oh man," I said with a sigh. "You have no idea."

CHAPTER 38

I walked home slowly. Tennis was over, Grandpa had left, and my mom would be home from work soon. If only I could fast-forward to tomorrow, when I'd get the translated letter back. What did it say? What do you say to the daughter you sent away and would never see again? It must be that proper goodbye Anna craved. It was easier to do that sort of thing in a letter, where you could take your time and make sure you said things the right way, without getting interrupted or derailed by emotions.

That's how it hit me: the ideal way to ask for my bat mitzvah present. While I waited for the letter from Anna's mom, I'd sit down and write one to my own.

I went to my desk the minute I got home. I took out a sheet of loose leaf and pumped my mechanical pencil. From there, the words just came. I guess they'd been there all along, but stuck behind my lips. Now they jumped at the chance to escape through my hand.

Dear Mom,

I'm sorry for what I said when we were dress shopping. I know it hurt you, and that is the last thing I want to do. I'm so afraid of hurting you that I've been afraid to ask for my bat mitzvah present, even though I've wanted it for a long time. I want to find my biological family.

PLEASE keep reading the rest of this letter so you can know why I'm asking for this. It's not because I don't love you and Dad and Jaime and everyone else in our family. It's not because I want to live with someone else. It's not because I don't realize how lucky I am to have you and a great life.

It's only because there's a big question mark inside me. Grandma Anna's diary was like a window to our family history, and it only made me wonder more about mine. Where do my birth parents come from? Why did they place me for adoption? What race is my father? It's hard to look different from your parents and everyone else in your town. It's even harder if you don't know why you look the way you do. I've been

327

wondering in secret (and looking, but only just a little, I swear) because I know it upsets you. But I can't help the wondering. The only thing that will stop me wondering is finding out.

I know it might be hard to find information about my birth parents, and I know what I find might be something bad or sad. But I still want to know. I am mature enough to handle it.

Since I'm under 18, I can't do a real search without permission from you or Dad. But even if I could, I'd want to do this with you and Dad anyway because you're my parents. No matter what I said when I was angry, you ARE my real mom. Learning about my biological past isn't going to change that. I love you.

Love,
   Imani

I read the letter five times. My plan was to rewrite it in pen, on nice stationery, but now that seemed inappropriate, like putting a frilly cushion on an execution chair. So I folded the piece of loose leaf in thirds, stuck it in an envelope, and wrote MOM on the front. I went into her room and placed it on her pillow.

Then I left for Madeline's house before I could change my mind.

CHAPTER 39

Mom didn't reply that night. She didn't mention the letter the whole morning either. She didn't even give any indication that she'd read it—no tearing up when she looked at me, no adoption files on my desk. By the time I got to school, I worried that she didn't actually get it. Had it fallen under the bed or behind the headboard? Did Jaime steal it as a joke? Did Dad get to it first and decide to spare her the pain?

Madeline did her best to distract me, but I was starting to freak out. Another day or two, and I'd have to ask her about it with words, which defeated the whole purpose of writing it in the first place. Why did I think it was a good idea to do this now, when I was also waiting in agony for the letter from Anna's mom? It made me seriously question my sanity.

Finally, between sixth and seventh period, Ethan bumped into me on the stairs.

"Watch it," I said jokingly.

"Sorry," he said with a smile. "Here."

My pulse sped up as I felt his hand press against mine. But then he was gone, and a folded piece of paper was in my palm, like Grandpa Fred's magic quarter. I ducked out of the crowd at the top of the stairwell, leaned against the wall, and opened it up.

Mme. Veronique has your letter. Meet at French room after school?

For a second I was disappointed that the note didn't say anything more personal, like a request to meet him somewhere else, just us. But then I was over it. Mme. Veronique had the letter!

I slipped Madeline a similar note during math, and the two of us met Ethan at his French room right after the last bell. Mme. Veronique was there, leaning on the teacher's desk and talking with Ethan's regular teacher.

"Bonjour," Mme. Veronique chirped. She said something in French to the teacher, who glanced at us and smiled. "I have your letter." She walked to the back of the room and began looking in her bag.

My fingers played with the bottom of my sweater while I waited. They were quivering. This must've been how Anna felt before she read this letter herself.

Months and months—maybe even years—with no news from her family, and then, at last, a letter from her mother. I could picture her holding it in her trembling hands, her heart thumping in her chest. *Keep your expectations in check,* I told myself. I imagined her doing the same.

"Voila," Mme. Veronique said. She handed me a piece of paper. It was folded in thirds. I stared at it for a moment and then looked up. Mme. Veronique's eyes were moist. "This is a very special letter," she said.

Perhaps my expectations were in line after all.

I thanked her and carried the letter, still folded, into the hallway. Ethan and Madeline followed.

"Do you want to read it alone?" Madeline asked.

Anna would've read it alone, I knew.

But I'm not Anna. On one side of me was my best friend, and on the other was my . . . whatever Ethan is.

"No," I said. "Let's read it together."

My most dearest Anna,

It has been twenty-four heartbreaking hours since I sent you with the smuggler. How can it be, with five other children still here, one of whom looks so much like you, that my heart can feel so empty? When I gave birth to you twelve years ago, I never could have supposed that I would not be there to see you grow into adulthood. It is my most sincere hope that I will, that we will be reunited shortly, and that I will never need to post this letter because I will be able to convey all of these sentiments with my kisses. But I have many sincere hopes, and I fear my heart will rupture if I do not put them on paper.

First, I hope you can forgive your father and me for letting you go on your own. It is a terrible thing to do, to send your child away. My second hope is that one day you will be a mother yourself, and you will understand exactly how painful yet necessary this decision was.

If someone had to go alone, Anna, I'm so very glad it was you. Kurt is strong, yes, but you are stronger. You have such kindness, such intelligence, such intuition. You are my thoughtful child, and my resilient one. You feel as deeply as your sister, but you don't let it waver you. I know that whatever comes your way, you will endure. No, you will shine.

Oh, Max and Hannah are so lucky to have you, Anna! I don't need to tell you to be good, but I do hope you will feel free to be bad sometimes. You and your twin complement each other so nicely, like little pieces in those jigsaws you love. Instead of feeling lost without her, my darling, find the missing pieces within yourself, for they are there. You are just as beautiful as Belle (you are identical, remember!) and just as bold and lighthearted and loving. You two are better together, yes. Know that you can also be whole apart.

I hope you will not just carry Belle with you, but all of us. I wish for you to see the best in people and situations, like your father. To be as selfless as Kurt, who sent you in his place. To view life as an adventure, like Belle. To be as determined and persistent as Greta. To connect with others like Oliver—and to remember how dearly he loves you. To be as innocent and happy as Mina, despite the cruelty of our current world. And to love others as deeply as I love you.

May we all meet again, but, Anna, if we do not: You are strong. You are smart. You are beautiful. You will be fine.

With all my love,
Mama

CHAPTER 40

What could any of us say after reading that? With an indescribable mix of happiness and sadness, I folded it up and put it in my backpack. I said goodbye to my friends and walked home. Somehow, I made it through the blur of sidewalks and passing cars. And somehow, with that same mix of happiness and sadness, Anna lived another seventy-three years.

At home, I paper-clipped the translation to the envelope with the original and placed it back into Anna's memory box. I left the open box on my desk and walked over to my bed. Another letter was there, sitting on my pillow. It was addressed in Mom's swoopy handwriting: IMANI.

I closed my eyes, questioning—again—why I decided to torture myself so much in one week. It was too late to undo it now.

Dear Imani,

I'm the one who should apologize. I've been very emotional lately, but not for the reason you think. Let me explain.

I knew this day would come, when you'd say you hate me or you wish I weren't your mother. All kids say something like that to their parents at some point. I suppose adopted kids are the only ones who have extra fuel, because they can say something so hurtful that is also true. I was dreading the day you'd hurt me that way, but not because I don't want you thinking about your biological family. I was dreading it because it means you're growing up, and as you probably realized, smart girl, I am in denial about that. (I'm sorry for making you shop in the children's department. We should have gone to juniors.)

It sounds sappy, Imani, but you are becoming a young woman. You're preparing for your bat mitzvah, you're spending more time with boys (yes, I've noticed!), and you're starting to ask meaningful questions about yourself and the world. When you were little, you adored me and Dad. It didn't matter that you don't look like us, or that our complexion is lighter than yours. We could solve your problems and answer all your questions. That's not the case anymore. It makes me worried and I get upset, because you have a lot of big, important questions. I don't want you to get hurt, but my power to protect you is shrinking.

If you are determined to search for your birth family, Dad and I will help you. But I don't think it's a good idea, and please let me explain why. It's not because we want you to have a big question mark inside. It's not because we're worried you'll like that family better or renounce your upbringing. (That is a fear of mine, but it's not the reason.) It is because I don't want you to get hurt. In order to prevent you from getting hurt, I'm going to tell you something that might cause you pain. (Thank you for the idea of writing a letter. This would be even harder to say out loud.)

Imani, your father and I received very little information about your birth mother because that was her choice. We were willing to consider an open adoption. She was not. I don't know why, but my guess is that it was a very, very difficult decision to place you for adoption. She made that decision for a reason. I don't know her reason, but it had to be very compelling, since it would affect many people's lives. Dad and I have always felt we must respect that decision.

*In some ways this has made things easier for us
(it would be tricky to navigate having her in our
family's life). I can only imagine that it makes
things easier for her too, and that that is why she
wanted it this way. (It would be very difficult to
watch your daughter grow up with other parents,
even if it is for her own good.) Maybe there
are things about her or your biological father
that would be hard for you to deal with, so she
wanted to protect you too—she is your mother,
after all. I'm including the letter we received from
the social worker about your birth parents. You'll
see that it reveals very little. (I'm sorry it took me
so long to write back to you. I had to go get this
from the safe-deposit box.)*

*I'm sorry if this makes you feel more
incomplete. Weren't things easier when you
were a little kid?! But you're not anymore, that's
for sure. So how about this: I'll stop pretending
that you are a child. Instead of being sad about
you growing up, I'll be proud. Imani, Dad and
I are very proud. You are turning into such a
delightful, smart, talented, and thoughtful young
adult. I'll make an honest effort to treat you as
such. In return, all I ask is that you please think
some more about your request. It's possible that
your birth mother has changed her mind in the*

past twelve years. The adoption agency might know more, and if you are sure that you want to know, we will contact them. But first, Imani: Please weigh the pros and cons. Ask yourself what exactly you're hoping to find, and if it's possible for you to find it later, or in another way. You said you've been wanting this for a long time, but now that you know a little bit more, all I ask is that you please think on it a little bit longer.

Whatever you decide, we will support you. We'll also give you another, more fun present, like a guitar or a trip or a lifetime supply of tortellini. You deserve it!

Love,

Mom

Wow. Boy was I wrong about Mom all this time. She wasn't mad at me, which was a huge relief. She was going to stop treating me like a baby (or try to, at least), which was big. And she decided to share everything she knew about my birth mother. That was the biggest thing of all.

My hands shook as I put aside my mom's letter and exposed the one behind it. It was typed and official-looking, and even shorter than I guessed it would be.

This 24-year old black woman stands 5 feet 6 inches tall and weighs 120 pounds when not pregnant. Her mother is living. Her maternal grandfather died young of kidney failure. She is allergic to tree nuts and has worn glasses for distance since the age of ten. Her pregnancy has been healthy and uncomplicated.

I turned the paper over. That was it.

I let out the breath I'd been holding. I had a weird, anxious feeling, kind of like when I lose a tennis match—let down, but still pulsing with adrenaline.

The information about my birth mother, it was so . . . clinical. Her height, her weight, her tree nut allergy. The empty space—the purposeful lack of information—said more than what was there. It seemed to drive home the point about my birth mother not wanting me to connect with her. It hurt. I'd always assumed she was wondering just as much as I was, maybe even posting on one of those message boards, looking for me. In my head, she's always regretted giving me up.

Why did she want a closed adoption? Was it because she was happy to get rid of me? So happy she'd never want to look back? Or was it because the decision was as painful as Anna's mother described, sending her daughter away out of necessity? Could she have just needed to put it behind her, to help herself survive? If so, how would she react if I *did* manage to track her down? Would I be some unwanted ghost from her past, messing with her life and ruining everything she thought she'd put to rest?

I thought nothing could deter me from my decision, not even if it crushed my parents. But all this time, they were way more resilient than I realized, and now *I* was the one hesitating. It could be that this five-foot-six black woman changed her mind, and she does want us to find each other now. But what then? I might get some answers, but, like Mom said, it could also make things very complicated. And what if finding her doesn't resolve anything? What if she doesn't have information about my birth father? The social worker's letter didn't include anything about him, not even his height or health or race or ethnicity. Was it worth making things complicated if I'd still be left with unanswered questions?

I rubbed my face with my hands. This was like a mental seesaw.

My eyes wandered to Anna's memory box on my desk, then to my closet. Stuffed between the dress I wore to Parker's bat mitzvah and the blue shirt I wore to the funeral was Anna's fur coat, heavy on its hanger. I remembered the way it felt when I tried it on, with the smooth silk lining on my arms and the warm, soft fur enveloping my body. I could see why Anna felt transformed in it, so glamorous and American. But I also understood her guilt, her desperate ache for information about her family in Europe.

I heard some clomping downstairs, and my mom shouting for Jaime to take off his shoes. Mom's phone rang with the ringtone reserved for Dad, and I heard my mom pick it up and say, "Hi, hon."

I stared at myself in the mirror. There was still so much to think about. I was nowhere near figuring out where I came from. But right now, I would join my family downstairs.

CHAPTER 41

After dinner, I chatted with Madeline online. The serious stuff would be easier to talk through on the phone after my thirty minutes of screen time, so for now, we just brainstormed ideas for my fun present.

You could ask for lessons with some pro tennis player or something, she suggested.

Yeah maybe, I said. *Or a trip somewhere. That could be fun.*

Can I come?

Yes! Where should we go?

"Australia," Jaime said from behind me.

"Hey!" I tried to cover the screen with my arm, then realized I was being stupid and just clicked to minimize the window. "I thought you were in bed."

"Snack," Jaime said. He held up a rice cake and

took a bite. He held it out to me, but I shook my head. Jaime nodded toward the screen. "Were you talking about your bat mitzvah present?"

"Maybe."

"You should ask for your own computer. Then we wouldn't have to fight over this one."

I'd thought of that too, though coming from Jaime, the for-me-for-you element was obvious. But I didn't say so. Maybe I was thinking that Jaime might have some good insight, or maybe this day had made me addicted to drama. Whatever the reason, I found myself saying, "I might ask to search for my birth parents."

"Huh?" Jaime's face contorted like his rice cake had gone stale. "Why?"

If I was looking for another shock, his reaction did not disappoint. "Just to find out who they are," I said. "Where I'm from. Don't you ever think about your biological family?"

"My biological family?"

"You know, your birth parents. In Guatemala."

Jaime's dark eyebrows rose up. "No, do you?"

"Um, *yeah*." I'd always imagined that the day Jaime and I finally talked about this, it'd turn into a heart-to-heart scene worthy of an Academy Award. As different as Jaime and I are, it never, *ever* occurred to me that we didn't feel the same way about this. Was it because he was a boy? Or because he was only nine, and like Mom said, I was growing up? Was it because he knew his ethnicity already? Or was there something in his DNA that made him less inquisitive, more willing to go with the flow?

"Are you serious, Jaime?" I asked. "You have no desire to know who you really are?"

Jaime shrugged. "I'm Jaime Mandel."

"Well, yeah. But you never even *think* about your genes? Your DNA?"

"What's DNA?" he asked through bites of his snack.

I was becoming exasperated. "DNA. You know, like, your genetic makeup."

He looked at me blankly. To be fair, I probably didn't know much about DNA when I was in fourth grade. But this whole conversation was not going the way it should, and I had the sudden, urgent need to make him understand *something*. I pulled up the browser and googled "DNA." A familiar picture of a twisted double helix appeared. I read aloud: *"A molecule that encodes the genetic instructions used in the development and functioning of all known living organisms and many viruses."*

Jaime looked more blank than ever.

"Okay, that's not helpful. But DNA is in your body. It's passed down to you from your parents— your birth parents. It's, like, the reason you look the way you do, and part of why you have the personal-

345

ity you have." I frantically scanned the search results, trying to find something that would explain it in simple terms. And that's when I saw the ad on the top.

DNA test kit. Discover your ethnic heritage with DNA testing. Simple and easy with accurate results.

"Oh my God," I muttered.

"What?" Jaime said.

I ignored him and clicked the link. There was a big picture of a woman and a breakdown of where in the world her genes came from: 53 percent Iberian Peninsula. 10 percent North Africa. 10 percent Italy/Greece. 27 percent other.

I scrolled down. A picture of a man, with a quote in large type: "People often look at me and wonder what I am."

"This is it," I said. "This is exactly it!"

"What is it?" Jaime asked, leaning in to look at the screen.

I scrolled back up to the top. It was a "simple saliva test that you can do at home." Ninety-nine dollars, and I could find out what I wanted to know, without having to decide anything about searching for my birth mother just yet.

I printed it out.

"This," I said, "is exactly what I need."

CHAPTER 42

*S*tep two . . ." Dad read aloud. It was early May, and the four of us were gathered around the kitchen table, preparing to spit. *"Fill the tube with saliva to the black line."*

I held up my tube. "Just spit into it?"

"Yep," Dad said, showing me the directions. "Spit until liquid saliva reaches the black line. Bubbles don't count."

Mom smiled at me. "You go first, Imani. This was your idea."

It was my idea, but Mom and Dad had really run with it. They'd spent a whole week researching which company's test kit to order, and then they ordered four: one for each of us. Once we mailed in the DNA samples, the results would take four to six weeks to arrive, so we'd waited to do the spitting until today, exactly six weeks until my bat mitzvah. If the timing was as advertised, I'd have this part of my present just in time for my big day.

"Let's all do it at the same time," I said. "One . . ."

"Pick up your tube, sweetie," Mom said to Jaime. "Two . . ."

"Prepare your saliva!" Dad announced.

Jaime closed his mouth and swished.

"Three!"

We all spit forcefully into our tubes. Then we looked around and laughed, because no one's was even close to the black line. It took a lot more swishing and spitting to collect enough saliva. When mine finally reached the fill line, I gave one final spit, for good luck. Then I screwed on the cap, which topped the saliva with some liquid to "stabilize the DNA." It really was in there, I guess. Amazing that this small collection of spit could hold such big information.

Into a plastic bag, then a padded box, and off to the post office.

I still hadn't decided if I was going to search for my birth parents or not. I went back and forth almost every day. Short of some sign from the universe about what to do, I was putting all my faith—my *imani*—in this DNA test. Either the test kit would answer enough of my questions, or I'd be more determined to find the people who'd given me these genes.

But for now, mailing that box felt like turning in a final exam at the end of school. I didn't know the results, but the questions were out of my hands, and for now, out of my mind.

CHAPTER 43

My Hebrew school class was shrinking every week. A few parents—like Ethan's—made their kids keep coming after their bar or bat mitzvah, but most didn't, so almost everyone whose thirteenth birthday had passed was no longer around. Parker showed up every now and then, but I wished she didn't, since she spent most of the time walking around and saying things like, "At *my* bat mitzvah . . ." It didn't seem to bother Mrs. Coleman, though. In fact, she seemed to grow younger with each passing week, as though every successful mitzvah reversed a wrinkle from her face. She must've been particularly worried about Jeremy Weintraub pulling it off, because last Saturday was his service, and today all of her gray hairs had been dyed brown.

I was in good shape for being three and a half

weeks out. I could read my Torah portion smoothly, and I could chant most of my haftorah without mistakes. My speech still needed work, but I couldn't add anything else until I got the results from my DNA test. I decided to search for some pictures to include in my Holocaust project, which was basically done. (Mrs. Coleman had relaxed her rules about using the computer too. She was becoming more lenient as she got younger!)

I googled *Luxembourg in the Holocaust,* like I'd done ten million times before. But before I could click to view images, I noticed something. There was a new page in the search results. One I'd never seen before.

Luxembourg marks 75th anniversary of German invasion.

I clicked on it. It was a newspaper article about a new memorial in Luxembourg to honor the Luxembourgers who lost their lives in World War II. One part of the memorial was dedicated to the Jews who'd died in the Holocaust. About three-quarters of the way down, there was a photo of the dedication, which I enlarged.

The memorial itself looked similar to the one at our temple, with a plaque under metallic flames, surrounded by Hebrew words. An old white man and two brown-skinned teenagers stood next to it. The caption read: "Holocaust survivor Oliver Christmas, 78, and his grandchildren, Regina and Theodore, traveled from England to help mark the 75th anniversary of Germany invading Luxembourg."

My heart twitched. I looked closely at the photo of Oliver Christmas. He was seventy-eight years old, exactly the age Anna's little brother would be today. But it couldn't be him. Anna's Oliver was Oliver Hirsch, not Oliver Christmas. Oliver Hirsch died more than seventy years ago.

And yet.

I scanned the article for any more mention of Oliver Christmas. I found it about halfway down.

Born in Luxembourg City, Oliver Christmas was just three years old when Germany invaded in May of 1940. His family was forced from their home and deported to Lodz shortly after his fifth birthday. Young Oliver jumped from the train on the way to Poland and found his way to a convent, where he was discovered on Christmas Day in 1941. The nuns took to calling him Oliver Christmas.

"A little boy shows up on Christmas Day, the sisters thought it was a miracle," Christmas says with a chuckle. "I suppose in some ways it was. I never saw the rest of my family again."

He stayed in the convent for a few months, then lived in numerous homes before settling with a family in England when he was seven. Christmas was raised Anglican, but he knows he was once Jewish because he is circumcised.

"I don't remember very much about those years. I was so young. But I know I am from Luxembourg," he said.

Christmas says he brought Regina, 15, and Theodore, 17, to the memorial to honor the memory of relatives he barely remembers. "It's important for my grandchildren to know about my past, and to feel a connection to it," Christmas said. "They are Christians who live in Surrey, but this is part of their heritage. We are all connected."

My blood was rushing so quickly, I thought it might gush out of my veins. "Oh my God," I muttered. "Oh my God. Oh my God."

Madeline slid into the chair next to me. "What is going on over here? You look like you're about to hyperventilate."

"Oliver," I spluttered. "He's—it's Oliver and—" I gave up and pointed to the screen.

I watched Madeline's jaw drop as she read. Soon it seemed like we were both about to hyperventilate.

"It's him!" Madeline cried. "It's definitely him."

"You think so, right?"

"It has to be."

"I thought he died," I said. "*Anna* thought he died."

"He didn't die! He jumped from the train." Madeline removed her reading glasses, looked me in the eye. "Imani, he's still alive!"

My thoughts were like firecrackers. "Should I contact him? I could contact him. How can I contact him?"

Ethan came over. "What are you guys so excited about?"

"Imani's great-grandmother—her brother," Madeline explained, sort of. "He didn't die in the Holocaust. He survived, in England!"

"What?" Ethan gasped.

Mrs. Coleman came over too. "What did you find?" she asked.

Madeline pointed to the screen, and both of them read it. "No way," Ethan said when he was done. "That's Imani's great-grandmother's brother!" he told Mrs. Coleman.

"I thought he died in the camps," I explained.

Mrs. Coleman put a hand to her heart. "You're sure that's him?"

"I really think so," I said. "If I contact him I can find out for sure. But how can I contact him?"

"Is there, like, an online directory for England?" Madeline said.

"You could google him," Ethan tried. "Get his phone number or address."

"You could write to the group that put up this memorial," Mrs. Coleman suggested. "Explain the story and ask for his contact information?"

Then it hit me. "His grandkids," I said. "I'll see if his grandkids are on Facebook."

I pulled up Facebook and logged in. Mrs. Coleman and Ethan and Madeline all leaned in. The few kids left in our class were gathering around too. It was pretty obvious that something big was happening.

"Regina Christmas," I said as I typed. It took a few seconds to load. But then half a page of results came up, and there she was. The fourth one down. The girl from the photo, her skin dark like mine (I might have cousins who are black!). Regina Christmas, fifteen years old, Surrey, England.

"This is *awesome,*" Mrs. Coleman said.

I clicked on her, and the first thing on her page was the same photo from that newspaper article, with a link to the story, and a note: "I love my granddad!"

CHAPTER 44

I spent most of that night drafting my message to Regina Christmas. I didn't want to sound creepy ("I have something your grandfather wants") or ditzy ("We might be cousins!"). I wanted to make sure my case was convincing, but I didn't want it to be so long that she'd get overwhelmed. My mom tried to weigh in, but I kept shooting down her ideas until she announced that I had to do this on my own and finally left me to figure it out. Close to two hours later, I had a one-paragraph message that wasn't perfect, but was as close as I was going to get. I closed my eyes, took a deep breath, and hit SEND.

I didn't expect a reply instantly. England is five hours ahead of Baltimore, so my message arrived in the middle of the night there. But I was bummed when there was no reply the next morning, or at lunchtime, or after school. Mrs. Coleman even called my house around dinnertime, and I could hear her disappointment when I said I hadn't heard back yet. Another day passed, and another. Had Regina deleted my message, or flagged it as spam? Did she think I was a lunatic?

On day four, I googled her brother, Theodore Christmas. He wasn't on Facebook, but I tracked down what was probably his email address. How much longer should I wait before trying my luck with him? Or would that only make me seem like more of a psycho?

As the days dragged by, my anxiety spilled over to the other decision I still had to make, about whether or not to try and find my birth parents. Would trying to contact my birth mother be like this? Waiting and waiting and checking and hearing nothing and losing hope drip by drip?

I went to the mall with Parker and Magda over the weekend, and Parker brought her *It's better to have loved and lost* tote bag with her. I seethed at those glittery letters. If Regina was never going to write back, it would have been better not to have found possibly-Oliver at all.

And then, exactly one week after I found her, Regina replied. It was like she was waiting until I could open the message at Hebrew school, surrounded by people who'd become invested in our story.

I wanted to read it privately first, just in case she totally shot me down. But Madeline was right next to me when I logged in, and she shouted, "She replied!"

Everyone came running, and Mrs. Coleman did a little excited clap. I clicked to open the message. It was short. I cleared my throat and read aloud:

Hi Imani,

At first I thought your story was rather nutty. My brother didn't think I should even tell Granddad about it. It could be upsetting to him, couldn't it? I finally decided we had to at least tell him . . . and he thinks it just might be true! He says he has a fuzzy memory of a sister who left for America, and the name Anna, but he wasn't sure if it was real or not. Can we all set a Skype date, to talk some more and get this sorted? Granddad wants to be there, of course. This weekend's no good, but we're available the following weekend. Saturday the 6th? Prepare your best evidence! You don't want to break an old man's heart. ;)

> *Regina*

The class erupted in cheers. I laughed. Who'd have thought my family history would turn into a group sport?

Ethan gave me a big hug. "You're going to Skype with her!"

Madeline hugged me from the other side. "You're going to see Oliver!"

This was all so surreal. How was I going to wait until June 6? It felt like forever. But my bat mitzvah was just a week after that, so Grandpa Fred would already be in town. He could be there to see Oliver too, which was perfect. If only it weren't too late for Grandma Anna to be there. Imagine *that* reunion!

My mental seesaw tipped strongly to the *find your birth parents* side. If finding them would feel half as good as this, I was all in.

Don't get too excited just yet, I told myself. *It's entirely possible that Oliver Christmas is not Oliver Hirsch.* But it was entirely possible that he was. Either way, I'd find out on June 6.

There was one last part of Regina's message, a P.S. that I didn't read aloud.

P.S. You said you're adopted. Where are you from originally?

It was entirely possible I'd know that by June 6 too.

CHAPTER 45

My mom licked her finger and rubbed it on my cheek. I brushed it away. "Mom, that's gross."

"Not as gross as having shmutz on your face. You're about to Skype with long-lost cousins!"

"I don't want my mom's saliva on my face either."

"Everyone relax," said Dad. "They're not going to think we're gross."

"Even me?" said Jaime. He stuck his finger up his nose.

"Jaime!" I yanked his hand down. "You better not screw this up."

"Listen to your sister," said Grandpa Fred. "We want to make a good impression." He put a tissue on his head and let it sit there. Jaime cracked up.

"Dad," my mom warned.

We were due to Skype in three minutes, and the

image of the five of us was in the center of the computer screen. Ready or not, this is what Oliver would see when our call connected. Me and my colorful family. It made me smile.

The speakers started ringing with the sound for an incoming call. "They're calling!" I shouted. "They're early!"

Everyone got quiet. My mom gave my arm a squeeze.

"Okay, here we go."

I clicked, and there they were. Regina and Theodore plus a white man and a black woman who must have been their parents. Front and center, seated right in front of the camera, was Oliver. Grandpa Fred gasped. "He looks just like her," he whispered. Mom put his arm around him. I knew she'd be crying before long.

"Hiya," said Regina. "I'm Regina. This is Teddy, and my mum and dad."

"I'm Imani," I told them, with a wave, and did our introductions.

"I'm told," said Oliver with a sophisticated British accent, "that you might have known my sister."

I held up the diary. I told them what I'd said in my message to Regina, about Anna's little brother Oliver, and the dates matching up. My voice trembled a little, and my hand did too, as I held one of the photos of Anna to the camera, nice and close, so they could see it clearly. "She thought you all died," I told Oliver. "She got a letter from your brother, Kurt, and it said something about you that made her upset. She doesn't say exactly what it was—and the letter's not here anymore—but maybe it said you jumped from the train."

"I told the newspaper reporter I jumped," Oliver replied, "but I'm not sure that's entirely true. That is, I don't think I jumped of my own accord. It could be that my mother threw me."

I inhaled sharply. From what I knew of Anna's mother—*his* mother—I could believe it. I felt tears building behind my eyes. My mom put her arm around me.

Oliver rubbed his cheeks with his hand. "I can't be completely sure, however. It was so long ago, wasn't it? I was so young." He told more of his story, the type of crazy-but-true story that filled all those Holocaust books. Once he was off the train, he wandered through the woods, alone, for as long as a week. When he finally showed up at a convent he hadn't eaten in days, had seen terrible things, had nothing but the ragged clothes on his back. "I could barely communicate," Oliver said. "I must've spoken Luxembourgish, and who understands that outside Luxembourg? But I'm told I barely spoke at all. My parents—the ones in England—they said it was years before I really started talking again. Shell-shocked, wasn't I?"

Regina's dad—Oliver's son—placed his hand on his shoulder.

"But my parents, they told me I used the French word for *train,* and I said 'America.' They initially thought my family had taken a train, left for America, and I'd gotten left behind by mistake. But I do think I remember a sister named Anna. You say I also had a brother named Kurt?"

"Yes," I said. "There were six Hirsch children. Kurt was the oldest. There was a baby, Mina, and a girl, Greta, who would've been about five years older than you. Then Anna, of course, and her twin sister, Belle."

"Twins!" Oliver said. Recognition flashed over his eyes. But then he looked sad, skeptical. "You're adopted, Imani? You know what's it like to wonder, to search your mind for memories. Twins sounds right, but it was so long ago."

"It seems like it could be true," Regina's dad said. "But how can we know for sure?"

"My son worries that you're after my money," Oliver said.

"Oliver!" Regina's mom said.

"He does," said Oliver.

His son raised an eyebrow, looked at us apologetically. "There are nutty people in the world. Con artists. They might have seen your article, sensed an opportunity."

In the corner of the screen, my whole family was shaking our heads vigorously.

"We want nothing of the sort," my dad insisted.

"See, Dad?" Regina said.

"Imani was just researching her great-grandmother's history," my mom said.

"We don't want anything from you," Grandpa Fred added. "In fact, if you're the right Oliver, we have a lot of things to *give* you."

"Give us?" Regina's brother asked.

"My mother's diary, to start," said Grandpa Fred.

"All her photos too," I added. "The letters she saved. There's one from your mother. Anna would have wanted you to have them. She wrote and wrote about how much she loved you. How close you two were. It's all in the diary."

The Christmases were looking at each other. I could tell that they wanted to believe, but some of them were still not convinced. The dad started saying something, and his family began to argue with him quietly.

"She kept your bear," I said loudly.

Oliver sat up straighter. He held up his hand to silence his family. "Pardon?"

364

I opened the diary and unfolded the photo I'd printed out of Bier. Isabel was going to bring it when they came next week for my bat mitzvah, but in the meantime, they'd emailed me a photo. I held it up to the screen. "Your bear. I'm not sure how to pronounce it . . . *Bier?* It was your favorite stuffed animal, and you gave it to Anna to bring to New York."

There was silence on both sides of the screen. I held my breath hopefully. When I lowered the picture, I saw that Oliver had started to cry. "Bier," he whispered. He began to laugh through his tears. "It's true," he said. A broad smile on his face, tears dripping down his cheeks, he shook his head with belief.

In my living room in Baltimore, my mom and grandpa wrapped me in a hug. They were both crying, and, I realized with a smile, so was I.

In England, my seventy-eight-year-old great-great-uncle gave a big, big sigh and said, "Anna."

CHAPTER 46

One week later, I stood in front of my family, friends, and Jewish community, becoming a bat mitzvah. I was nervous at first, and Rabbi Seider had to whisper to me to speak louder into the microphone. Then I messed up some Hebrew words in the beginning of the service—part of a prayer I knew back to front. But instead of making me nervous about the tougher readings to come, it was actually a big relief. I was bound to make a mistake at some point, so at least I got it out of the way. Even better, nobody noticed or cared. My parents were still beaming with pride in the front row, with my dad's video camera on a tripod in the back. My brother was still fiddling with his yarmulke and drumming his hands on his prayer book. And Madeline and Ethan were still there, silently cheering me on.

I only stumbled once while reading my Torah portion, and I chanted my haftorah perfectly. After that, the last big hurdle was my speech. I stepped up to the podium and stood up very straight.

"In the Torah portion I just read, Naso, the Israelites are wandering in the desert, and God asks Moses to take a census. He needs to count all the men between the ages of thirty and fifty, to determine how many there are from each of the families. The family that they're from determines what their job is in moving items from the Tent of Meeting, or the Tabernacle. I'll admit I was kind of disappointed when I learned that this was the subject of my Torah portion. Taking a census sounds pretty boring."

I got a few laughs here, which made me blush. I took a breath and continued. "Then I realized that being part of a census means identifying yourself as one group or another. In this story, being a Levite or a Gershonite determines what job you have, but in real life, identifying as one group or another can mean a lot more.

"In researching my Holocaust project, I learned that Hitler invaded the small country of Luxembourg in May of 1940." I looked up for a second here and glanced at Grandpa. He winked.

"The Germans wanted everyone there to join the Nazi party and identify as German," I read. "But in the 1941 census, 95 percent stated that they were Luxembourgish. In this small way, the Luxembourgers showed their resistance. This made the Nazis angry and led to mass arrests. Of course, it was even worse if you were Jewish. Starting in September of 1941, the Jews had to identify themselves by wearing the yellow Star of David. This made it easier to deport and kill them. We often hear the final count—the census—of how many Jews died in the Holocaust. But it's important to remember that each number in that census represents a real person, like my great-grandma Anna's parents, and her grandparents and siblings, even her twin sister.

"Because of the color of my skin, people are always surprised when I identify as Jewish. They often ask me what I really am, or where I'm really from, just like they're taking a census. Being adopted, I've always asked myself these questions too, and not knowing the answers is hard. Where you come from is a big part of who you are. That's why my family and I decided to take a DNA test, to see where our ancestors are from. I just got the results to mine, and it turns out I'm a real mix. My genes are 40 percent Nigerian, 10 percent North African, 13 percent Eastern European, 13 percent Western European, and 24 percent Middle Eastern—maybe those ancestors were wandering the desert with Moses!"

People laughed and started whispering to each other. I wondered what they were saying. When I'd opened the package, my own reaction was just as mixed as those results. The African percentage was something of a confirmation, and it was definitely interesting to see so much was from Nigeria. It was cool to think I was part Middle Eastern, too—maybe my ancestors were Jewish, though who knows. And European! Maybe a small strand of my DNA had roots in Luxembourg.

I still had so many questions, though. Were my European ancestors like Anna, who came to America on a boat full of refugees? And my African ancestors—did they come on a boat too? Did they make a choice, or was their ship full of slaves? When and how did those strings of DNA intertwine, and what did that say about my past, and my present?

I didn't know the answers, but in a way, it made no difference at all. I still came from a long line of people who made the difficult choice to send away their child. One was smuggled across the ocean, one was thrown from a train, and I was placed for adoption. But that doesn't mean those parents didn't love those children; I know that for sure. The best part is that all those children lucked out, because I also come from a long line of people who take in strangers and make them part of their family. Max and

Hannah, Oliver's parents in England, and—beaming with pride in the front row of the synagogue—my mom and dad.

I didn't need to find my birth parents. Not yet, at least. It's not like I'd ever forget about them, and I might still decide to look for them someday. But right now, the people who mattered most were all in this temple, listening to me read this speech. And once I read the ending, I'd be minutes away from becoming a bat mitzvah.

"My DNA results answer some questions about *'what'* I am," I read, "but they don't really change *who* I am. I am still me, and my family is still my family. Whether or not Judaism is in my blood, it is in my history, and I can still feel a connection to it. Before I read from the Torah today, my family stood in a line and passed the Torah down, from my grandparents down to me. I only wish my great-grandma Anna could have been here to be in the line. If I were to take a census of all the things that make me proud to be who I am and connected to my Jewish heritage, Great-Grandma Anna and her story would be high on the list."

CHAPTER 47

Everyone came back to our house after the service. It was strange to think that the last time my mom's side of the family was all together, it was for Grandma Anna's funeral. The vibe was much happier today, obviously. Grandpa Fred performed some magic tricks. Jaime and Uncle Dan talked about baseball for, like, two hours. My cousin Isabel drew a giant family portrait out of chalk on our patio. Mom even let Aunt Jess take me around the block on her motorcycle. (Mom buried her face in Dad's chest, and I screamed as loud as Grandma Anna did when she rode the Cyclone!) Everyone lavished me with compliments and hugs and presents. My face started to feel sore, I was smiling so much.

By the time the sun set, most of my relatives had trickled out to their hotel, and things had started to wind down. Madeline's family stayed late, though. Our parents chatted out on the deck while Jaime and Henry tried to see who could catch the most fireflies. Madeline and I joined them for a while, then moved to the hammock, my head by her feet for ideal balance.

"What was Ethan's present?" Madeline asked me.

"A gift certificate to the movies," I said, glad that she couldn't exactly see my face.

"So you guys can go together?"

"That's what he wrote in the card."

If Parker and Magda were there, they'd have shrieked in unison. But Madeline just sighed. "This trip from your parents. Your DNA results. A *date* with Ethan. I probably shouldn't even bother giving you my present."

I lifted my head. "What is it?"

Madeline shrugged.

"Come on!"

"It's inside with all the other presents. Yellow gift bag."

I got off the hammock as quickly as I could without making Madeline fall out. Then I sprinted into the house and started sorting through the cards and boxes piled on the kitchen table to find her yellow bag.

Grandpa Fred was standing by the wall, looking at the results of all of our DNA tests. My dad had printed them out on big pieces of paper and taped them up for all our relatives to see. He and Mom had similar makeups: mostly European, but with a few surprises thrown in, like my mom being 10 percent Pacific Islander, and my dad having a trace of Central Asia. Jaime was mostly native to the Americas, but he had West African and even Irish roots too.

"Fascinating," Grandpa said.

"Yeah," I agreed. I found Madeline's gift bag and went to the door.

"Hang on a minute," Grandpa called. "I want to give you my present."

I came back to the table. "Which one is it?"

He pointed to a small box. Then, like a little kid who's too excited to wait, he blurted out, "It's an iPhone."

My eyes bulged. "No way."

He smiled. "You'll enjoy it?"

"Are you kidding me?" I said, practically screaming. I wrapped him in a hug. "Thank you, Grandpa!"

He squeezed me tight. "Thank *you*, Imani." When he pulled back, his eyes were shining. "You gave me the greatest present, finding my mother's diary, and then finding her brother. To think that we're all going to go to England in a few weeks. And I'll get to meet him. . . ."

Grandpa trailed off. It was like my cheeks were superglued up, thinking about the trip. We were going to England—me, Mom, Dad, Jaime, Grandpa, and (since this was my present) Madeline! Our first stop would be Surrey, to meet Oliver and his family and give all of Anna's stuff to its rightful owner. I especially couldn't wait to hang out with Regina; she and I had been messaging back and forth like crazy. After that, we were going to spend a whole week in London. My mom even bought tickets to a match at Wimbledon. Just three, for herself, Madeline, and me. I wanted to see Luxembourg too, and to get some tortellini in Italy, but Mom and Dad said they don't have the vacation time or the money to go on an entire European tour. That's okay. Maybe Jaime can ask for that for his bar mitzvah. I've got a few years to convince him.

"Okay," Grandpa said. "Go back to your friend."

I gave him a kiss, grabbed Madeline's gift bag, and ran back to the hammock. The outside lights flicked on, one after another, as I ran past.

"Ta-da," I said, holding up the bag.

Madeline shifted as gracefully as possible in the hammock, until her legs hung over the edge. I lay down carefully beside her so that my legs dangled too. I reached inside and pulled out a small box. "Chinese checkers!" I announced.

"Travel size," she pointed out. "So we can bring it to England."

"Oh my God," I said, "that's perfect."

"There's more."

I reached back in the bag and pulled out a thick book with a soft fabric cover and a long red ribbon to mark the pages. A blank journal.

"So you can record your own story," Madeline explained, "whether you decide to find your birth family someday or not."

I didn't think it was possible for my grin to get any bigger, but I was wrong. "Thank you," I said. "This is awesome. And if I do look for them, I'll be sure to give you an exclusive interview for your radio show."

"Really?" Madeline asked, excited. "I mean, only if you want to." She tapped my new journal with her knuckle. "Just make sure you tie up all the loose ends," she joked. "You don't want to upset *your* great-granddaughter and *her* best friend."

My eyes widened at the thought. Me, old, with a great-granddaughter of my own. Would she be anything like me, look anything like me? Would I hand down a Torah to her on the day of her bat mitzvah? Would she *have* a bat mitzvah? Maybe she or her friend would be adopted too. Who knows. It's such a long way away.

I hugged the journal and stared up at the darkening sky. A few stars were just starting to appear. Those were far away too. But they were brilliant just the same.

ACKNOWLEDGMENTS

I'm often asked if my characters are based on real people. Imani, Anna, and everyone else in this book are fictional, but I couldn't have created them without the help of many, many real people who shared their own stories and experiences with me.

Imani would not exist if it weren't for my first friend and lifelong companion at Jewish holiday dinners, Larisa Mannino. Her openness and honesty brought Imani to life, along with input from Mariel Phillips and Roberta Gore. I'm also endlessly grateful to Sarah Hannah Gómez, Chelsea Lemon-Fetzer, Kaila Neipris-Gross, and Barbara Gross, sensitivity readers extraordinaire. Anything that rings true about Imani and Jaime is thanks to the people listed here. Anything that doesn't is my fault alone.

Anna would not be from Luxembourg if I hadn't had the incredible fortune of befriending Jennifer Breithoff and Christine Hansen. They both answered countless questions, and Jennifer put her amazing language skills to work reviewing Anna's broken English. Amanda Ashe reviewed Anna's English as well, while Reese Ashe kept me sane and sharp. Most importantly, thank you to my grandparents, Joan and Marty Baron and Terry and Lee Weissman, for sharing their stories about growing up in New York City, working in the fur business, and saving hot dogs for later. As with Imani's story, anything I got right about Anna and the 1940s is due in large part to their help. Mistakes are my own.

Thank you to the United States Holocaust Memorial Museum and all the survivors who volunteer their time to speak with visitors, especially the survivors who spoke with me: Henry Greenbaum, Marcel Hodak, and Martin Weiss. Among the many books I found useful, I must acknowledge *A Dimanche Prochain: A Memoir of Survival in World War II France* by Jacqueline Mendels Birn and *Surviving the Nazi Occupation of Luxembourg: A Young Woman's WWII Memoir* by Marguerite Thill-Somin-Nicholson.

Elisabeth Dahl, Shawn K. Stout, Laura Amy Schlitz, Erin Hagar, and Stacy Davidowitz provided early and incisive feedback, not to mention invaluable encouragement. Anne Bartholomew provided reassuring pep talks and much-needed comic relief.

Flip Brophy, Holly Hilliard, and Nell Pearce helped this book find a home—and what a home! I could not have dreamed up a more dedicated, perceptive, thoughtful, and supportive editor than Dana Chidiac. We most definitely would have been friends in middle school. Thank you to everyone at Dial for embracing this book and getting it ready for readers, especially Lauri Hornik and Namrata Tripathi, Regina Castillo, and Jenny Kelly. I couldn't be happier with the beautiful cover with art by Olaf Hajek, designed by Tony Sahara and Kristin Boyle.

Finally, much love to all the Weissmans, Barons, Rudnicks, and Roches, especially Grant, Karina, and Lev. Imani and Anna lucked out with their families, but not more than I did with mine.